BEVERLY
KILLS
AGAIN

SEAN McDONOUGH

Welcome to
domestic hell.

D & T
PUBLISHING

To Kristy, from California to New York.

BEVERLY
KILLS AGAIN

———————————

CHAPTER 1

BEVERLY

The party sucked.

Rich old man parties usually did.

Executives.

Politicians.

Suck ups.

Trophy wives.

Predators.

I downed another gin and tonic, my third in the last hour, and waved my empty glass at the clotted tumor of botox, fake tits, and bleached hair that had entangled me in one-sided conversation for the last twenty minutes. "Excuse me for a moment," I said. "I'll be right back once I top this off."

And after I spike the broken glass stem through my eye.

My first stop was the bar. I did need a refill, that much was true, but then I made a beeline for the balcony for an equally necessary refill of fresh air and some fucking peace.

The heat, oppressive and all-consuming, hit me immediately as I opened the glass doors, but it was a welcome change from the sterile, frigid climate of the air-conditioned estate. The drink in my hand was already sweating from the sudden change in atmosphere.

I leaned against the polished brass railing and breathed in the Alabama night. It wasn't the silence I savored, but the noise. The endless bickering of crickets and katydids. The bullfrogs croaking with throbbing life. And the others. Weasels. Bobcats. Alligators. You couldn't hear them, but you could sense them prowling just beyond the edges of the manicured estate. Lording over the waterways and underbrush. Hunting in the darkness just beyond what we could see. Out there in the real world. Not in this twenty-acre monstrosity.

Peace.

"Quite a view, isn't it?"

The bobcat would have bared it's teeth. So would the alligator. All little old me could do was clench my glass until it creaked in my grasp. I turned to face the interloper. The man was sweating more than my drink, but he had also put in more effort than most of the other wealthy men gathered inside. He had the look of a former football player (Roll Tide, y'all). About thirty years past his prime, but not going quietly. His teeth were white, his hair was still jet black, and his suit shirt was crimson. A rarity in a crowd where powder blue was considered daring.

He really was sweating, though. It seemed like no matter what you did, everybody in this state couldn't help but sweat constantly and copiously.

Everybody except me.

"Have you been here before?" he asked.

I shook my head. "First time."

His smile widened, and I clearly read the thought burning in his greedy little eyes.

She speaks.

I understood how this could seem like a monumental victory. I was famously mute at these parties and yet here I was, speaking freely with the full moon hanging overhead like my own personal spotlight, leaning against the railing and luxuriating in its light. My lips glowing. My cleavage straining out of my dress as if my breasts wanted to see a little bit of that moonlight for themselves.

And I was smiling at him.

"Matt Bolton," he said. "And you're Pamela, right? Pamela Paxton?"

"Just Pam is fine," I lied.

Matt got more comfortable, settling in alongside me at the railing. "Well, Pam." He sipped at his bourbon. "If you like the view, take my word for it and make sure you accept the invite for the Fourth of July party. Best fireworks display in all of America. Swear on the bible."

"I don't know," I said. "The show over the Hudson River is pretty hard to top."

He shook his head. So, the rumors were true. "A northern gal," he lamented.

"New York born and bred," I said. As if confessing a crime.

He scowled good naturedly. "Well, the important thing is you're here with us now. And I for one am just thrilled to make your... acquaintance," he drawled, deliberately adding a little extra twang to the last word,

"I guess you've been around here awhile?"

"Here in Green Mountain, or here in Haig Manor?" he asked.

"Either. Both."

"Both," he confirmed. "Sid the Third and I go all the way back to when Sid the First was still alive. I've been drinking beer in this house since I was thirteen years old."

My smile curled with a slightly more genuine twist. "I had friends like that once," I said.

"That so? Still keep in touch with any of them?"

Instead of answering, I looked back over the dark estate, tucking a long strand of blonde hair behind my ear with seemingly careless grace.

"Thirteen years old," I said. "What is that for you? A hundred years ago?"

He didn't appear bothered by the jab, which was a point in his favor. His old man's face twisted in a wry grin. "The way I feel most mornings, it may as well have been. I'm not starting power forward for Alabama anymore."

I raised an eyebrow. "Really? Basketball? I would have guessed football for sure."

"My three brothers, my pappy, and my grandpappy all said the same thing. Three generations of Boltons, all of them star receivers. I had the hands for it, but what can I say? We're all born wired for something, and I was built for the basketball court."

I tipped my glass in his direction. "I'll drink to that. To knowing what you're built for."

His glass clinked against mine with careful discretion. A gentle *ting* of glass hitting glass.

"To walking away gracefully," he added.

I tilted my head. "You're not still involved with the game?"

"Would that I could," he said. "These days it's just profit reports and board meetings. A man's got to make money." He sipped again at his own drink. "What about you? What do you do for work?"

I watched his eyes move down my body, and I knew what he was expecting me to say. Model. Influencer. Singer who doesn't write her own songs. But he was smart enough to stay quiet and let me fill in the blanks.

What I did was turn away from him. Turn away from his sly fox gaze and the slim gold band on his drinking hand. Turn back towards the night beyond the railing. To the dark edges of the manicured property and the small shack just visible in the gloom beyond the landscape lighting.

"What's that there?" I asked him.

Matt peered out, following the line of my pointing finger. "That's the chicken coop," he said finally. "This ain't been a working farm for forty years, but Sid still keeps a small clutch of hens on the property. There's no substitute for fresh eggs. No substitute for fresh milk either, mind you, but cows are a mite tougher to keep around."

I wrapped a strand of blonde hair around my finger. "Not too many chicken coops in New York City. Wanna show me around?"

The old fox was only too happy to oblige.

CHAPTER 2

We walked side by side, but Matt never crossed the invisible border between his body and mine. His hand never strayed to the curve of my hip or the hollow above my ass. It would have been easy to look at us walking the grounds and imagine us as father and daughter. A gentle older man with no interest except sharing some local history. We reached the secluded structure at the edge of the grounds and Matt gave the old timbers a hearty smack with the flat of his hand. "They don't make 'em like this anymore," he lectured. "Aluminum is too cheap these days, but I maintain that eggs taste better when they're birthed in God's cedar."

I craned my neck, as if that would somehow let me see inside the coop. "Are there chickens there now? Can we go inside and see them?"

Matt fought to smother a grin. The kind of grin that likes to cross borders and grab some hip. "We're not supposed to," he said. "But I reckon ol' Sid might have a few other things to keep him occupied for the moment." He bent and swept his arm towards the short ramp leading up into the chicken coop as if it were a red carpet. "After you, ma'am."

I hated being called ma'am, but I had other things on my mind. I walked along the slope of creaking beams to the door of the chicken coop. There was no lock. There wasn't even a doorknob. I tugged at a simple iron door pull, fighting nothing but the friction of a swollen door too big for its frame, and stepped into the chicken coop.

I had a moment to take in my surroundings in the dim light – a wooden floor permanently darkened by stamped dirt. A row of empty wooden boxes filled with musty straw against one wall. On the opposite side stood a ladder-like latticework of 2x4 beams hosting a clutch of mottled hens blinking their beady, marble black eyes at this disturbance to their sleep.

Matt's hands touched me then. He pushed, plenty of strength left in the old fella, and sent me stumbling against the row of empty boxes. I caught myself at the last moment, wooden splinters biting into my palm, and then I nearly fell into the box anyway as his bulk enveloped me from behind. I felt his hands again. Under my dress now and working higher.

"Nothing like a chick in the nesting box," he hissed. His whiskey-soaked breath hot and reeking against my ear.

I reached back and caught his wrists. Stopped his hands from going higher, but I laid my touch just right. I wasn't refusing him, I was just... savoring.

I spun around. It was a tight fit, but I managed to lean back in one of the nesting boxes. I grabbed his low hands and brought them higher, let him graze the sides of my breasts, and then pulled them higher still. I nipped at one of his fingertips, tasting the ice off his glass and coaxing out a low, eager moan from his throat.

"Good hands, that's what you said, right?" I asked.

He groaned. I gently kissed the spot where my teeth had left indentations. "Good hands," I repeated. "Is that right?"

Matt nodded. "Yeah. I had the touch. Boards. Steals. I was good. I was very, very good."

I could believe it. Wide palms. Long, nimble fingers. I took one into my mouth and ran my tongue along the length of it. "I'm very good, too," I muttered.

And then I bit down hard. Skin was easy. Meat was easy. Bone would have been hard, but I came down right on the knuckle. Tendons were chewy, but not hard if you knew what to do. I braced against his wrist, pulled back with my teeth, and twisted in a single motion. I felt the finger rip loose before the taste of his blood flooded my mouth.

He did have good hands.

Matt retreated with a shriek and clutched his bloody hand to his suit shirt. Crimson on crimson. There was fear in his eyes at first, but something flipped quickly in his gaze. Anger fueled by his bank balance and memories of his big man on campus glory days. How dare I get blood on his suit after I was lucky enough to get picked for a turn in the nesting box? His hand that still had five fingers coiled into a fist.

"Look at what you did, you sloppy little cunt!" he snarled.

But Matt was too slow on the rebound this time. I had already picked up the other thing I'd noticed before he tossed me around the chicken coop.

I'd gone for the pitchfork.

If Matt saw what was coming through his haze of self-righteous fury, it was only for a moment. I thrust forward with unerring accuracy, skewering his eyeballs on the central tines and gouging a pair of bloody furrows into his temple with the outer points. There wasn't much resistance, not in his eyes and not in the brain meat behind them. I pushed until I felt the back of Matt's skull and then I kept pushing, driving his jittering, twitching body backwards. His feet skittered beneath him, no grace or agility now, but I maneuvered the pole back and forth to keep him vertical until I finally slammed the back of his head against the far wall of the chicken coop. His skull hit against the wood with a *thud* like a Mormon on a mission.

I held him there until he stopped twitching, and then I let go of the handle. Matt swayed on his feet for a moment and then slumped forward with the pitchfork still embedded in his brain. The pole propped him up like a tripod leg, leaving Matt hanging in a grotesque triangle. Perfectly balanced.

The chickens, understandably agitated by this disruption to their evening, raced in circles on the floor, filling the air with errant straw and indignant clucks. A rogue feather drifted in the air, just in front of my face.

"Relax," I said. I puffed out a breath, blowing that lone feather back into the wild from whence it came. "It's just us girls now."

But, ah, what to do with the old fox? I could have left Matt there. I'd have to wipe my fingerprints off the pitchfork, but the way he was propped up made the whole thing look like some bizarre accident. A drunken fall and a freak twist of geometry.

The thing you have to understand is that men of Matt Bolton's status don't get murdered. It makes the rest of the gentry nervous. Better for everyone if it could be swept under the rug as a morbid oddity. The sort of weirdness Anthony would have –

No.

The problem was the finger. The one currently getting pecked at by one of the bolder hens. The severed digit was currently lying so that it was pointing right at me. That felt like bad luck, so I stepped to the side.

The finger complicated things. There was no writing that missing finger off as a freak accident, even if somebody wanted to. I was going to have to move his body.

His *heavy* body.

Carrying him was out of the question. Cutting him to pieces had its own issues. Time and mess. Christ, maybe there was a wheelbarrow or a motorized cart around. There had to be a gardening shed somewhere around here. I truly recognized what a headache this would be at the same moment that I realized exactly how many drinks I'd downed since I walked into this ugly-ass house.

"Oh, Beverly," I muttered to myself. Another bad sign. I only talked to myself when I was drunk. "Oh, Beverly. What the hell are you going to do about this?"

The door opened behind me then with an accusatory creak of old hinges. I spun around at the sound, frustratingly naked with the pitchfork still wedged in my victim's skull.

The newcomer was so tall he had to duck down to enter the chicken coop. "Is this where they're having the after party?" He asked.

Matt had been past his prime. The man who had just discovered me was decidedly still in his. His shoulders stretched the expanse of the open doorway. He was sheer granite muscle muzzled by a Brooks Brothers suit. Hands the size of beer mugs hung at his sides.

There was no chance of lying to him. No hope of deception. His eyes were too sharp – hawk's eyes swiftly digesting every detail before him. The dead man with the pitchfork in his face. The woman with bloodstains smeared across her chin.

He took another step forward. The top of his head brushing the roof of the coop.

A smile cracked across his face. Like a rock thrown through a thin layer of ice over a lake.

"I'm sure I would've gotten an invite eventually," my husband said. "Ain't that right, darlin'?"

CHAPTER 3

————|————

I remember being eighteen and coming over the George Washington Bridge at two o'clock in the morning.

I hadn't planned it that way. At ten PM I was still in northern Maryland and wasted from a full day on the road. I was low on gas, food, and funds. My back ached. My calves hurt. The fucking wig itched like crazy. I needed to call it quits. Sleep a few hours, get something to eat. Cut somebody's throat and take whatever cash they had on them.

Keep moving.

When I started, I had thought this road trip would be fun. Los Angeles to New York. An entire country of open roads laid out in front of me. No schedules or deadlines. Nothing but the freedom to do what I wanted, when I wanted.

And it had its highlights. I watched the sun come up over the Rocky Mountains after driving all night. I stopped in Kansas and shoved a farmer into his own hay baler. I sat outside at a faded wood picnic table and ate Missouri barbecue by the light of an antique coke sign. A few miles later I stopped for a hitchhiker on the side of the road and left him where I found him. I left his head another few miles further down.

There were some valleys to go with those peaks, of course. Nights where I couldn't find a hotel and slept curled up in the backseat. Walking twenty miles to the nearest gas station after the car I'd stolen blew its engine.

But worse than the valleys were the fucking flatlands. Literally and figuratively. Miles and miles of forcing myself to just claw forward for more of the same. No fast forward, no way to skip past the monotony of moving. Seven days of driving, and the book closing on the eighth. I kept long blinking. The humming of tires over asphalt was a tranquilizer that no Top 40 generic rock station could counteract. It was time to pull over before I rammed my car up the ass of an eighteen-wheeler, but I couldn't catch a break that night. I scanned every interstate sign that buzzed by, desperate for a blue "Lodging" sign with a smorgasbord of discount motel logos to choose from, but I kept coming up empty. A match for my hollow stomach, but a marked contrast from the increasingly full state of my bladder.

Nothing.

Nothing.

And suddenly, directly over the highway, there it was. Not an exit sign. Not a lodging sign.

There, racing towards me, larger than life, the sign for the transfer to Interstate 95. Baltimore, 25 miles away it read.

And then, below it, Manhattan… 200 miles.

It had taken me eight days to cover the last 2,700 miles. When I started, an entire nation had stretched between me and the one thing I wanted most in this world. It didn't seem so long anymore. The city, the *life,* that I had chosen for myself, and it was only a mere 200 miles down the road.

Another sign came zooming up shortly after I passed the interstate sign. This one announced that in 2 miles there was a Pinewood Motel, a Khaki Palms Motel, and a Hotel Del Coronado.

I just pushed down harder on the gas pedal and kept moving.

I remember very little of the next three hours on the road. No meal break. No cat naps at a rest stop. Sheer adrenaline kept me wired for the first twenty minutes, but the road works on you after too many hours. I pushed through those final few hours of driving in a soupy fog. I may have been asleep for five-mile snatches here and there.

But I remember reaching the bridge. I'll remember how that felt for the rest of my life.

It came up out of the cloudy night. Nothing but dim lights in the haze and then, suddenly, huge and looming in front of me. And so bright. The lit-up cables, dazzling orange, were like runway lights calling me home.

Welcome home, Beverly.

I needed that. I needed that so badly.

Crossing that bridge, driving over Fort Washington Park and crossing Broadway, it was the first time that the throbbing pain in my left hand went away. That stab wound in my palm had been a constant companion ever since I left LA, flaring up every time I shifted gears or clutched a knife. The bite was more than physical. It was a constant reminder of Alicia. Lyndsay. My parents.

Anthony.

No take backs, that pain said. *If you're wrong about where you're going, there's nothing to turn back to. You made sure of that.*

It was the truth. I'd killed my best friends. I'd killed my parents. I'd left Anthony with nothing except reasons to think I was dead. I'd left the only home I'd ever known and drove to the opposite side of the country, confident that it was the place where I belonged.

But there were nights where that scar hurt more than others. Nights where I lay in a shitty motel bed and my hand screamed at me that if I was wrong then I'd ruined my entire life.

Those doubts all died screaming the moment I crossed the dark waters of the Hudson and finally reached New York City.

The aging Nissan Maxima I'd picked up in Ohio was flirting with empty. I ditched it on West 179th, taking nothing with me but the dark brown wig on my head and my shoulder bag with a few essentials inside. I walked away without a single backwards glance at the car, or the two bodies left behind in the trunk.

I was a New York Girl now.

The first subway station I found was 181st Street. Dirty metal steps and rust flecked green paint. A white number one wrapped in a bright red circle told me what train line I was on.

I made my way down those steps. My same knees working up and down each riser. My California hands sliding along the metal banister, still warm with the touch of thousands of New York strangers.

You're not the same, I told myself. *You're new.*

I made it to the bottom of the stairs. The downtown platform. Twenty minutes until the next train according to the digital schedule board, but that was fine by me. I sat on the uncomfortable wooden bench and soaked in my surroundings. A cavern of brown and beige stone and ceramic tiles. Weathered and dingy, but who gave a shit how it looked? A hundred years later and that stone and ceramic was still there.

Eventually, a dull rumble began to gather in my ears. It got louder as a flare of light appeared beyond the curve at the end of the tunnel. The light was getting stronger too, eventually revealing itself as a single burning flare in the dark of the tunnel.

It was an older train. I would learn in the fullness of time that there were newer ones, polished chrome trains with LED lights inside and digital readouts to tell you exactly which stop you were at, but this was not one of those trains. This was a grinding, laboring battle tank forced to work until its dying moment. Chairs in ugly, alternating shades of yellow and orange. Plexiglass windows cloudy with age and scarred with graffiti scratches. It was a relic. It was an iron behemoth, looking for a place to die.

And it was all mine.

I took a seat in an empty car and stretched my legs out, savoring the rocking motion of the car. Turning my head, I could see the list of stops on a fading sticker overhead. 135th Street. 96th Street. So on and so forth, down and down. On a whim, I decided I would get off at Times Square.

I had the train to myself until 59th Street station. That was when the doors opened, and the girl stumbled on. She was in her early twenties. T-shirt tied high to show off an admirable strip of flat waist. Long, dark hair ruffled with the signs of a long night out. She was swaying a little and had to grab onto one of the poles for balance long before the train started moving again. She seemed most interested in just staying vertical, but her eyes swept past me once and then suddenly brightened and swung back to me for a second look.

"Felicity!? You *bitch*! Why didn't you tell me you were coming to New York!?"

I smiled. "I think you've got me confused with somebody else."

She peered closer, bleary eyes trying to focus, and then she sprayed me with a drunken burst of laughter.

"Oh shit! I'm so sorry, you look just like my best friend!"

I shrugged. "All good."

She sat down next to me, redolent of whiskey, citrus, and vape smoke. Apparently, her feelings towards me had not changed despite having never met me before. "Where are you coming from?" she asked.

"West," I said.

"Hardware Bar?"

"No. All the way west." I tilted my head, nodding past the steel and stone to unseen sand and waves. "California," I clarified.

Her eyes got big. "Are you new? I mean, are you here for vacation or did you just move here?"

A wide smile slunk across my face. I couldn't stop it if I wanted to. "Yeah, I just got into town."

"You're going to love it here," my new friend gushed. "It's such an amazing city. I mean it. Totally fucking incredible. I'm new too. I just moved here from Osh Kosh. Do you know where Osh Kosh is?"

"Can't say that I do."

"Of course not," she said. "Nobody can. Osh Kosh is a fucking hole in the ground. But it doesn't matter because I'm *never going back*. New York is my fucking home and now it's yours, too." She gave my leg a friendly squeeze. "You're going to be so happy here."

My smile got wider. I reached out and stuck a screwdriver in her knee.

She had time to scream once, not that it mattered in the empty subway car, and she didn't have time for a second one. There was a grapefruit-sized chunk of cement in my jacket, carried with me all the way from Ohio. I brought it out and around into her throat with enough force to crumple her larynx like a soda can. The first swing was probably enough, but I added another just to ensure her throat was totally collapsed. She was already turning purple as she sunk to her knees and I got up off the bench.

I guess I was getting off at 50th Street instead.

CHAPTER 4

————|————

I ascended up out of the subway station. It was closer to 4 AM now. The first morning delivery drivers were stirring. The sidewalk coffee carts were prepping to start the day. Their bright fluorescent lights flared unnaturally with dawn still just far enough away to feel unlikely. Solitary, unshaven men played an uneven melody of cutlery and plastic cups as they prepared for the rest of the world to catch up. The humid summer air sweetened with the scent of fresh brewing coffee.

I stood at the top of the stairs, letting it all sweep over me. Los Angeles is built out, not up. There are some skyscrapers dotting the landscape here and there, but for the most part the city spread long and low like creeping moss. It was nothing like this. New York City towered over me. The highest windows overhead were nothing but vague smudges in the sky. I looked at those high windows and found myself feeling like a bug crawling along the trunk of a massive evergreen. My hand went to the cascade of dark hair falling over my shoulders. My wig. I'd traveled this whole way under the cover of this false shroud, worried that even in some godforsaken corner of Tennessee I might be recognized as the missing blonde. Beverly Kilbourne, the only unaccounted victim from what the news reports called the LA Prom Massacre.

Now, under the towering New York sky, it suddenly felt unnecessary. My friend on the train was right. This was my fucking home now. I belonged here. I tossed the wig into the trash and flipped my head back.

I let my blonde mane free to breathe the warm morning air, and I stepped out into my city.

I was hungry. Ahead of me on my side of the street I saw a 7

Eleven, but I hadn't come all this way to eat a taquito. I looked further down. I saw a shuttered shoe store. Then an Italian restaurant with a storefront of glass and polished mahogany.

And there, at the far corner, a towering theatre marquee surrounded by old fashioned halogen bulbs. The massive poster featured two young people staring soulfully into each other's eyes. A woman with pink-streaked hair and a young man with black-rimmed glasses and an olive scarf.

The Bousman Theatre was playing *Lofts.*

I stopped dead in my tracks and fought the shudder running down my back. I spun abruptly and turned in the opposite direction.

Not retreating, I swore to myself. I repeated it again and again.

Not retreating.

————————

I didn't stop walking until I found a deli. Not a part of a chain. Not a convenience store. A cramped NY deli with dirty floors and fluorescent lights badly in need of new bulbs. The cup of coffee I ordered came in a blue, white, and gold paper cup that said it was, "happy to serve you." I took it back to a small, circular table of chipped linoleum and sat on a chair with a cracked red cushion and a dull chrome back. I took a big gulp as soon as I sat down. It scalded my tongue, but that was fine. The pain was grounding. I was here. I was ready to start my new life.

I had a free newspaper from one of the racks out on the street. The Daily Midian. It was one of those alt papers made of flimsy recycled pulp plastered with articles about revolutions in Venezuela, indie band reviews, and dominatrix advertisements. But they also had apartment listings squished between the ads for weed gummies and an hour with Mistress Mary ($125 an hour. Jesus Christ). I was here. I was home. But I also needed to put an address on that.

I ran my finger along the paper, scanning the listings, filtering out the ones outside my price range.

...I did a lot of filtering.

Jesus Christ. I had tried to manage my expectations from the beginning, well aware of how few bloody twenty dollar bills I had in my bag, but this was *bad.* Manhattan was out. Ditto Brooklyn. Queens and the Bronx seemed possible, and it wasn't like I was afraid of rats or bad neighborhoods. I circled a few likely contenders and then went back to the counter for an egg sandwich with Canadian Bacon. I glanced at the clock on the wall behind the counter. It was only 5 AM, way too early to make any calls, so I ordered my sandwich to go and took back to the streets.

I walked a couple blocks down and found a fountain shooting streaks of water up into the lightening sky. It was getting to be real dawn now, orange life rising up at the horizon where pavement met sky. I sat down with my breakfast and enjoyed watching Sixth Avenue blossom to life in front of me.

The construction workers came first. Men in orange and neon yellow t-shirts shaking the sidewalk with heavy boots and tools slung over their shoulders or swaying at hip level. A couple favored me with a leer but, to be fair, my eyes were crawling over them too.

Hammers. Wrenches. Power saws. So many possibilities.

And then the office workers. A legion of them in a city without a highway system to hide their sheer numbers. You wouldn't believe that so many people could exist in one place.

My sandwich was done. I crumpled the wrapper up and swung back to my feet. I stretched my arms over my head, trying to roll out the last of the stiffness from the long drive.

Then, I slipped seamlessly into the current of victims.

I walked among them. Maybe a little slower than the ones looking to be first at their desk, but not so slow as to be an obstacle. Just a beautiful young woman with her long hair pulled back in a sensible ponytail. Not going to a financial firm or a law office, not dressed in jeans and a checkered t-shirt, but maybe an intern at an ad agency or a freshman taking summer classes at Columbia. Another up and comer with places to be and people to impress.

But they'd be wrong. None of those leashes were around my neck.

I was free. I was the predator. Some of these people with their cellphones and briefcases might meet me again after a couple drinks in the middle of the night. Meet me with a butcher knife or a dead carpenter's hammer, and then their deadlines and conference calls wouldn't mean a thing anymore. I was here to do what I was built to do. I was the killer. I was the weapon. I was...

I was outside my mother's New York branch.

I stood outside of 1345 Sixth Avenue. There were a couple corporate logos on the obsidian monolith outside the building, but West & Brundle Pharmaceuticals was easily the largest. As well as it should be, they owned four floors after all. My mom came here about twice a fiscal quarter. You'd think I would have tagged along at some point, but... no. This was my first time here.

I stood my ground this time. I didn't walk away like I walked away from the *Lofts* sign outside the theatre. Or the way I kept switching off the radio in the car every time the Kincaids came on.

I stayed right where I was. I stayed who I was.

I'd killed Lyndsay.

I'd killed Alicia.

I'd killed my parents.

I hadn't killed Anthony, but he was just as gone.

I'd killed them all once. I would kill them as many times as I had to, to live the life I'd chosen.

I didn't care what time it was. I took the burner phone out of my bag and started calling landlords.

———————————

The elevated train took me out to the Queens Bridge. I stepped off the platform and into a section of town that looked like maybe it was starting to turn around but still had a ways to go.

The address I'd gotten over the telephone in broken English was three stories of faded brick clinging to life between an autobody shop and a corner grocery. Narrow windows surrounded by chipping white paint like foam on the mouth of a dying dog. One of them had a hand drawn sign that said, "Apt for Rent." I knocked on the door and the answer was almost instantaneous, as if the landlord had been waiting there ever since I called. The man at the door looked like everything else in this neighborhood. Old and worn down, but still standing because the frame underneath was rock solid. He was short with wide shoulders and graying hair. One of his ears had been raggedly ripped away, crude work in my opinion, but there was nothing wrong with his eyes. He took the measure of me in one casual glance and grunted.

"You call?"

I nodded. "Yeah. For the apartment."

Another grunt. He spun back inside, leaving the door open for me to follow. I trailed behind him up bare wooden steps.

"When you want to move in?" he asked.

"That's the thing," I said, walking fast to keep up. "I'm looking to find a place as soon as possible. I was hoping if I paid cash I could maybe skip the whole thing with the application and the credit–"

"Rent is first of the month," he said. "You pay, you stay. You don't, I change the locks. You try to be cute? Hide in apartment? I know every delivery driver in zip code. You starve first. Fair?"

Y-yes," I said, trying to hide my elation. "That would be fantastic."

Each level only had two doors made out of wood like popsicle sticks. As we reached the top floor, the righthand door opened and a small Hispanic woman came out with a laundry sack over her shoulder. "Morning, Mr. Giallo!" she called.

He grunted in her direction. It was slightly more cheerful than the ones I'd gotten so far. The woman offered me a small smile before scurrying down the steps with her clothes.

The Landlord turned the key in the front door. He let me enter first.

The apartment was totally empty. So empty that my every step echoed off the scratched wooden floors. The rooms were painted dingy white like a stained trash bag. The toilet and the bathtub were mauled by water stains. The bedroom could probably fit a sleeping bag, but it would be a tight fit. It didn't take long for me to lap it and end up back in the living room. There was only one window, covered by curtains thin as peeled skin. The glass behind it was dirty, but beyond that glass, there was a single slice of the Manhattan skyline blooming between encroaching buildings. A dandelion sprouting between concrete.

"I love it," I said.

I handed over the first month's rent in wrinkled tens and twenties, leaving me without enough money for groceries, never mind a couch or a TV. I'd figure it out. In return, I got a pair of tarnished brass keys and the trash schedule. And then that was it. I was alone in my apartment.

My apartment.

I had no chair to collapse in, but I leaned against the wall with my chin up and eyes closed. I slid down along the drywall until my ass was on the dusty floor. My floor. My dust.

It was June 28th. Less than a year ago, this had all been just an idea in my bedroom.

But I had made my choice. It wasn't going to just be an idea. It was going to be my life.

And I had done it. Getting here had been harder than I'd expected, but I had willed it into reality. I had done it – all by myself.

I was in New York. And I was never going to leave.

CHAPTER 5

I woke up to Owen's hand cupping my breast and his teeth gnawing at my neck.

I groaned, but not in the way he wanted me to. My fucking head was killing me. My mouth tasted like swamp mud. I didn't even know what day it was. Trying to open my eyes felt like a task better suited for the next century.

Owen chuckled. His broad hand stayed on my chest, but his urgency lessened to a gentle squeeze. "Did you enjoy the party?" he asked.

I answered with a sound like a pained hyena. "Whyyy..." I cried.

I still hadn't opened my eyes, but I felt my husband shrug. "I told you to slow down. You're not a kid anymore." The bed creaked as he sat up. Then, with cruel disinterest, he casually added, "My mom's going to be pissed at you by the way."

My eyes launched open. I sat up faster than my pounding head could tolerate, but that was no longer the issue. "What do you mean?" I demanded. "What is she pissed about. Why?" Jesus, if I'd blacked out at one of their fucking high society events and offended one of that woman's seven hundred and forty unwritten rules of etiquette...

Owen's normal southern drawl thickened and rose an octave. "Pamela, Matthew Bolton is a dear friend and a pillar of the community," he mimicked.

"No," I said. "No, no, no, no. Are you fucking kidding me!?" I yelled.

"The next time you can't restrain yourself, please think of the rest of us and at least limit yourself to a valet or one of the more deviant

Witherspoon children."

I collapsed down and covered my own face with a pillow. "Oh my God. Why didn't you *warn* me?!"

The pillow was suddenly pulled away from my face. Owen was there, his tussled blonde hair unkempt and hanging over his eyes. "The damage was already done by the time I found you," he drawled. His lips again. Now at my clavicle and kissing lower, "Besides, why would I want to go and spoil your fun like that?"

I pushed him off. "I should just say that you were the one that did it."

"Nice try. I just carried his remains out into the swamp like the gentleman I was raised to be. This is all you, babe."

"Go eat breakfast," I groaned. "I'll be down in a minute."

Owen laughed. "Best to get it over with, eh? I'll see you down there."

The mattress groaned at the loss of his weight. Internally, I groaned too, but I was not so hungover or worried about my mother-in-law that I didn't appreciate the sight of him disappearing into the bathroom. He was so large, so brick-solid, but he moved like his feet were padded with memory foam. I never got tired of seeing it.

I waited until I heard the toilet flush, then I forced myself into the bathroom to make myself halfway presentable. My hair was a disaster area, and I hadn't had the energy to wipe off my makeup after staggering home. I did it now, sweeping away layers of foundation and eye shadow until it was just me staring back from the mirror.

You're not a kid anymore. That was what Owen had said, and there was no pretending that he was wrong. Only thirty, no cause for panic yet, but it was a grown woman's body looking back at me. Not the hot shot kid who'd lived in Queens on a grocery budget of $40 a week. (Dozen eggs and a pack of Canadian Bacon. Loaf of bread, a pound of salami, two pounds of ground beef, pack of cheddar, and a gallon of milk).

Not the kid who thought she had everything figured out. It was an adult-ass woman with all the minor decay that went with it. An adult-ass woman living in Alabama.

I slapped on a cursory layer of fresh makeup and presentable shorts and a t-shirt before going downstairs. I had enough shit to deal with without my appearance coming into play.

I opened the bedroom door and immediately regretted it. The summer sun poured down from the skylight, and my eyes flared up like they were pickled in gasoline. I nearly went back to bed, but there were too many voices filtering up from the kitchen below. There was nothing to do but make my way down into the belly of the beast.

I thought the house I grew up in was big, but Paxton Manor was something else entirely. An ancestral monstrosity dating all the way back to great, great grandfather William Paxton I, who ate a Union cannonball before he ever saw it completed. Our bedroom was on the top floor. Real tallest room in the tallest tower shit. A massive spiral staircase was the only way down. This morning, it didn't do me any favors.

I made it into the living room. A massive cavern of polished, dark wood walls, heavy furniture, and a gigantic stone hearth fireplace. The nearest wall was covered in family photos, plaques for civic engagement, and a mounted antelope head. Tawny fur. Ribbed, black antlers as long as my forearm. Polished, black marble eyes staring blankly ahead. Great Grandfather William Paxton II had brought it home from Kenya and it had been in that spot ever since, a silent witness to decades of celebrations and arguments. Reconciliations and recriminations. Birth and death. Mostly death, including William Paxton II, dragged to death by his favorite horse.

"Wish me luck, Auntie," I said as I passed. I could hear the rest of the family in the kitchen. Their drawls twanging together in perfect harmony. A family band, just starting to warm up.

But the music stopped as soon as I entered the room.

The Paxton family. Gathered around an antique oak table chopped down by Grandpa William Paxton III. A man killed in a card game over a royal flush with two aces.

There were five of them all together. Some of them looked right at me, others pointedly looked anywhere else. For my part, I crossed the kitchen with my head held high and went to the fridge for the pitcher of fresh squeezed orange juice.

"Pam, do you want some bacon?" Reese asked with exaggerated solicitude. "There's plenty."

"I'm okay," I said.

"It's that wuss bacon you like," clarified Luke, the man who looked exactly like my husband but wasn't anything like him. He floated the platter of Canadian Bacon in my direction with taunting solicitude.

I took a deep breath. "I think I'll keep it light, thanks."

"Everyone, please. I'm sure Pamela needs a minute," my mother-in-law proclaimed. That was how Charlize always spoke, loudly and to nobody in particular. Just trusting that her message would get to where it needed to go. "After all, she had a *very* late night from what I understand."

The tension around the table was thicker than the maple syrup on it. Owen and Luke traded snickers behind their coffee mugs. My sisters-in-law were more sympathetic. Reese and Jennifer were both used to similar treatment from their mother for wearing the wrong dress to a party or bringing home a boy unworthy of the Paxton family. Or for killing the wrong person.

I closed the fridge and leaned against the kitchen island, doing my best to look casual. For her part, Charlize tried to do the same. She was a big woman with cheeks like uncooked biscuits and small eyes with pinprick pupils. She was still in her nightgown, but her short, blonde hair was already perfectly coiffed. It looked to me like a small, foreboding mountain range. One that she would be all too eager to push me off.

I lifted my chin with careful poise and a little humility, but not too much. "I apologize, Charlize. If I had known he was a friend of the family…"

"Matthew Bolton was a dear friend and a pillar of the community!" Charlize snapped. She was looking at me fully now. Blue eyes blazing with cold fire. "There is a way things are done here, Pamela. And you've been in this family long enough to know that!"

I didn't flinch, but I didn't snarl back either. There was a deft touch to dealing with Charlize. There was no winning an arms race. If you escalated, she escalated back. But if you rolled over, then she would just keep ravaging you.

"As I was trying to say, Charlize," I continued with patient dignity, "I would never deliberately disrespect the family like that. But Mr. Bolton lured me away from the party, knowing full well that I was married to your son, and made untoward advances on me. With that kind of behavior, how could I possibly have known that he was considered kin to us?"

Charlize harumphed. "I don't see how else a man can be expected to behave when you go out dressed like you do."

But she said it with no real vehemence. She couldn't back down, not in front of her children, but obviously such disrespect to her son couldn't be tolerated.

"You at least disposed of him properly, I hope," she continued.

"Deep in the swamp, momma," Owen piped up. "That's why I left the party early. By the way, I'm going to need some money for a new suit before the Dourif wedding."

She favored him with a look of such fawning. "Of course, my son. We can't have you looking anything but you're absolute best. That's what you deserve after all."

Her gaze pivoted towards me, making sure that I agreed.

I tried to make it clear that I knew exactly how lucky I was.

CHAPTER 6

————————|————————

By 9 AM, a search party was forming to scour the swamp for that benevolent titan of industry, Matthew Bolton. The Paxton family was naturally expected to make an appearance. For my sisters, that meant new outfits. And, obviously, you couldn't go shopping without a few brunch cocktails first. That's how we wound up at the Dixie Pig, overlooking the Conecuh River from an air-conditioned topiary and working our way through our second pitcher of southern champagne.

Reese raised her glass. Holding it up and looking so stupidly elegant that it was a goddamn sin she wasn't on a magazine cover. "To Pam," she toasted. "May she always remain such a shining example of temperance and patience!"

Jennifer hoisted her glass too fast and jerked it to a stop with none of her sister's grace. A generous dollop of bubbly splashed onto our plate of deviled eggs. "Fuck that," she crowed. "To Pammy, may she finally do what we're all rooting for and make a fur coat out of that miserable old wildcat!"

They both drank. Reese, a single, demure sip. Jennifer, draining half her glass in a single swig. I rolled my eyes before taking my own generous mouthful. The morning's headache was already a distant memory. It was hard not to feel good with the sun shining down and Owen's sisters on the other side of the table. I never bothered to use "in-laws" when referring to them. They took me in without question the moment I showed up on their doorstep.

They were opposite sides of the same coin, the two of them. You didn't need to know them for years like I did, you only had to be sitting across from them for five minutes at a brunch table. They were both blonde, tan, and effortlessly gorgeous. But Reese was a magna cum laude who favored black-rimmed glasses and typically kept her woven gold hair restrained in a sensible up-do. She was tall, composed, and never seen with a single hair out of place. Meanwhile, Jen was just as smart but hadn't been inside a classroom since high school. She wore her hair loose in a thick mane that rarely saw a comb and favored grueling workouts that left her arms toned and her legs bound with muscles like firewood. She smiled like a Venus fly trap as she leaned in close to me.

"Owen didn't say," she breathed. "...How did you do it?"

I took a quick look around. The closest table was unoccupied and nobody seemed to be paying us too much attention. "Pitchfork," I whispered. I held up four fingers and jabbed the middle two at my eyes.

Reese favored me with a thousand-watt smile. "You're so bad," she said.

Jen leaned back in the chair. "I love pitchforks," she said dreamily. "Troy Efron in his daddy's barn sophomore year. That was a good party."

"Matthew *was* fun at parties though," Reese lamented.

"Someone else will play the part of him," I quoted, only to receive blank stares in return.

"What?" Jen asked, but Reese's phone pinged before I could elaborate. She snatched it up with compulsive speed and started tapping out a response.

"Ree, it is a Sunday morning and we are in Sunday *mourning.*"

"Matthew was a long-time campaign contributor, Jen. The Senator needs to make a statement."

"He needs to do it now?"

"You don't take breaks when you want to be Governor."

"Or First Lady of Alabama," Jen snickered. Reese scowled at her in return. I had my own thoughts, but kept them to myself. Personally, I thought that Reese was more interested in one day sitting in the Governor's Mansion herself. That would make it a real red state.

Reese took a bite of one of the deviled eggs and made a face.

"Excuse me, waitress!" she shouted, not caring that our waitress was nowhere to be seen. "We need more paprika over here, these deviled eggs wouldn't even make it to purgatory!"

Jen and I locked eyes. Both of us tried not to laugh.

"We should get the check," I said.

"Good point, the lunch crowd is always so loud."

"We also need to get to the search party."

"Oh right, that too," Jen said.

"Let's look at the dresses at Morningside. It's closest."

I laughed. As if they needed new clothes at all. Reese and Jen could show up on the riverbank wearing a dead catfish and every boy in five counties would still fight for the chance to cook it up for them. They had been terrors on the pageant circuit in their younger days. Reese, in particular, could have been Miss Alabama if she had set her mind to it.

But both of them had been free to pursue other passions.

———————|———————

We made it to the search party fashionably late, but not so late that there was any shortage of team leaders jockeying to recruit Jen or Reese to their search groups. I drifted to the side and caught the eye of one of the organizers, a matronly dear in a neon hunting vest, and she huffed towards me. "Pamela, sweetheart, thank you so much for joining us. Every little bit helps." I took her hand, smiling with easy sincerity, as if I had any clue who this woman was. "Of course," I said. "It's what Jesus would do." I cast my eye around, surveying the gathered crowd milking their coffee before setting out into the swamp. "Have you seen my husband?"

The woman pointed towards the edge of the property. "Is that him or is that Luke?" she asked. "For the life of me, I still can't tell those boys apart."

I could. And it wasn't some platitude about marriage or about how you can tell your soulmate apart from anyone, even their identical twin. It was just that the men who wanted to fuck you and the men who were already fucking you just had different energy about them. It was Luke on the riverbank, standing there in a muddy t-shirt and jeans and looking at me like a hungry dog on a leash. And it was Owen emerging out of the swamp in a small outboard boat. He navigated to the edge of the bank and then hopped nimbly onto shore, coming towards us with a look of somber disappointment.

"Still no sign of him, Mrs. Wilson." Ah, Wilson. That's who she was. Owen had grown up with these people and knew them all by name. Seven years later and I still hadn't mastered the trick of it.

Mrs. Wilson sniffed and brushed a tear away from her ruddy face. "Lord forgive me. I'm praying and praying that he comes back unharmed, but half a day later... I just don't see it. I don't understand how such a thing could have happened."

Owen looked appropriately sympathetic. "Matt was a great man, but we both know he enjoyed himself a party. And if you get out to the edge of that swamp without the mind to be careful..." he shrugged rather than finish his thought.

"God willing, I hope that you're wrong, Owen. I hope maybe he just took it in his head to call one of those Ubers and find himself a riverboat casino. I pray he'll be rolling in any minute now with a stack of roulette winnings."

Owen squeezed her hand. "That would beat all, wouldn't it? We'd all be winners then. But let's not give up hope yet." He turned to me. "Pam, I came to get a blowhorn and then I'm gonna check the north tributaries. Wanna come along?"

I matched his earnestness as I nodded and squeezed his arm. "Of course. Whatever I can do."

———————!———————

We didn't open the beers until we were safely away from the other search party volunteers. I lounged in the stern of the boat, watching Owen navigate lazily through the waterway. A light breeze and the tree canopy overhead combined to protect us from the worst of the early afternoon heat. "You ought to be an actor," I remarked. I mimicked his woeful tone. "If you get out to the edge of that swamp..."

"You're one to talk," he came back. "I've seen you bring the house down plenty of times. Are you sure I didn't steal you away from a career on Broadway?"

I watched the algae swirl in the water by the boat. "Too much like work. I think the pace of living here suits me better."

Owen swigged his beer. "It's all too much like work. Pretending to care. Pretending to be like them. Walking around like I'm holding a damn hat in my hand. Bad enough I already I had to do it last night at the party without having to do an encore today."

"Mad at me?" I asked.

He didn't bother to turn around. "No, darlin'. I'm not mad. I think you've got it exactly right. You do exactly what you want, no matter what anybody else thinks."

The waterway opened up into a circular pond. The trees cleared and the noon day sun hit us like a meteor. We floated in an open circle of water. Overgrown trees and swaying tall grass all around us. My own beer was empty and I dabbed a fresh cold one against my forehead before cracking it open.

Owen was still in an introspective mood. "Soulmates are bullshit, Pam, but for the two of us to meet like we did... It's the closest I've ever come to believing in God. You're beautiful, you put up with my family's shit... You are so incredibly, amazingly fucking deadly. I love you, Pamela. You're the best thing I've ever found."

"I'm sorry," I said. "Were you saying something?"

He finally turned around. I'd taken the liberty of removing my top while he was talking. I laid there in the back of the boat, naked except for a pair of jean shorts that barely reached the top of my thighs. I didn't need a mirror to know how I looked with the sun shining in my honeycomb hair and heating my golden skin to the temperature of a warm bath.

Owen came to me. My jean shorts didn't last long much longer.

It was hot. Literally. We were already sweating even before we kissed, his bare chest slipping and sliding against mine. I loved it like this. I loved when heat outside mirrored the heat between us. I screamed at his first thrust. My hands went to his back and twisted into thorns in his flesh.

"Fuck me," I urged. "Fuck me, baby."

Owen obliged. The entire boat shook, but that was nothing compared to the waves crashing inside of me. It wasn't going to take long for either of us. I tilted my head back and closed my eyes, letting the world behind my clenched eyelids turn atomic red as I screamed my ecstasy into the swamp.

"You're the best thing I ever found."

I hadn't expected to find him either.

CHAPTER 7

————|————

It was a real 'meet cute' how the two of us got together.

I was trying to murder him. He was trying to murder me.

We started at a bar. It was my first night out in a month and I was so desperate for a release that I was planning to slaughter the first person that gave me the opportunity.

That first person happened to be a muscular guy in a polo shirt and a camo cap. A guy with dark eyes and a crooked nose who stuck a shot in my hand two seconds after I walked into the bar.

Ten minutes after that, we were making out in his apartment.

Even then, I was thinking it was a shame to kill him so quickly. His mouth was a pool of whiskey and heat that I would have been happy to luxuriate in all night.

But Momma had more important needs to satisfy that night. I had the hook holstered on my rear thigh, the one that wasn't currently rocking back and forth between my new friend's legs. The hook was just about slipped free when I felt the point dimpling against the front of my dress, just above the hip. I briefly glanced down before looking back up into eyes as green and inscrutable as the darkest jungle.

"What kind of knife is that?" I asked. The tapering, triangular blade looked familiar, but the handle was swallowed by his clenched fist.

"It's a Fairbairn Sykes," he said. "Authentically certified from 1944, not a reproduction."

I rolled my eyes. "Oh dear. Am I about to be killed by a fucking History Channel commentator?"

He didn't laugh. "And what's that you've got there?" he asked. He couldn't glance down and see for himself. Not with the hook's metal point digging under his chin.

"Twenty-aught shark hook," I said. The barbed point was under his jaw. The other end of the massive hook curved all the way behind his ear. He looked like he was about to make a phone call.

He laughed as I put a little more pressure on it, just enough to draw a thin stream of blood. "Do a lot of fishing?" he asked.

"Caught you, didn't I?" I shot back.

The knife stayed where it was, but I felt his other hand come forward, underneath the hem of my short dress.

"Were you gonna go straight up into my brain?" he questioned.

I started to shake my head, but his fingers slipped past the lace band of my underwear and the motion of my head shifted to a gentle roll from one shoulder to the other. "No," I moaned. "I was going to stick it under your jaw and then out through your cheek." My free hand moving now too. A little more hassle with buttons and a zipper, but I got where I wanted to be. "And then," I whispered, "Once I had my hook in you... I was going to drag you to that stone counter and smash your head against it. Again. And again."

I stroked faster. So did he. "And what about you?" I questioned. "Were you going to cut me from hip to hip?"

"Diagonal," he groaned. "Hip to tit. You would have poured out all over this floor."

"Sounds like fun," I breathed.

"It is," he panted. "But you already know that, don't you?"

Yes," I said. And then, "Yes! YES!"

I surged forward against him, kissing and panting as he groaned into my ear and clutched me tight as he started to shake and spasm. The knife had broken skin. Warm blood coursed down my thigh. Something else hot and wet filled my hand.

That was just the opening act. We blazed a path to his bedroom, trailing discarded shoes, clothes, and killing tools along the way.

The rest of that first night with Owen passed in a warm haze better than any high. They say you're supposed to remember every second of a night like that. You're supposed to be able to look back years later and see every moment as clearly as if you were living it all over again. That was how it had been for me the first time with... before.

But this was different. This was a perfect blur. A beautiful, thick haze that sent the whole world out into the hallway to wait patiently until I was ready for it to exist again.

There was sex, yes. God, again and again. But we also talked about first murders and favorite pizza places. We debated the savage power of chainsaws versus the precise intimacy of a good slicing knife. We talked details that I'd never had anybody in my life to share with.

"I like to go by the East River," I said, laying against his chest at two in the morning. "Yeah, I'll do bars sometimes. But my favorite thing to do is be by the water at like 4 AM. You ever watch a corpse float away? It's peaceful."

"I know the feeling," he said. "But that's gotta be slim pickings by the water. You could go to any midtown bar and get your pick of sniffing dick in five seconds."

"Sure, that's always there. Doesn't mean I always feel like choking on beer breath and 'fleek' last words either. I've got more tricks than a short skirt, you know. I can stalk and ambush just fine."

He favored me with a look I would come to know well. It wasn't quite a smile, more of a twitch of wry, tomcat amusement. "So hard to be taken seriously as a *sexy* serial killer," he teased.

I reared up and slapped him in the chest. "Don't give me that! Like you're any better with your shoulders, and your eyelashes, and your fucking *drawl*!"

"You like my eyelashes, darlin?" he asked.

I straddled his torso and pretended to smother him with a pillow.

Of course, then I was straddling him, so we stopped talking for a while.

A little while later, sweaty and absolutely de-boned, I glanced out the window and saw the first glimpse of coming light.

"I've got to get home," I said. "Cat's gonna need breakfast."

Owen sat up. "You mentioned the river. Only rivers I know are back home. Want to show me yours sometime?"

I shrugged. "I might."

I did.

I came to New York expecting to be completely alone. Then, I expected it to be just me and Cat.

I never dreamed that my life would have somebody like Owen in it.

It wasn't just the killing. New York is full of people who kill because they're angry or greedy or desperate. Criminals and psychopaths who killed as a means to an end or because their meds weren't right. But Owen was like me. He understood.

"We're built for it," he told me one night. We'd made friends with an investment banker who'd invited us up to his apartment for some blow. We'd taken a little to be polite, and then we took his heart out of his chest. We were together in the dead man's shower, washing off his blood, when I asked Owen the question that I'd never had anybody to ask before.

"You ever wonder what makes us like we are?" I thumbed some stray white grit from my nose and let it rinse away with the blood staining my arm. "Why couldn't we just snort some coke, double team him, and call it a night?"

"Because we weren't built for that shit," Owen said. He answered immediately. No hesitation or consideration. "A thousand years ago we would have been Viking warriors cutting heads off on the battlefield, and we would have been celebrated for it. You could have been a queen and I would have been your king. We were just born in the wrong time is all."

———|———

Months later, I dreamed of what Owen said. I dreamed my hair was behind me in braids and I was on the field of war with a battle axe. Men fell before me in never ending waves of blood. I hacked through bone and slashed open meat and veins. I killed and killed until my furs were drenched in red and when I was done; the people saw me for what I was and they cheered my name. I sat down to a feast and nobody averted their eyes from the bloody axe leaning against my chair. Instead, they looked at it with something like worship.

I woke up feeling exulted. I woke up with the warm afterglow of knowing what it was like to be seen and loved for exactly what you were.

And then I threw on my winter clothes and went to work.

It had snowed three days earlier, but the temperature was finally high enough to start turning the mounds of ugly, dirty snow into puddles of frigid, grey soup trying to seep through my boots and drench my socks to wet rags.

I showed up to work in a foul mood, but my client didn't seem to mind. It was hard to tell of course, because he was already wearing a ball gag when I let myself in with the key he'd left out for me, but his eyes lit up with fervent worship as I sauntered into the living room and dropped my overcoat to reveal a black leather corset and fishnet stockings. The scowl never left my face, but the fervent mumblings from behind the apple-sized chunk of plastic wedged between his lips told me that I looked just fine to him. If anything, he appreciated the extra savagery I threw into every swing of the paddle.

At least one of us was enjoying it. I slammed the studded piece of wood against his bare flesh again and again, but there was no *thunk* of steel through skin. No gush of hot blood, no matter how hard I beat him. I threw everything I had into it and received nothing in return.

My client obviously didn't feel the same way. He was strung up like a slab of beef at a meat packing plant, his arms stretched over his head and hanging so high that his toes barely touched the cashmere rug. He groaned and writhed with every blow, squirming in his shackles like a silkworm on the string.

"More," he mumbled through the gag. I had no idea what he did for a living, but I recognized a gold Rolex when I saw one. "More!"

You want more? I'll give you more.

I laid into his flabby ass again and again, but I knew all too well that there was no real damage being done. I needed to bring the paddle down on top of his skull was what I needed to do. Or smash the narrow end into his trachea and watch the eyes bulge out of his head as he struggled to breathe. Even his ribs. Enough damage would break bones and drive the jagged edges into his lungs until he died choking on his own blood.

Not if you want to make rent.

Of course. I gave this man what he paid for. Savagery that tasted like twenty-year-old scotch to him, but curdled in my throat like warm Coors. At least I didn't need to hide my disgust as I took the crumpled wad of bills and left his penthouse.

That dominatrix ad in the Midian had been prophecy. I had no ID. No social security number. I had managed to get a job as a waitress at a diner willing to overlook those details, but the tips barely covered the costs for the subway, never mind rent. I needed to get creative if I was going to survive, but all this time later that's all I was doing. Surviving.

I stopped for a cup of coffee between appointments. The same blue coffee cup, no longer so magical after five years. I sighed and fixed the buttons on my coat, making sure none of my leather outfit peeked through. There were no conversations, complimentary or otherwise, that I felt like dealing with.

I had two more appointments before I could go home. Mistress Julie, that was what they called me. I hurt them. I made them afraid. I made them feel less than human. I put them through suffering like nothing they'd ever known and they paid me very handsomely for the privilege. It was the closest thing I could find to making a living with the gifts I'd been born with, and I hated every second of it. I felt like a tiger playing with a ball of yarn.

I nearly lost control once. Took a man's finger off during some razorblade play. I thought I'd have to kill him. But if the $500 tip was any indication, he seemed fine with the situation. But still, I recognized that I'd gotten lucky. Missing appendages wasn't the job. The job was playing softball.

I took another sip of coffee from the "Happy to Serve You" cup and tried to shake the soreness out of my arms after twenty minutes of treating some rich asshole like a batting cage. I was tired of it. I was tired of New York in general, really. I didn't want any more pizza. I didn't want to fight for space in the subway. I didn't want any more winter, period. I'd never actually lived this far north, and I'd learned quickly that there was nothing fucking magical about trekking through grey snow up to your knees.

It had all seemed so easy five years ago. I'd chased this life and I made it happen. Like every other idiot eighteen-year-old, I believed that would be the end of the story. Dream achieved! The End! Roll Credits!

But then another day happens. And another. Until eventually it seemed more and more like I didn't know why I was even bothering to stay here.

That was why I asked Owen to come over that night.

"Tell me again about your family," I said. "Your home."

Owen swigged from his beer. "Green Mountain, Alabama. Forests. Swamps. Plenty of fresh air so long as you stay clear of the bleach factories. The Paxton's have lived there for over two hundred years. Hunting. Fishing."

"Killing," I said.

He regarded me carefully. Took a second, more cautious, sip from his drink. "Yeah. All the way back to great, great grandpa William. Lumber made us our money, but murder was always the family business.

"The whole family?" I pressed. "No conscientious objectors? Nobody abstains?"

"There may have been one or two white sheep over the years, but none in this generation. Me. Momma. My twin brother. Both sisters. Killers all."

"No judgment?"

He laughed. "Oh no, there's plenty of judgment. Get sloppy with an axe or leave a co-ed screaming for too long and you'll catch holy hell for it. Nobody in my family is shy."

"Is that why you came to New York?"

"No," Owen said firmly. "I left just to get some space for once in my life. I've spent the last twenty-five years surrounded by the same four people. Nobody works. We all live in the same house. We eat together. Sleep together. Not like that," he said, catching the amused smirk on my face. "But yeah, we do kill together. My entire life, I've never seen anything that the same four people didn't see at the same time. I came here so I could see some things by myself. Make my own experiences. But I always assumed eventually I'd want to go home."

He reached out to squeeze my knee. Looked me dead in the eye.

"But you know that the old saw about assumptions and asses. I want to be wherever you are. If that means dying without ever seeing Green Mountain again, that's fine by me."

I didn't flinch away from his gaze. I laid my hand over his. "I've made some assumptions of my own over the last few years too, Owen," I said. "I assumed I'd never want to leave this city."

He got it. I saw it immediately in his eyes, but he worked to maintain his reserved composure. "How do you mean?" he asked.

"I mean maybe New York isn't everything I thought," I said. "I had my time here, I did what I wanted to do… and maybe now that's done. Maybe it's time to think about someplace else. Or maybe someone else."

He moved closer to me. "That so?" he asked. "Anyone I know?"

"Shut up," I said. "Would you do it?"

Again, that bare hint of a smile. "With you? Absolutely. But you better be sure before I tell my momma her baby boy's coming home."

I answered by kissing him.

CHAPTER 8

———————|———————

I smelled the smoke coming off the fire. Applewood and the lingering vestiges of roast sausages. There was a speaker nestled between some stones at the edge of the fire. Country music, naturally, but at least it was a deep cut and not more pop bullshit about pickup trucks and solo cups.

The real music was the sounds accompanying the speaker. Ice shuffling in a cooler. Can tabs popping open. Laughter and happy chatter.

There were six of them, evenly split between boys and girls. Tennessee license plates on a crew cab pickup. Three tents, even though they all could have fit into one if they wanted to. Not hard to do the math there, but hard to blame them for it. They were a good-looking bunch of kids. Athletic boys with cutoff sleeves and tan muscles. Girls with fantastic figures squeezed into five-inch shorts and t-shirts that fit like saran wrap. One of the girls wore a leather crop jacket for a little extra style.

And they were all happy. So extremely and clearly relishing one of the finest nights of their young lives. I watched them and imagined what they were doing out here. Early May, probably college graduates. Maybe they were out here on a celebratory camping trip. Given the relaxed chemistry between them, it was easy to imagine the group of them forming up freshman year and locking each other up tight. Inseparable.

But maybe not forever. Maybe this was it for them. Maybe the boy with broad shoulders and the Craven University t-shirt was going to a brokerage firm in New York in the fall. Maybe the blonde with the amazing tits and the bookish glasses was going to Florida. The boy with the cute dusting of freckles had a position in daddy's construction company waiting for him. This may have been the last time they would all be together.

But that was a problem for another day. Tonight, they were here in a circle. There was beer. There was music. There was each other.

There was Luke, and a length of chain as thick as my wrist.

He went for the blonde with the glasses. Luke always went for the blondes first. He whipped the chain horizontally, smacking into her skull with a sound like a truck collision. The chain kept going, completing a half wrap around her head. Smashing skin, bone, and those clever little glasses all to pieces. She pitched to the side, pouring blood into Craven U's lap. He screamed and fell backwards over the log, inadvertently throwing Blondie off his lap and into the dirt. Freckles lunged over to check on her. The world had come apart too quickly for him to truly understand what had happened. The flying chain and the spray of blood were too much for him to process that quickly. The most important thing was his friend. His friend had suddenly fallen over. His friend must have had a seizure or something. His friend needed help.

"Brandy!" he yelled. "Did you-"

She didn't. And he didn't either. Owen answered first. He was suddenly there at the fire with them too. He had a massive earth auger. A t-shaped cross bar and a long, swirling drill shaft of black steel. There was no sound as the tool sprung to immediate life, just that leg-sized corkscrew spinning into a silent, deadly blur before Owen plunged it through the boy's back. The kid screeched, but he wasn't alone for long. The others were up now. Screaming and tripping over themselves to get as far back as possible.

Owen kept going. He shoved the boy facedown into the ground and kept pushing until the drill broke through his chest and into the earth, kicking up blood and soil as Owen screwed him down like a garden stake.

Panic set in then. The remaining four of them scattered, screaming like and flailing like birds with a wildcat in their midst.

Two boys and two girls left. I had my eye on the boy with the long auburn ponytail trailing behind him as he ran, but Reese beat me to it.

Not that she's faster, mind you, but it turned out to be a damn shame for me that we didn't have an archery team at Robert Englund Memorial. As he ran, Reese sprang up from behind one of the tents with an arrow already notched. She pulled back on her compound bow and let the first shaft fly without even seeming to really aim.

A running target in only firelight and Reese made it look effortless. One in his gut, just for fun. And then a second arrow through his mouth just as he tried to scream.

I put my disappointment aside quickly. There was a redheaded girl stumbling and staggering at the far side of the fire, making her way away from the campsite and into the dark refuge of the woods as fast as she could. Which is, to say, not very fast at all. I'd watched this girl kill half a handle of Bacardi by herself. There was no terror in the world that could sober her up quickly enough. I paced her from the shadows, running alongside her through the screen of trees, trusting my body to avoid root snares and gopher holes. I drew even with her first, and then I pulled ahead. I cut around a tree and stepped smoothly out of the darkness and into her path.

She saw me coming. Her face was only shadows in the backlight of the fire, but I saw it in her body language. The desperate, last-minute attempt to slow her momentum before she was in my grasp. Her feet skidding through the dirt.

It was too late. I swung my machete like a baseball bat. The blade and her chest came together with the momentum of a head on car crash. Blood flew from her mouth with propulsive force as I chopped through ribs and deep into her lungs. I yanked back with the blade, equally smooth, and drove it up and under through her gut. I didn't need to check to know she was dead. I left the machete where it was and turned back to make sure the family was in control.

I didn't have to worry. Jen had already taken down the leather jacket girl. She had her prey face-down in the dirt and she had a flaming log in one hand, the makeshift torch casting alternating light and shadow over her snarling grin as she brought that flaming log down onto the other girl's head again and again. Bashing and burning with every blow.

Craven U was the only one still standing. While my family was butchering his friends, he had made a mad dash for the truck. I saw him fling open the passenger door and scramble over into the driver's seat. Through the windshield I watched him fumble frantically in the cup holders and yank down the visor, searching desperately for the keys.

He should have looked in the back seat.

I saw a pained grimace wipe the fear away from his face. The Craven University shirt stretched away from his chest, stretched and then split open, sending a spray of blood across the glass and blocking my view of the interior in a red privacy curtain.

The back door opened a moment later and Mama Charlize lumbered out, huffing for breath the entire time. The bloody alligator harpoon in her hand now doubled as a walking stick.

"Boys, one of you come help your mama," she said.

Owen dutifully came to her side. He took an elbow and carefully helped her navigate the shadowy path to the fire.

The rest of us focused on cleaning up. Reese retrieved her arrows. Luke methodically coiled the chain back up around his arm. Shifting the auger into reverse, I muscled Owen's drill out of the corpse and the earth. The tool hummed and the long shaft stuttered, refusing to exit the flesh as willingly as it drilled through it.

"Alright with that, Pam?" Owen asked.

"I'm fine," I grunted, earning a couple chuckles from around the fire as the auger finally came loose from the coffee-can sized hole in the teen's back.

"I could use a hand!" Jenn huffed, dragging the cooler of beer a little closer. Luke obliged her without missing a beat.

Moving the corpses took a little more time, but we got it done together.

I sighed as I sat down on a long log and sidled up next to Owen. Jen tossed me a can of beer from the dead kids' cooler. I caught it and cracked it open. I lost about half the can in a spray of suds, but who was keeping track? There was more where that came from.

While we spread the beers around, Luke busied himself skewing a row of sausages onto a scavenged arrow.

"Asshole!" Reese yelled. "Don't stick my arrows in the fire!"

"You're the one who forgot the skewers!" Luke shot back.

"Hush, both of you," Charlize scolded. "Luke, don't take your sister's things. There must be a dozen sharp points in that truck of yours. Pick the one you like the least and bring it over before I get so famished, I start gnawing on one of these poor souls on the ground here."

Grumbling, Luke retreated back to his own truck, parked a few hundred feet off in the underbrush.

I tuned out his muttering and teased Owen about trying the electric auger for the first time instead of gas. "Isn't it so much nicer when things just *start*? No screwing around with a ripcord or primer?"

Owen rolled his eyes in return. "I still say it doesn't drive the same."

"Oh my," I said with exaggerated surprise, "Are you trying to claim that the motion matters more than power when it comes to drilling?"

Reese blanched. "Keep that talk in the tool shed, please."

We all laughed. Even Mama Charlize. Luke returned with the sausages spiked on a stray post of iron fencing, the tip still spotted with dried blood. There were no objections as he squatted by the fire, slowly rotating the meat links over the flames.

We settled into companionable silence. No sound except for the crackle of the fire. I leaned against Owen, and he put his arm around me. I sighed and nestled in amongst the red stains on his shirt, enjoying the warmth from the fresh blood and the live chest below it.

My angle was across from Mama Charlize and slightly to the side. A good angle to watch her without being seen in return. She sat there on a log stump with the harpoon leaning between her thick legs. The firelight captured the beginning of creases in her cheeks and around her eyes, the shadows deepening them to the ravines they would become as she grew older. It struck me that her eyes looked more engaged than the others'. The rest of us were lazing, sleepy and content in the warmth and the growing haze from the beers. Mama Charlize's eyes were still sharp, roving the circle of her children. Taking everything in, down to the last sparking from the fire.

She's memorizing this, I realized. *This is a night she never wants to forget.* And I saw it wasn't just firelight burning in her eyes. It was pride.

"Pamela," she said casually. "Would you mind getting me a beer?"

I shrugged. "Sure, Mama." I played it cool as I got up, but I caught the barely concealed giggle from Reese and Jennifer. This might as well have been my fucking coronation. I retrieved the can and brought it back across the campsite, maintaining a veneer of casual ease, but inwardly cautioning myself. Don't drop it. Don't shake it. Oh God, what if she didn't actually want a beer?

But I kept all of that to myself. I stood in front of my mother-in-law and held the icy beer out for her to take, and Mama Charlize took the can with the same refined ease.

"Thank you, dear," she said. She smiled.

SHE SMILED.

I only nodded in return, not trusting myself to speak. I retreated back to my spot next to Owen. He added an extra squeeze to my knee as I sat down.

"It really is a shame we couldn't throw you two a proper wedding," Reese said. "If nothing else, the pictures would have been gorgeous."

I felt Owen shrug. "Not our style," he said.

Plus, I technically don't exist. What they knew about my past was a lie, but some details were the same. In both fact and fiction, I was legally considered dead. Not exactly a candidate for a major society wedding.

"Yeah, I know. I'm just saying that it would have been a good one." Her eyes took on a dreamy sheen. "I do love weddings. The food. The decor."

"The bridesmaids," Luke piped in, overlapped by Jen saying,

"Groomsmen," at the same time. The two of them subtly touched knuckles.

Reese ignored them. "What do you think you would have picked for a first dance? Do you know?"

I threw a hand over my eyes. "Oh, God."

"Come on," Charlize prodded. "You must have talked about it."

We had. I saw Owen smother a grin, and I wasn't the only one to see it.

"You have!" Jen pounced. "Spill it!"

"All right," I relented. "If we had a real first dance, it would have been *New Old Word* by The Five."

"I don't even know who that is," Charlize said. "Wouldn't it be better to pick something classic?"

"Most people don't know them," Owen said. "They were this weird little rock band out of Texas. They broke up a bunch of years back. "

"Didn't a bunch of them get shot?" Jen asked.

Charlize brightened. "Now *that* I remember!"

"It's not a romantic song," Owen said. "But Pammy played it for me one night and it said a lot about what it felt like before we met each other. There was an old world."

I squeezed his hand. "And now there's a new old world," I said.

To my surprise, Reese hummed a few high bars.

"Welcome to the world and everything in it," she sang in a slow, high voice.

I couldn't hide my amazement. I knew she could sing, but never thought in a million years that Reese, Miss Teen Alabama turned State Senate aide, would know some obscure rock band's final song.

But apparently, she did. *"You might be in a place where the old skin won't fit. You might feel as worthless as a cup of spit."* She sang on, weaving a spell around the circle. The lyrics rose up, mixing with the sparks from the fire and flying to the stars above.

Owen shifted beside me, rising up to his feet. He held a hand out to me and I took it wordlessly. He lifted me up until we were looking at each other in the glimmer of the fire. He gripped me gently by the waist. I crossed my wrists behind his neck. We swayed together in the firelight, occasionally stepping over a sprawl of dead legs. Owen's arms around me felt secure as iron. It felt like we were the only people in the world, even as I was aware of Reese and Jenn's warm gazes as they watched us. Even Mama Charlize cracked a smile.

"So welcome to the world and everything that's in it.
It'd be a poor old world, described in four minutes."

But it was good that they were here. That was why weddings had guests. You were alone, and then you weren't anymore. You were a part of something new. Something new and something old.

"Today the new old world
Was the old world
Today the new old world."

A family that I never thought could exist. A family with blood on their hands. Sisters. A mother.

A brother-in-law who scowled and ripped a chunk from sizzling sausage with his teeth.

"Try and try, grow and thrive,
Because no one gets out of here alive.
Try and try, grow and thrive,
Because no one gets out of here alive."

They clapped when we kissed.

————————|————————

We drove home a few hours later. Across state lines from Tennessee back to Alabama. We couldn't take trips like this often, wholesale massacres were flashy like that, but I never felt as fine as I did on the drive back home from a family slaughter. All of us together, four or five hours in the car with bellies full of beer and hot meat. Some people caught a few hours' sleep, but I always stayed up to watch the sky turn pink and purple as the sun struggled to climb over the Cumberland Plateau.

It was cloudy this time, the forecast threatening rain, but that was its own kind of beauty. And the storm was kind enough to hold back on our account. The thunder had only just begun to rumble in the distance as we crunched over the red dirt road leading up to Paxton Manor.

We got out of the truck, risking the rain to stretch our joints in the cool morning air. The sisters lugged the empty cooler inside. Owen helped Mama Charlize get inside while Luke gathered up the weapons. They would need to be washed in water and bleach before getting put away.

I went into the house, but not up to our bedroom. I stopped one floor lower and cautiously poked my head into the bedroom there. Cat was still asleep. I crept inside and ran a hand along her back. The window was open as the thunder growled louder and the first sprinkling of rain started to fall. I reached across her sleeping form and gently pulled the window closed.

I didn't want my daughter to get wet.

CHAPTER 9

I set the pregnancy test down alongside the others. A pink plus sign glared back at me from each one. Identical triplets.

Don't speak that shit into the universe.

I sat down on the toilet and pressed my fingers into my eyes. I wasn't surprised. I knew my body. I knew something was wrong weeks before I was late; this just confirmed it. I heaved a heavy sigh that echoed back at me off the ceramic tiles. Alone in my cramped, shitty apartment bathroom.

Except that was the problem. I wasn't really alone, was I?

I could be though. I could be alone again very easily if I wanted to be.

That was true. There wasn't anything stopping me. I'd gone with Lyndsay to the clinic once before. I certainly wasn't "pro-life" by any definition of the term. This early on, a pill and a glass of water was all it would take to put my life back onto the track I wanted.

The bathroom felt too cramped. I went to the kitchen and fixed myself a salami sandwich. There wasn't much else to eat, money was tight and dead men's wallets weren't going to keep me going forever.

It's going to be even tighter with a baby to feed.

Absolutely right. To say nothing of time. My first three weeks in New York had been everything I hoped for. So much to see. So much death. A screaming baby would put an end to all of that.

I knew what the right thing to do was. I knew what the smart thing to do was.

But the need wasn't there.

I understood need. I knew what it felt like to have something pounding in your blood; an urge demanding to be satisfied. Something that wouldn't stop screaming inside your head until it had what it wanted. That was the feeling I'd built my entire life around. The need to kill. The need to leave Los Angeles. The need to be free.

The need to feel Anthony inside of me.

Anthony. It was his baby, there was no doubt about that.

It was Anthony's sperm, another voice weighed in. *He's not changing diapers anytime soon.*

I finished my sandwich and laid down on my meager twin mattress. No money for a frame yet. I laid there and saw Anthony more clearly than I had in weeks. His ruffled hair. The glasses that never sat quite properly on the bridge of his nose. The way he would look at me. First, with almost superstitious awe that we were together. Then, later, with more confident satisfaction. I was incredible. I was otherworldly. I was untouchable.

And yet, he could. I let him inside of me in ways that I never let nobody else. I wanted him for reasons I had never wanted anybody else. His stupid little wordplays. His weird taste in music.

"They're called The Five. For the record, I liked them before somebody started killing them. Goddamn tragedy what happened. They could have been big if they stayed together."

I had never reflected on what we had together. I was just inside of it, content to luxuriate in the knowledge that I had found somebody unlike anybody else I had ever met. Somebody special.

But not special enough to keep.

…But would it be so bad? Experimentally, I touched my flat stomach. Yes, Anthony was gone, but would it be so terrible to keep a part of him with me?

A part that screams and eats and shits? A part that needs to be taken care of 24/7? Are you going to wear a baby bjorn while cutting some drunk's head off in an alley? How does that work, Beverly? Please tell me, because I'm genuinely curious.

I didn't know. But what I felt now was the need to find out.

It could very well turn out to be a disaster. I had no illusions about that. Trying to live my life with a baby in tow could be absolutely fucking catastrophic.

But, in the end, the reason I decided to chance it was that pregnancy didn't come with the same stakes for me that it did for other people.

Permanence. That was the fear for most people. "Don't get pregnant," their parents warned. "Don't get pregnant. You'll be living with the consequences for eighteen years."

But me? I could be pregnant as long as I wanted. I could be a mother for as long as I wanted.

And, if at any time I decided it wasn't for me, I could end the situation just as quickly.

It wouldn't even take me eighteen seconds.

———————

I wouldn't call pregnancy fun. By the end I was moving around like a blimp full of ball bearings. My feet hurt constantly. I got Carpal Tunnel Syndrome for some fucking reason. My skin itched constantly and I ate twice my weight in pickles. Axes, machetes, wrenches, anything that required any kind of wind up was a lost cause. I had the turn radius of an eighteen-wheel truck, so I stuck with knives and stabbing implements for the last few months.

But I endured.

I gave birth in my apartment with the aid of some charity organization doula. I called upon my skills as Robert Englund Memorial's finest actress to conjure up a passable Slavic accent and let the agency fill in the details. Poor little undocumented immigrant girl, scared to go to the hospital. They also helped with the birth certificate without asking for any identifying documents.

When the time came, my water broke at four in the morning. Fourteen hours of pushing, sweating, and screaming later, along came

Catherine Kilbourne.

Cat.

The first thing that struck me about her was how little she cried. By the time she was swaddled and handed over to me, the baby was already silent. She just stared at me. This tiny little face peering out from a knit cap and a cocoon of blankets. Dark brown marbles for eyes, peering intensely at me, trying to take in the measure of this woman with the splotchy red face and the tangled mess of blonde hair. No tears, but her small lips were twisted skeptically to the side. *You're what I got, eh?*

Anthony's eyes. Anthony's dubious twist of the mouth.

The doula left, and then that was it. Me and Catherine.

I bathed her. I nursed her. I put her to sleep.

And I went out. I worked. I murdered. I was still who I was. If I was going to be gone all day, I had Senora Rodriguez across the hall keep an eye on her. If she was asleep and I was only going to be gone an hour or two, I left her in crib. I'd go out, have a few drinks, slit someone's throat, and come back home. Most of the time she was still asleep. Other times, she would be crying with her little fists clenched up like rubber balls. If that was the case, then I picked her up. I changed her diaper if I had to, and then I rocked her until she fell asleep with her cotton-soft cheek pressed against my shoulder. No harm, no foul.

That was our life. Milk and murder. Snuggles and slashings. Once she outgrew the crib, I'd sometimes come back at two in the morning and find her sitting in the living room. Dark brown curls around her ears, studiously looking through a picture book she wasn't old enough to read yet. Her eyes would light up the second I came through the door. "Mommy you back!" she'd exclaim, and toddle over to me on chunky little legs. If there was a spatter of blood still on my cheek, she never mentioned it. All she wanted was a hug and a kiss before agreeably going back to sleep in the tiny bed I'd gotten off Facebook Marketplace.

Once she was three and talking in sentences, I started to look for signs my own mother didn't know to look for. Signs that maybe she was like me.

There was nothing. She used plastic play-knives for spreading imaginary butter. She asked me to read her stories about bunnies and princesses and whimpered at even the kiddiest of Halloween stories. She never so much as pushed another kid on the playground.

She wasn't one of us.

It didn't bother me. I was born a murderer, and all I wanted was the freedom to be that person. Catherine wasn't the same as me, but she would find her way in time and I would give her the freedom to become that person, whatever that meant.

She was five when Owen came into her life. Watching them meet was like putting a wolf and a juniper bush in the same enclosure. Not predator, not prey, just two living things coexisting and not giving a single, solitary shit about each other. They occupied different parts of my life, and that was how they both wanted it.

Two years later, I brought up the idea of moving to Alabama and Cat just shrugged. "More room would be nice," she said. "And it's good weather for growing."

The last thing to take care of was Owen.

"She's not like us," I told him. "And that's the end of it. We don't talk about it around her. We don't let her know what we do. And we never, ever, kill in front of her. Not you, not your family, nobody. Promise me or it's over right now."

Owen held his hands up. "She's your daughter," was all he said.

My daughter.

———|———

She woke up about three hours after we got back from Tennessee. Most of the family had gone to sleep after the long night, but I never needed much sleep. I was cracking open some eggs when Cat came down the steps, already wearing her glasses and still blinking sleep from her eyes.

"Hey, mom."

"Morning, Cat." I didn't bother asking if she was hungry, I just added a couple extra eggs into the bowl. "How'd you sleep?"

"Fine. How was the race?"

Nascar. That was excuse we gave Cat whenever we planned a killing trip, knowing that she absolutely wouldn't want to come because she "saw enough circles in geometry."

"Slow," I replied.

She grinned at me. A cracked, amused smirk that still caused an ache of memory that I pushed to ignore. "Were there any right turns?" she asked.

I laughed. The pan was hot enough. I poured in the mass of scrambled eggs and listened to the immediate crackle of yolks sizzling.

"There's a Lunch and Learn at the botanical gardens about native perennials today," she said. "Can I go?"

The botanical gardens were a 40-minute Uber away. The twelve-year-old girl thought nothing of asking to go by herself. That was our relationship. Cat knew she was free to chase what she wanted, and I knew that she was smart, confident, and cautious enough not to get into trouble by herself.

And if she wasn't, then that was her problem.

But the rain had already moved along, and the sun was glistening off the mist in its wake. There were worse ways to spend my day than strolling among the early summer blooms.

The eggs were about done, I divvied them up onto a pair of nearby plates.

"Mind a little company?" I asked her.

Cat shrugged. "Sure. If you want to."

I set out a plate. Sat besides her.

"Sounds good to me. Eat up."

We ate in silence. She had a Loretta Sage book she was working through, and I was content to drift along mentally. Life was good.

"Are you gonna drive?" Cat asked.

"Gotta earn my keep somehow. What do you think? Wanna take the Cadillac?"

"How about the Raptor?" another voice cut in.

Luke sauntered into the kitchen. No blood, thank God. But he was still sooty with campfire smoke and dirt. He leaned on the counter, fully aware of how his shoulders and biceps looked in a dirty A-frame shirt. "The tank's full, and the kid loves the way the engine rumbles. Don't you, Cat?"

Cat chuckled. "Sounds a lot better now that I helped you chase out that leak in the transmission line."

I stood up. The fork was still in my clenched fist. Not that you would have guessed from the casual pleasantness in my tone. "There's no point in that big truck just for the two of us," I said.

"Looking for a third?" Luke drawled. "Might as well tag along. All that time I spend hunting in the woods, I should learn what I'm walking through."

"I'll bet you could find out what plants attract deer and wild turkey," Cat piped up.

"Luke's got his days mixed up," I said sweetly. It was Luke I kept my gaze fixed on, not Cat. "He told Owen that they'd work on the airboat today. Remember that, Luke?"

I waited to see if he was going to remember, or if I was going to have mix up his innards.

It wasn't a long wait. "Oh, shit," he deadpanned. "That's true. Raincheck, kid."

He heaved himself up off of the counter and sauntered out of the kitchen. I didn't unclench the fork until I heard the back door open and close.

I went back to my food first and chewed up a few forks full of eggs. Letting the moment pass.

"Does Luke ask you to look at things like that a lot?" I asked, doing my best to sound casual.

"Only once or twice," Cat said. Actually sounding casual. "I usually say no. He's kind of got an underwear sniffing vibe. But I do like the truck."

I snorted. Amazed that I'd forgotten for even a second that she could take care of herself. "Finish your breakfast and let's smell some flowers. I'll drive the Raptor."

Cat laughed. "I thought you said that was too much truck for just the two of us."

I shrugged, responding with a mischievous smirk of my own. "Like you couldn't fill a truck bed like that two-times over."

She responded with a display of feigned ignorance that belonged in the Louvre. "You can never have too many native plants, mother."

Cat had discovered Botany by chance. I dropped her at the New York Public Library so I could slip off and slice up somebody I met on Tindr. I came back, two hours later, and found her, six-years-old, digging *through Dr. Verrill's Guide to North American Flora.* After that, the Brooklyn Botanical Garden became one of our regular stops. I'm sure half the reason she went along with the move to Alabama was the promise of entire acres where she could plant whatever she wanted.

I wasn't surprised when she asked to stop at the garden center after the lecture. I obliged and we got back on the road with the truck overloaded with flowers so bright they made your eyes hurt.

"You've got money at home, right?" I teased.

Cat rolled her eyes. "It's already in your wallet," she said.

Back on the highway, Cat plugged her phone into the dash and asked if she could put on a playlist. I said fine, expecting Ashley Cyrus, or maybe the Sharpays. She was on a major pop kick.

What I wasn't expecting was the high shudder of guitar chords and an even higher whine of castrated male vocals.

I instinctively stepped harder on the gas.

"You turn thirty and forget to say something?" I asked, trying to sound like I didn't care much one way or another. Like the song wasn't twisting an icicle down into my chest.

"Everybody's listening to this song," Cat said. 'They used it in the trailer for the new season of Crystal's Lake. You know it?"

"It was popular back when I was in high school."

Cat giggled. Unusual for her. "It's weird thinking of you in high school," she teased. "Catching a ride home on a tractor and stopping at the general store for taffy with your friends."

"We got electricity my junior year," I deadpanned. "That's when things got really wild."

That was the lie I told her. My childhood in Beaverkill, New York. Some nowhere town I picked off the map at random. I'd decided early that avoiding my past would just make her more curious, so I came up with an answer for any question she might ask. My father was an accountant. Mom worked the counter at a diner. We didn't talk anymore. My grades in high school weren't great, but I was more focused on moving to the big city. I told her that her father was a travel league baseball player, just a guy passing through town. We were at the same party because of a friend of a friend and we got careless. No, Cat, I don't know his last name.

"So, were you a big fan?" Cat asked, pulling me back to reality. She nodded towards the radio. "What was your favorite Kincaids song? Which one did you want to marry? Brucey or Wesley?"

I wrinkled my face. "I didn't like them that much. My friends did."

"I've got a couple songs in here I like. Some of the live tracks are really good."

I shrugged, and we lapsed into silence. Brucey Kincaid's melodramatic warble filled the air between us. How it sounded live, I couldn't tell you. My school's exclusive prom performance was canceled after the Prom Queen disappeared and all her best friends were chopped to pieces.

"See if they're on tour," I said to Cat. "You can go with your friends."

Cat rolled her eyes behind her glasses.

"Mom, what friends?"

"Isn't music supposed to help plants grow?" I asked. "Put a few into wagon."

She laughed like it didn't matter, but that was the end of the conversation. A few miles of silence later, I turned the volume down low so we could hear each other clearly.

"Cat," I began.

"I don't need any parental intervention, mom."

"I know that. I'm just making sure you realize that you're doing everything right. You're chasing what matters to you, and you don't care if anyone thinks it's weird, or stupid –"

"I get the point. Thanks."

"You're who you want to be," I finished. "Years from now, that's going to matter a lot more than anything these idiots think. It took me awhile to find my people, too."

"You really are a millennial, mom. Does that speech come with a participation trophy?"

"Such wit," I said. We were back at the Manor. I shifted the truck into park. "Go," I said. "Grow something."

Cat hopped out and went to unload her plants.

I stayed where I was in the cab. I turned the volume back up and listened to the Kincaids as I watched Cat in the rearview mirror. She ran to the barn for the wheelbarrow and loaded flowerpots in an ungainly heap. I watched her trundle around towards the side of the house, where there was a bed of freshly turned earth with plenty of vacancies.

Puberty hadn't hit yet, but she was knocking on the door. Starting to get some of my height. A sparkle of clever humor in her eyes, glowing brighter every day. She was bright, and confident, and utterly unafraid of anyone or anything. I watched her until she was out of sight and Brucey Kincaid's mournful ballad whispered to an end.

Then, I got out and went to kill my brother-in-law.

CHAPTER 10

I stalked in the other direction. Away from the house and towards the land around the property. I didn't bother with the rusty red barn hovering close to the driveway. Cat had just been there, and Luke undoubtedly would have come sniffing out after her if he'd been inside. But that barely narrowed it down. The Paxton plot was the size of a nature preserve, and just as wild. There was no shortage of nooks and crevices he could be hiding in. I doubted he'd be out hunting deer, not so soon after hunting co-eds, but maybe he was down at the dock by the river, checking his shrimp traps or working on the boat engine. Wherever he was, I was going to find him.

Fuck that. Let me be clear. Wherever he was, I was going to kill him.

Kill him and that might be the end for you here.

Maybe so, but I'd warned Owen when I came out here. Cat was off limits. As predator or prey. Luke knew that. They all knew it. And a warning unenforced wasn't a warning at all, it was a fucking request. I didn't make requests.

I didn't find him by the water. There was the hill where they shot at bottles, but I didn't hear the crack of rifle fire. I cut through the tall grass in that direction anyway. Even if Luke wasn't there, the hill offered a hawk's eye view of the entire manor. Maybe I would get lucky.

"Ah, Pamela. You're back."

Mama Charlize was there at the crest, sitting beneath a tree with far-stretching branches teeming with white flowers. Cat probably knew exactly what kind. All I knew was that it provided plenty of shade for an old woman to sit in a wicker chair. She had a small table set beside her, topped with a bowl of walnuts and a small hammer.

Thunk.

She cracked a walnut open, plunked the choicest morsel into her mouth, and fanned herself. Even in the shade, sweat was already forming on her upper lip.

"It's hot today," she remarked. "I hope there was plenty of shade at the Gardens."

For me, it suddenly didn't feel so warm. The breeze making the long grass sway crawled across my back like spider legs made of ice.

"Luke mentioned it," Mama said, answering the question I didn't need to ask.

Thunk.

She smashed another walnut open. Broken pieces of shell fell soundlessly into the grass.

"I hope Cat had fun. I think it's good you let her go seekin' out whatever makes her sun shine."

Thunk.

"Now, my Lukey. That boy liked *bugs* when he was her age." She shuddered, but the theatrical dread never seemed to quite reach her flat eyes. "Do you know what that boy did? He used to dig up this entire property. Drove the landscapers crazy. Kept whole jars of spiders, cicadas, and Lord knows what else in his bedroom. One time, forgetful like little boys are, he left one of those jars open. Spiders the size of silver dollars all over the manor!"

She laughed, showing off a mouth of small, square, yellow teeth. "I made him search all over the house until he swore on the Bible that he'd found every last one... but I didn't tell him to stop with his collectin.' And I think you understand why. We all want what's best for our children, don't we?"

She watched me from her comfy chair. An old woman with heavy thighs and a thick middle. But with eyes sharp enough to pick up a speck of pollen on my eyelash. So incredibly sharp.

Thunk.

"Would you like a walnut, dear?" she asked. "You can borrow my hammer... that little knife tucked into your bra won't do a darn thing."

"...I'm okay, thanks," I said. Speaking with careful, deliberate slowness. "I'm going to go back and check on Cat."

Mama Charlize shrugged as if it didn't matter to her one way or another. "Have it your way, dear. But I'm sure she's fine, and that's the only thing that matters to a mother, wouldn't you say? That our children are kept safe?"

"Exactly right, Charlize," I said. My lips were numb, but I formed the words perfectly clearly.

Then I turned back around. Towards the house.

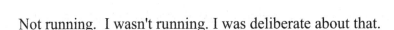

Not running. I wasn't running. I was deliberate about that.

I was walking. Because I wasn't afraid of her. I had my line, but Charlize had hers, too. We'd met at the border. I saw the price Charlize would make me pay for Luke's head, and I declined to foot the bill. It was an understanding of cost. Simple as that.

I wasn't afraid of her.

Yes, my heart was pounding, but that wasn't fear. I'd just amped myself up for the kill and now that energy was bottled up inside of me. The bloodlust hadn't magically gone away just because I wasn't able to kill Luke. I needed to cut somebody open, and soon. That would clear everything up. That would make this rushing sound in my ears go away.

I repeated that to myself. Head down. Eyes fixed firmly on my feet tramping through grass and underbrush. I just need to kill. I need to kill and this feeling will go away. I'm fine. Fine.

The ground beneath my feet transitioned back to hard packed dirt. I was almost back at the house. I lifted my gaze and, mercifully, something had broken in my favor.

We had a visitor.

There was a man at the front door. A stranger, slender and undersized, with a knotted tangle of dirty hair down to his shoulders and rumpled, threadbare clothes. The car parked at the top of the driveway was a dirty brown sedan with headlights clouded with age. A collector for one of the small churches in the hills. Or maybe just a scrapper inquiring about the stack of metal fence posts nobody had taken to the dump yet.

It didn't matter. It didn't matter what he wanted.

What mattered was I'd seen him first.

I sauntered closer. "Help y'all?" I called out. Loud enough for him to hear, but hopefully not loud enough for anybody in the house to hear. The knife against my chest suddenly felt warm. Ready for use.

The solicitor turned at the sound of my voice. I met his eyes, and suddenly my smile of a false welcome slid away like sand through a clenched fist. My casual stroll towards him stopped dead. I ground to a halt as suddenly and violently as a tractor trailer slamming into the side of a mountain.

Cat's face peered back at me. A little older, a lot more haggard and sullied with dirt, but Cat's face all the same. Her eyes. Her chin.

"...Beverly," Anthony said.

CHAPTER 11

ANTHONY

I had plans for the summer after senior year. Curtis and I were going to play through the entire Halo Trilogy on co-op in one day. There was a new John Marinville novel coming out in July. I wanted to finally give the show *Falling Skies* a try.

And I was going to spend every waking second that I could with Beverly Kilbourne before I went to Caltech and she went to Columbia.

I loved her. God, I was so madly, stupidly, in love with that girl. Already, the idea of staying in California while she went to New York sat in my stomach like three courses of broken glass. It took every IQ point I had to remind myself that I couldn't blow up my entire life and follow her to New York.

At least, not yet anyway. But that was an issue for my transfer application. Falling in love with Beverly was a lesson in savoring every second. I didn't know what the rest of our lives would hold. I didn't know if we were going to get married or if we would eventually split up like most high schoolers did. But whatever happened, I loved her now, and we had three perfect months stretching out before us like the line for a creator signing at Golden Apple comics. I wanted to let her drag me around the shops on Rodeo Drive. I wanted to hold her hand as the screen lit up at the Hollywood Forever Cemetery. I wanted to feel Venice Beach sand on my back and Beverly's soft cheek against my chest.

I wanted my prom night to be anything but the nightmare it became.

That was the night all my plans burned to ash. Prom, the night I waited outside of a locked house for twenty minutes, leaving thirty missed calls, about a hundred texts, and debating whether I should smash down the front door.

I ended up going through the back door. I went around that way just to see if I could look into the house and see if anybody was inside.

I saw inside alright. I saw a massive pool of blood in the foyer.

I took a deck chair and used it to smash open the glass sliding doors. I cut my leg good on a shard of broken glass, but I didn't even notice that until the paramedics pointed it out to me an hour later.

Not Beverly, I thought frantically at the time. I wasn't even ashamed of it. The blood I saw was too much for any to survive. So fuck it, let it be her mom at the foot of the stairs with a smashed open skull. Let Lyndsay be on the floor somewhere with a butcher knife in her chest. Let me find anything except my Beverly.

Technically, I did get my wish. I found Mr. Kilbourne. I found Lyndsay. I found my best friend's head.

I didn't find Beverly. Nobody did.

There were no movies for me that summer. No trips to the beach.

There was therapy. Lots of therapy. Doctors and medication and a few weeks at an actually really nice in-patient facility near Lake Arrowhead.

I started college on time. My parents wanted me to defer a semester, but I was going to go insane if I spent any more time dwelling on Beverly and Curtis.

More insane anyway.

I moved into my dorm orientation weekend, right on schedule. My roommate was a business major from North Carolina. "We're going to have the *best* year, bro" he enthused.

Maybe he did. I wouldn't know, he put in for a transfer after I spent a week screaming my throat raw every night, flinging myself out of bed and punching at air as if I could physically drive away the images of my best friend's severed head lying next to a Salma's Secrets gift bag.

It didn't get much better from there. I couldn't focus in class. I didn't shower. I gained twenty pounds of bad weight, compulsively stuffing myself with pizza bagel bites and soda.

I would have kept going, school was at least something to do, but three weeks into the semester I saw some blonde girl in the hallway. A random blonde, not even the right shade or the right haircut, and I freaked out. I sprinted after her in a crowded hallway, shoving people aside left and right, and I flung my arms around her from behind. I meant it to be a hug, but I wound up wrenching her across the hall and smacking her head against the wall.

"I knew you were alive," I sobbed into her ear. "I knew it. You had to be."

Tina Lohan of Lincoln, Nebraska didn't appreciate the mix-up. Neither did the administration.

There was a formal disciplinary process that we were supposed to go through, a few weeks of hearings and appeals, but I didn't see the point in wasting anybody's time. I had my bags packed about twenty minutes after the incident. Much easier to be efficient when there's nobody stopping by your door to wish you a fond farewell.

My phone buzzed a few times. My mother, trying to get in touch with me so we could figure out what to do next.

I ignored her. My car was on campus. I could make my own way home.

If going back home was what I wanted to do.

The thought must have been sitting in the corner of my mind for months. Ever since prom night really, sitting there like an elephant hiding behind a house plant, waiting to finally be acknowledged. It finally pushed forward now:

You don't have to go home, Anthony. You're eighteen. You can go anywhere you want to go.

And where did I actually want to go?

After Beverly of course.

Her body had never been found. Not Beverly and not her mother's. The cops' working theory was that Mrs. Kilbourne had snapped. Killed her husband, killed Lyndsay, Alicia, and Curtis, and then taken off with her daughter for reasons unknown.

Beverly was still presumed dead. No signs of a struggle, too much blood left at the scene. She wasn't being treated as a missing person by anybody except me.

And that was the knife-tip wedged inside of me. The thing that would never, ever, let me move on to some semblance of a normal life. I believed, truly believed, that Beverly was still alive. I didn't care what the police said. I didn't care about evidence. I believed it in my bones. She had to be alive.

I truly believed that, and yet here I was. Living my life like she was dead. Trying to focus on Analytical Geometry instead of spending every waking second trying to find the woman I loved. What kind of man did that make me? Certainly not one that deserved to be loved by the most perfect woman on God's earth. I was suddenly ashamed that it had taken me that long to do the right thing.

Well, that ended right now. I threw my bag into the car and pulled off campus. No more diversions. Not school, not my mom leaving her fourth message in fifteen minutes. It was time to be the man that Beverly deserved.

I got onto the highway. Not the 110 North, back towards Los Angeles. I got onto the 210 and headed East. Towards Beverly. It was mostly a symbolic gesture. I didn't expect to find Mrs. Kilbourne hanging in Santa Clarita (or maybe I would. How the hell did I know?) but it was someplace to start. I threw my phone out the window after about five miles. No explanations. Nobody coming to find me. I would come back when I had Beverly with me.

I drove for about five hours, into Nevada, and pulled off into some nowhere town called Desperation. The name was appropriate, but I swear I wasn't being dramatic. I chose it because I was a good saver. I had about ten grand in the bank and I made another fifteen unloading the El Camino for cash. A room in Desperation went for about $400 a month. Other than that, all I needed was Wi-fi and a computer.

I already had a computer. And it turned out Desperation still only had dial up internet, but I could make do.

For six weeks, that was my life. I ate Hot Pockets, drank Monsters, and poured over every news article I could find. Not the big websites. I wanted the local shit. Small town newspaper websites with terrible web design chugging along on ad revenue from the local funeral home. I factored in a baseline of 70 miles an hour, eight hours a day, and calculated how far Beverly and Mrs. Kilbourne could travel a given day in any direction. From there, I took that radius and back tracked every calendar day from the prom, looking for any clues that I could find.

———————|———————

I barely slept. When I did, I had the same nightmare. A nightmare of late morning sunlight struggling to make its way through thick honeycomb shades. I was sitting up in a king-size bed, comfortably nestled in a goose down comforter and reading a Sindey Prescott book.

I was older. I couldn't see myself in the nightmare, but I felt it. My muscles were too tight. My stomach felt heavier.

It didn't bother me though. Nothing did. I had a book and I had nowhere to go.

My room had an adjoining bathroom, and I could see through the open door. Sand-colored tiles. A thick slab of a marble vanity and a massive mirror.

In that mirror, Beverly Kilmeade.

She was older, too. A little paunch pushing against her sleep tank top. She was critically holding out long strands of blonde hair and examining them in the mirror.

"They're gray, Anthony." She plucked at more long strands. "Gray, gray, gray."

I shrugged. "You still have your hair. I can only be so

sympathetic."

She shot me a dirty look in the mirror. "Bev," I continued, "You know what Curtis tells Lyndsay? You're not the porn stepdaughter anymore. You're the porn stepmom. That's the circle of life."

Except she wasn't anyone's step-anything. The proof came thundering down from the hall outside and into our bedroom with only a cursory knock. Our son stood in the doorway, taller than I ever was. Broader in the shoulders. A lacrosse bag hung from one meaty arm. "Mom, Archie's here. I'm gonna hang out with him after practice."

"Call if you're gonna miss dinner," she shouted from the bathroom.

Our son rolled his eyes. "I will. Later, dad."

A cursory wave in my direction and he was gone, slamming the door behind him as he disappeared.

The slamming door was my cue to bolt upright in bed like there was a hydraulic piston in my spine. I woke up that way every single morning, my sheets soaked with sweat like they just came out of the washing machine and my eyeballs straining out of my head with the force of my screams.

It made it easy to stay awake. Easy to keep working.

But it didn't make it easy work. There's a lot of murder in America. *A lot.* I did my best to weed out the kind of thing I was looking for. No domestic disputes. Nothing where the victim and the killer knew each other. Nothing with a suspect in custody, and no shootings. I remembered vividly the scene at Beverly's house. I didn't want bullets. I wanted sharp edges and the most senseless, savage crimes imaginable.

The first likely hit was in Utah. I read in the Geiger Gazette about the late June death of beloved local DJ Adam Barrymore. His body was found at a rest stop along Interstate 70. His throat had been slashed so severely that his head was almost cut clean off.

His van was missing from the scene.

I read that on a Sunday. The next day, I was in a 1994 Toyota Camry, wheezing along for the Beehive State. No worries about my 9

AM class, no concerns about missing whatever job my parents would have lined up for me if I'd gone back home. The only thing I cared about was how quickly I could chew through the 400 miles between me and the first real clue I'd found about what had happened to the love of my life.

———————|———————

Calling this place a "rest stop" was almost too much of a fiction for a reputable newspaper. It was a square patch of asphalt and a ramshackle pavilion with no walls. There was no gas station. No Baja Burger. There was a vending machine and some bathrooms that looked like they got cleaned once every six months. There was desert on one side. On the other, there was the beginnings of a forest of towering evergreen trees. The tree line quickly became so thick that visibility was gone after about a hundred feet past the first trunks.

This was months after the murder. The police tape was gone. Anything that might have happened here was just a faded, rusty stain in the parking lot. And not the only one. Not by a long shot.

And then there was me, standing in the empty lot, probably looking like just another twerpy true crime podcast guy.

Honestly, that was giving myself too much credit. True crime twerps at least had some idea what they were looking for. I was an idiot kid sitting in the middle of nowhere, hoping to see some sign that said, "Beverly Kilbourne This Way!" with a giant neon arrow.

Lacking one of those, I tramped off into the woods.

To be clear, I had no gear. No compass. No flashlight. I didn't even stop at the vending machine for a water bottle. All I had was the need to find something, *anything*, to proof that Mrs. Kilbourne had been here. There was nothing at the rest stop and I could see clearly that there was nothing to look at in the desert. Therefore, there must have been something out here in the trees. Something far enough from the crime scene that the police had missed it. Something waiting all this time, just for me to find.

If you haven't picked up on this yet, I was not doing very well mentally at this point in my life.

I blundered on through the carpet of dead pine needles, the shade from the trees doing nothing to stop the growing sinkhole of sweat at my back. I tuned the nagging need for food and water down into background noise. None of it mattered. *Focus, Anthony. Focus.*

I didn't find anything, so I kept walking.

Two hours.

Three.

My legs burned like nuclear rods. I wiped my cracked, arid lips continuously, coming away with a bloody smear on the back of my hand every time.

And then, eventually, I found it.

It hadn't actually come from the rest stop. That would have been impossible. No car could have trekked through the terrain of rocks and trees I'd blundered through.

That was the mistake that rational people had made. Rational people had assumed that Adam Barrymore's killer had come from the highway when, in reality, the killer had started from the ridge high above us. The ridge where the highway cut north instead of West. Somebody had started up there and guided their car down the treacherous slope, abandoned their vehicle in this narrow ravine in front of me, and then walked *backwards*, back to the rest stop. Somebody perfectly comfortable with ripping the innards out of their car as they coasted down over rocks and tree stumps. Somebody who didn't need it anymore.

It must have been there for months, the windshield coated with dust and pollen. A bird's nest in one wheel well.

California license plates.

I had memorized every detail of Beverly's disappearance. The prom victims and parents were the ones who got most of the spotlight. Less attention had been paid to their missing neighbor. Kathryn Fey. A seventy-year-old studio exec's widow. No surviving children. Nobody to raise her profile. But she had disappeared that night, too.

So had the Cadillac from her garage.

I knew that car. I'd seen it drive away that night, too much of a lovestruck fool to think that anything might be wrong, but I'd recognized it then. And I recognized it now.

"Oh shit," I croaked. "Oh holy, motherfucking shit."

It was here. Right in front of me. Mrs. Fey's Cadillac. The Cadillac everybody assumed that Mrs. Kilbourne had driven away in with her daughter.

True Crime Podcast guy would have kept his distance and taken some pictures. He would have made sure everybody knew who found it, but he would be careful not to get too close. Careful not to taint any potential evidence.

Fuck that.

I tripped over a root scrambling down to the car. Twisted my ankle pretty good, but I barely felt it. I was too determined to get down there and run my hands over the car. Confirm it was real.

It was. I felt the finish beneath my hands. The car. *Her* car. I could see inside through the dusty windshield, and I saw more than the car. I saw signs that Beverly had been inside it. I saw a Hobbs Cola in the cupholder. Her favorite brand. I saw a crumpled Baja Burger bag in the foot of the passenger seat.

She was here!

I saw it. I saw a million little details that all screamed out to me. Beverly! BEVERLY!

The only thing I didn't notice, refused to notice, was the prevailing stench that hung heavy in the air around the car.

There was too much else to notice. Too much to thrill over.

I'd found it!

Nothing to see in the backseat. No more clues there. I fumbled to the driver's side door. The handle turned easily in my hand. Not locked. The trunk button was in the first place I looked. Down at the bottom of the door. I smashed it in and heard the dull *thunk* as the trunk opened.

The smell of rancid hamburgers got stronger too, but I ignored that. I wanted clues to where I could find Beverly, but that stench wasn't a clue. Neither was the buzzing swarm of flies that came pouring out from the trunk as it opened.

None of that mattered. Three bags. A suitcase and two duffle bags That's all I saw in the trunk. Three bags with clues to where Beverly might be found.

Three bags with ugly brown stains settling at the bottoms.

I ripped the first one open and reality, at last, punched through my haze of mania.

A dead face howled silently back at me from within that bag. A dead face swollen and green from the summer heat. Eyes sunk deep in permanent dread. Mouth hanging open in a final scream crawling with fat, lazy flies that couldn't be bothered to fly away with their siblings.

I recoiled, tripped over a root, and threw up all at the same time. Vomit spraying upwards as my ass thudded down. But I bounced back up like a boxer refusing to take an eight count, even as my own puke came down on me like rain. I didn't even bother wiping my face.

I had to see. I had to know.

I stared at the corpse and, at first, I thought it really was Beverly. The thought was impaling, devastating agony, but there was a small twinge of relief buried deep within it. At least then I would know.

But it wasn't her. An easy mistake to make, though. Same blue eyes. Same blonde hair. A lot of the small differences obscured by decay.

They always looked so much alike, Beverly and her mother.

Mrs. Kilbourne. It was Mrs. Kilbourne screaming out at me from the bag.

Part of her anyway.

Her legs, I would discover, were stashed in the second bag.

Mrs. Fey was in the last suitcase, the smallest one. Her body smashed and folded over like a Bonestorm fatality.

But no Beverly. She could still be alive. She was *likely* still alive. The dead had been left here, but not Beverly. Somebody had killed her mother and her neighbor, but they'd kept her alive. Switching cars to stay ahead of the police. They'd gotten this far and then switched here with the DJ's van. A perfect vehicle for moving a hostage.

I went back to the driver's seat. I needed more. I needed something to tell me where to go next. Who had Beverly? Where had they taken her?

You're not an idiot, I chastised. I tried to throttle my brain back. I was trying to see a million things at once. I needed to be smarter. Beverly's life was at stake. I couldn't help her if I wasn't thinking clearly. *Focus, damnit. Figure out how to keep after her.*

I stared inside the car until my eyes ached. I examined the stitching on the logo etched into the steering wheel. I fumbled underneath the driver's seat and came up with nothing but lint.

But there was something here I wasn't seeing. I knew it. I *felt* it.

Maybe you're looking too closely. Maybe you're so busy counting leaves that you're missing the fact that one of the trees is really a cell phone tower.

Maybe. Something was wrong. That much was certain.

Suddenly, it struck me. It hit me so hard that I may as well have been standing on the highway while that Cadillac ran me over at a hundred miles an hour.

One drink in the car. One Baja Burger cheeseburger wrapper. One order of fires.

There was only ever one person in this car.

But then… where was Beverly?

She was here. She was in this car.

Bullshit. What the hell was she doing joyriding around with her mother's remains? Why hadn't she called anyone?

Because she did it. The thought settled on top of me like a rock.

She did it. That would be the only reason. Beverly killed her mom and Mrs. Fey. Beverly drove away in that Cadillac.

Another boulder dropped down. *That would mean she killed everyone else too. Her dad. Lyndsay. Alicia. Curtis.*

Fucking ridiculous. They were all butchered. Beverly wasn't some kind of psychopathic monster.

And then more rocks. *Thud, thud, THUD,* falling faster inside of my head. I thought about the night of the school play. The night that Clay was found sliced open with a slur carved into his chest. Beverly had been there, supposedly slammed against a wall by whoever had murdered Clay.

Never solved.

THUD. THUD. And then there had been the big party right before the start of senior year. I hadn't been there, but I had hurt about it. And I had heard about how Rob Cummings from John Carpenter High left that party and got gutted by some maniac.

Never solved.

One time when we were first dating, Beverly was supposed to meet me at the movies. She showed up a few minutes late. I thought she'd been running, because there were droplets of sweat beading along her forehead. I swooned at the thought that she'd been running to meet me.

She kissed me and my brain was so flooded with fireworks. I barely noticed the mall security car racing across the lot – stupid yellow bubble light flashing on the top.

When we came out of the movies, there was a SUV at the end of the parking lot all by itself, roped off in a square of yellow caution tape. There were real cop cars there now.

Somebody had been found in that SUV. Stabbed to death.

Never Solved.

Until now. Until *me.* Looking for the woman I loved.

Too many rocks, more and more until I couldn't take the weight in my head anymore. I dropped down onto a log. It was suddenly too hot. Too bright.

All this time, I thought I had been chasing a victim.

The walk back to the rest station took twice as long. It was pitch black by the time I made it back to my crappy motel, desperately clutching the packet of Xanax I'd bought from the sketchy dealer always hanging around the motel lobby. I took both of them and prayed desperately that my sleep would be dreamless.

It wasn't. Beverly was still in the bathroom, but her hair wasn't blonde. It wasn't gray either.

It was red. So was her face. And her shirt. The entire bathroom was soaked in blood.

And I wasn't alone in the bed anymore. Suddenly, I barely had enough room to fit.

Her parents were in the bed with me. Her father with a gory ravine between his eyes. Her mother with broken glints of white bone jutting from the stumps of her legs.

Alicia was there too, bloody vomit clotted over her lips.

Lyndsay. Split in half.

And Curtis' head. Not his body, just his head, doughy and acne-ridden, but otherwise unblemished. It stared up at me from my lap, balanced between the pages of a book soaked in blood. His eyes looking up at me with frightening life.

"Anthony?"

She was at my bedside. Beverly, her blonde hair drenched strawberry. Her eyes chips of diamond sparkling with savage glee. She had a meat cleaver. Maybe the blade had once been silver, but it was too drenched in blood now for it to make a difference.

She raised the blade over my prone form. No chance for me to move, not because I was tangled up in the bodies of her victims, but I didn't want to move. I just watched the cleaver rise.

Watched it rise and come slicing back down.

I woke up in a cramped motel room in the godforsaken wastelands of middle Utah. I woke up with sweat soaking the thin mattress until it squelched with the shift of my weight.

I woke up still in love with Beverly Kilbourne.

CHAPTER 12

———————|———————

In the last year, I'd gone through three major traumatic incidents. The night Clay was murdered at the play. The night my best friend was murdered and Beverly disappeared.

And now tonight. The night I learned that Beverly had been the one to kill them all.

Each time, I had gone to bed shaking, disturbed, and feeling like the world was a nightmare I didn't want to live in.

Every time, I woke up madly in love with Beverly Kilbourne.

This was no different. I woke up thinking that it might be. I woke up expecting to feel revolted, or maybe even relieved. That maybe this would change the way I felt about her and I could wake up and go home. Pick up some kind of life without having to cradle the idea of Beverly in my heart.

I was wrong. I woke up and absolutely nothing had changed. I was hers. I would always be hers. I'm sorry if that makes me a bad friend, Curtis.

I get it, man. I only saw her in a tank top and I get it. You saw her naked.

I laughed in my empty hotel room.

I was crazy. Oh Jesus, I was so fucking crazy.

Yeah, no shit.

But I'd already fallen in love with Beverly before I discovered this part of her. I loved the light in her eyes when she laughed. I loved her intensity. I loved everything about her.

Apparently, murder had already been a part of the package the entire time. If I loved it in her before I knew it was there, why should I stop now?

Hell, especially why should I stop now? I knew that she was alive. I knew it for a stone cold fact. I could find her. I could hold her again. Kiss her. Love her.

If she went out by herself sometimes, I didn't need to ask questions.

I stepped out briefly for a breakfast taquito and then I was back on the computer, searching for more murders. Axes. Decapitations. Impalings. The senseless. The inexplicable. I started to get a feel for what might be Beverly's work, and what could be dismissed as a drug killing or a crime of passion. Things that might be Beverly weren't just demented or tragic, they were... masterful. There was a grudging admiration in the news coverage.

" 'In a stunning display of brutality, the victim's face was forced into the food processor.'

'I've never seen anything like this,' one source said. 'It wasn't random. Whoever did this, they knew exactly how to do the most damage possible with a circular saw.'

'Manhunt continues in Haddonfield for the perpetrator of the horrific Poker House Massacre. Officials insist there is no sign that this shocking, appalling murder of six is at all related to the town's history of masked assailants...'

She wasn't just a mindless killer. There was a deliberateness to what Beverly did. An extremely fucked up sense of... artistry.

It felt like getting to know her better.

What it didn't do was get me any closer to her. Months had passed between now and when Beverly had abandoned the car in Utah. Had she settled somewhere? Was she on the move? I forgot about the prom window and started looking closer to the present day. I-70 led into Colorado, and last month a varsity swimmer in Alma Junction had stayed late to do some laps. They found her floating the next morning, strangled to death with one of the gold medals from the trophy case.

It seemed as good a place to start as any. I spent a week there, waiting to see if a pattern formed, and then it came out that a rival swimmer had done the deed.

From there, I looked into a decapitated hair stylist in Como. And a butchered butcher in Blue River.

I started to run low on money then, so I spent a month working in a laundromat in Bennett. Then a math teacher was killed with a pair of hedge clippers in Deer Trail, and I spent two weeks there working as a landscaper.

And those were just the leads I pursued. The whole country sprawled around me. So much land. So much death. It felt like searching for a single bloody knife in a cutlery warehouse.

I spent three months in Kansas shoveling grain and checking a three-state radius for the right murders. I turned to social media during two months washing dishes in Salie, Iowa. Backtracking through photos from murder victims and crime scenes, looking for a blonde laughing in the background at the fair. A girl who was both impossible to miss and impossible to find.

I turned 22 in Hawkins, Indiana.

I turned 25 in Arkansas, looking into a triple murder that seemed promising.

I drank a lot. I ate very little. People offered me spare change if I sat down on a park bench to drink a cup of coffee.

One night, particularly drunk, I got a tattoo of a white whale on my hip.

Amazingly, in all this time, all these years of chasing killings and atrocities, I had never seen a single drop of blood.

Not until I got to Ohio.

CHAPTER 13

———————|———————

It happened when I was 29. For the last few years, one of my background gambits was posing online as a true crime podcast producer. I said that I was looking to do a series about the greatest unknown serial killers in America. I left posts on Craigslist and other seedy, barely regulated corners of the internet. I promised total anonymity for anyone willing to sit for an interview.

I refreshed the posting every few months to keep it fresh. I got a lot of freaks. A lot of weirdos. A couple of responses that chilled me to the bone. Those were the ones I would string along for a while, trying to get more information, but it was never Beverly. It was always a man, or somebody who grew up in North Dakota, or someone old enough to remember watching The Love Boat.

They could have been lying, fudging personal details until they were sure they could trust me, but I didn't believe it in my heart either. I knew Beverly. I knew how she talked. I knew her text shorthand. Make me deaf and blind and I would know her hand if it slipped into mine.

I hadn't found her.

And then a message came in one night while I was living in a rented trailer.

Ohio winter. Icy wind rattling the shitty aluminum walls. The lights were off and I was close to drifting off to sleep when my phone *pinged* and dim blue light filled the room.

The message had come in on Blind-I, the encrypted app I'd made a profile on for any serial killers looking to talk.

Vodka Straight: So you wanna get to know a serial killer?

…Beverly had drank vodka. I cautiously messaged back.

Baja Boy: Well, "know," sounds a little too intimate. I'm just trying to talk about what a serial killer does and I'm looking for a good source. Not trying to be BFFs.

Vodka Straight: Smart boy. Killers bite.

Baja Boy: ...You speak from experience?

Vodka Straight: And you're saying you don't wanna get intimate? I only just swiped right here and you're getting pretty personal.

Baja Boy: Well, then I guess the obvious question is what can I do to make you more comfortable?

Vodka Straight: I'll think about it and let you know.

Radio silence after that. I figured it was just another crank, but then another message came in the next day.

Vodka Straight: So, are you a burger fan or a surfer boy?

It seemed for the best that she didn't suspect I was anybody she knew. *Baja Boy: Burgers, unfortunately. The only time I've seen the ocean was one family trip to Virgina Beach. Other than that, it's just been the Rust Belt for me.*

Vodka Straight: Too bad. Nothing like a day in California.

Baja Boy: Is that where you call home?

Vodka Straight: Once upon a time. But you never really leave. At least that's what I like to tell myself when I'm freezing my ass off.

As if in agreement, the wind rattled my thin windows in their frames.

Vodka Straight: Cute move, by the way. Trying to suss out where I am.

Baja Boy: Can't blame me for trying, right?

Vodka Straight: I could kill you for trying.

Vodka Straight: Cut your head off.

Vodka Straight: Fill a bathtub with your blood and soak up to my neck in it.

Baja Boy: ...I guess you don't want me to get aHEAD of myself.

Two long minutes passed without response. I lay in bed with my heart thudding until my ribs cracked. Terror and anticipation mixed inside me until I didn't know where one started and the other ended.

At last, dots on the screen.

Vodka Straight: I could kill you for that pun too :)

I was smiling and shaking as I typed back. This was the closest I'd ever been. She hadn't given anything away, she hadn't even confirmed she was a "she," but I felt it. I felt Beverly in the tone.

Baja Boy: I don't mean to be aggressive, but I think this could be an amazing project. I want to hear whatever you have to say.

Vodka Straight: Do you want me to start with my birthdate and social?

Baja Boy. LOL. Strictly anonymous. I swear.

Vodka Straight: So where should I start?

With where you went to high school. What was your favorite book. Did you ever really love me? Could you love me now if I didn't want to change you?

Baja Boy: Let's start with the basics. Are you actually a serial killer?

Vodka Straight: Since I was ten years old. 10-13 is a common age for True Bloods.

Baja Boy: ???

Vodka Straight: True Bloods are born killers. A lot of switches get turned on at puberty. Murder is one of them.

Baja Boy: Is that a proven fact? Do you guys talk shop with each other?

Vodka Straight: LOL. No, but I read a lot of true crime. You find patterns.

Vodka Straight: Also, we're not all guys.

Vodka Straight: Rude.

Holy shit.

HOLY SHIT.

Baja Boy: If I promise not to make any more assumptions, can we keep talking? Maybe a phone call?

Vodka Straight: No call. Not yet. But we can keep texting.

Vodka Straight: Wanna know the best way to drive a tent stake into someone's brain? You'd think eye socket, but you'd be surprised.

I didn't. I absolutely did not.

Baja Boy: Yeah, let's start there if that's what you want.

Vodka Straight had plenty of stories to tell. Gruesome, nightmarish stories. Stories that made me cold in ways that had nothing to do with the winter raging around my uninsulated trailer. She was a monster. She was neither proud nor ashamed of what she was. She just existed, purely content to be someone who found murder to be as essential as eating.

That was what struck me the most. The *need* that she felt to kill. It would be impossible for her to live without death.

She was also funny. And clever. And sometimes she would divert from bloody massacres and ask about music or Chinese food.

The first murder she told me about was a lifeguard at her local pool growing up. She caught him getting out of his car early one morning, first one in the lot. She crippled him with a lead pipe to the knee and then brought the same pipe down on his head, splattering chunks of skull and brains all over the asphalt.

Vodka Straight: I'm not that big, but I'm fast and I know what I'm aiming for.

She killed a busboy behind a restaurant. Cut his throat while he was emptying the trash.

Vodka Straight: I think of a kill like that as fast food. No time to get drawn out or fancy. Just scratch the itch and go home.

Some drunk girl leaving a college party. Wrapped a chain around her neck, dragged her into the bushes, and squeezed until she turned blue.

Vodka Straight: Better me than some date rapist, right? Dead is better. Not enough people respect that.

I remembered what I felt when Clay was killed at the play. I wasn't just horrified, I was mad. I was furious that somebody bright and kind had had his future taken away. I thought of that happening again and again, at the hands of the person I was talking to. It was revolting.

But all of that went away every time I remembered that it might be Beverly I was talking to on the other end.

Vodka Straight: I usually wear a cap when I'm "strolling." My hair's very light and blood shows way too easily.

The more we spoke, the more certain I became that it really was Beverly.

Blonde.

Born in Southern California.

Roughly my age.

Likes Canadian Bacon.

There couldn't be that many serial killers who fit that kind of profile. Especially not that many who were this clever, funny, and charming. (Yeah, yeah. Ted Bundy. Fine, you fucking marry him.)

It was her. It had to be.

Baja Boy: Alright, I'm convinced of your authenticity. When can I interview you for the podcast?

Vodka Straight: Anytime. Send me a Zoom link.

Baja Boy: ...What would you say if I told you I wanted to meet in person?

Vodka Straight: I'd say you were a cop.

Baja Boy: You pick the place. You tell me the time. You tell me what to wear. I'll get there first and you can case me. If you don't like what you see, just walk away and I'll be none the wiser.

Vodka Straight: What's wrong with Zoom?

Baja Boy: I need to know for real. I don't want to meet you across a screen. I want to look at you and see what's in your eyes. I want to understand you.

I was typing so hard my fingers were ringing like falling hail by the time I hit send.

Vodka Straight: Ok, one more question. What if I'm the last thing you ever see? Did you forget what we've been talking about?

Baja Boy: Well, if you ask to meet at midnight at the abandoned railyard, I'm probably gonna pass.

A lie. I'd meet her anywhere.

Baja Boy: You must want to talk to someone, otherwise you wouldn't still be here. One meeting. Anywhere in the country. I'm waiting on you.

I waited.

A day passed by. Two. I ached to message her again, but I fought the urge. *Have a little goddamn dignity,* Phantom Curtis urged.

Then, it came.

Vodka Straight: 6 PM tomorrow. Hobb's End, Tennessee. The Shop is called Around the Corner Books. Wear a red shirt with black jeans and a backwards baseball cap. Go to the coffee bar and sit with a Catherine Zellweger romance. Wait for me.

I didn't waste time responding. Tennessee was a ten-hour drive. I just hoped I could afford the gas.

CHAPTER 14

————|————

I got there at 4:00 PM, just to be safe. Which left me with plenty of time to sit there, consumed by anxiety that bristled up and down my spine like a strip of thumbnails. I should have taken the time to shower before getting in the car. I should have tried to buy a nicer shirt. I was second guessing everything down to my freaking shoelaces.

I didn't see her when I arrived. Even allowing for twelve years' time, I was confident she wasn't here. Nobody else seemed to be paying attention to me either.

That was fine. It was early. I ordered a cup of coffee and sat down with the Zellweger book. I was wearing what Vodka Straight had requested, but I'd also added a pair of sunglasses. When or if Beverly saw me, I didn't want her to recognize me too early and run off.

If she even recognizes you after all this time.

She would. She had to.

She loved me.

I waited, my heart creeping higher into my throat with every flip of the clock on my phone. The book in my hands was starting to warp, drenched with sweat from my palms and twisted with every anxious wrench of my hands.

Five fifty-eight.

Five fifty-nine.

Six o'clock.

Six oh five.

I knew that she wasn't coming, but I stayed anyway. I ordered a few more cups of coffee. I read a few chapters of this Zellweger romance. Damnit, maybe it was just my head space, but the dialogue was breezy and the characters had rich, developed inner lives. The LA Times had it right, she really was the queen of frothy, charming beach reads.

I had to use the bathroom, five cups of coffee lined up and impatient to get out, but I stayed in my chair. What if the thirty seconds I spent in the restroom were the same thirty seconds that Beverly came through the door? She would come in the moment I was gone, cheeks tinted pink from the chilly night air, her beautiful blue eyes scanning the room for the man in the red shirt, and then she would be gone while I was still shaking it off at the urinal.

Yes, she wasn't coming, but I still had a chance if I stayed in my seat.

That was how we met, after all. I didn't quit. I didn't accept that I was a loser with no business even talking to the most beautiful, popular girl in school. I took my chance, no matter how unlikely, and it paid off.

Someone tugged at my sleeve. I jerked out of my daze, heart racing, but it was just the barista with pink and blue hair. All of twenty years old.

"I'm sorry, sir. But we're about to close up. Did you want to buy that?"

I couldn't really afford it, but what the hell. At least I could see somebody's happy ending.

"Yeah, sure. Is it okay if I use your bathroom first?"

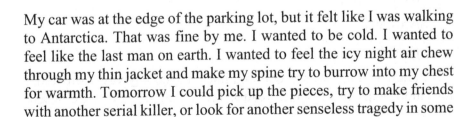

My car was at the edge of the parking lot, but it felt like I was walking to Antarctica. That was fine by me. I wanted to be cold. I wanted to feel like the last man on earth. I wanted to feel the icy night air chew through my thin jacket and make my spine try to burrow into my chest for warmth. Tomorrow I could pick up the pieces, try to make friends with another serial killer, or look for another senseless tragedy in some godforsaken corner of the country. Tonight, I'd walked into a gut punch. It was stupid to do anything except wait to recover.

I made it to the car. These days I was driving a 1993 Nissan Maxima. The passenger side door was almost rusted through and would fly open if you pushed it too hard, but the driver's side door made up for it by frequently wedging shut. Tonight was one of those nights, and I had to grunt and tug at the handle two or three times before the car reluctantly let me in.

The engine was as dejected as I was. I cranked the key and waited a good thirty seconds before it sputtered to cranky life. I shook my head, visualizing how corroded the pistons must be. I'd be lucky to make it back to Ohio.

While I waited for the heater to start wheezing lukewarm air, I fished out my phone and fired off a pathetic text.

Baja Boy: I guess there was somebody who looked like a cop wearing the same outfit. Crazy, right?

I didn't expect any response at all. Certainly not one so quick. I'd barely hit send before the responding notification blipped across my phone.

Vodka Straight: Sorry, there was just somebody I had to kill. Let's reschedule.

Like an idiot, I was all too eager to respond.

Baja Boy: Okay, what time?

Vodka Straight:10:12 tonight work for you?

I checked the neon green clock on my car dash. 10:15.

"I think that clock is a little fast."

I heard the voice in my ear, a split second before I heard the sound of tearing fabric and felt the flare of sharp, agonizing heat in my lower back. Heat that whipped away the chill in my bones far faster than my beat-up V-4 engine. I instinctively tried to writhe away from it, but a dry, chapped hand grabbed my chin from behind, holding me in place.

"Get comfy," the same voice hissed. "You're going to be here for awhile."

Fresh pain as something slid into my back again. *Beverly,* I thought. *Beverly's last kiss.*

And was it worth it? Oh yes.

She skittered up from the backseat like a spider. Long limbs. thick torso. Short, dark hair hung over her eyes, but I could see her mouth of grinning wolf's teeth all too clearly. The knife in her hand was darker still, too thick with my blood to catch the street light's glare.

Wordlessly, she snapped out again with the knife. This dark, grinning thing. I brought my hand up to block the blade and lost a pinkie for my troubles. Blood squirted across the upholstery. My severed finger turned end over end, impossibly slow, and dropped into the cupholder, only to be snatched up by the wraith in my passenger seat. She flipped her hair back to get a better look at her prize. Her pale skin a sickly orange in the sodium light. Her eyes, dark and sunken, inspected my severed finger with casual expertise.

"Thanks for the keepsake," she said.

Not Beverly, I realized. *Oh, my friend. You are so fucking dead.*

She stuck my finger into the breast pocket of her flannel shirt and lunged at me with the knife again.

I lunged with the book.

My arm was longer. I landed first, driving the spine of the book into the bridge of her nose. Her knife kept coming, but my strike made her wince and threw off her aim. The blade that would have gone into my throat carved a gash across my shoulder instead.

What happened next might have seemed clever. It wasn't. It was blind, stupid, reactionary bullshit. I flailed out with both hands, squealing like a stuck pig as I did. I caught Vodka across the chest and managed to push her back against the passenger door. My shitty passenger door that I never bothered to fix because there was never anybody in it. In a more reliable car, I would have bought just a few more seconds to bleed before she got around to cutting my throat. In my piece of shit car, the rusty latch gave way and Vodka Straight kept going. The door flew open and she tumbled out onto the asphalt with a bewildered squawk.

I took my chance. I shifted into reverse and backed out of the parking spot with a squeal of burning rubber. I jerked the wheel in a hard, violent arc and slammed to a stop with her sprawled figure caught dead center in the murky glow of my dim headlights.

Hyperventilating, soaked in my own blood, I shifted into drive, smashed the gas, and ran right over her. I bounced in my seat as I hit the speed bump of her legs. Her scream echoed across the empty parking lot as I plowed over her.

I slammed on the breaks and shifted into park. Got out of the car.

I wasn't acting blindly now. I knew exactly what I was doing.

That's not to imply I was in my right mind. I staggered towards Vodka Straight. She was screaming and writhing on the floor. Her legs were shattered. Kneecaps pulverized. She was screaming until the eyes nearly bulged out of her head.

Too much screaming. I had to act fast. I reached for her arm, and she lashed out like a viper with the knife, cutting another gash into my arm.

I kicked her in the ribs. While she was groaning, I stomped on her hand holding the knife. I brought my foot down again and again until I heard bones break. Eventually, the knife slipped from the ruins of her hand and I kicked it across the parking lot.

I knelt down beside her as she kept screaming and thrashing and punched her in the face as hard as I could. I was hoping to knock her out with one punch, the way it usually worked in the movies when the hero needed to knock somebody out. And then I punched her another time just to be safe.

Vodka Straight hadn't gotten the studio notes. I'd punched out two teeth but she was still conscious, and she was just so fucking, excruciatingly *loud.* Screaming and screaming in an ever growing pool of her own fluids. Shrieking until the sound made my blood vibrate with its force.

"Please," I panted. "Please stop." I cocked my fist back again, but something in me broke. Her mashed, bloody body was too much. I couldn't do it again.

I shuffled behind her and grasped her under her armpits. She didn't resist.

She didn't stop screaming either.

I kept waiting to see police sirens. Either hurtling past me towards the scene of the attack, or howling at my bumper because somebody had reported what I'd done.

None came. I kept driving, making my way at a steady forty miles an hour through the dark streets of this small southern city.

Just me and the serial killer pounding relentlessly in the trunk of my car.

CHAPTER 15

"You're going to bleed to death," the voice said from the trunk.

She was right. I'd tried to patch myself up as best I could with fast food napkins and ripped up strips of my undershirt, but my hand with the missing finger was totally numb. I couldn't seem to catch my breath, no matter how hard I tried, and mysterious pains gnawed at my stomach even thought I hadn't been stabbed there. I was in desperate need of medical attention. We both were.

"I need something else more," I said. It hurt to raise my voice, but I did it anyway. I wanted to be sure she could hear me in the trunk, and I didn't have to worry about being overheard. I'd parked behind an abandoned grocery store. I didn't see any rats scouring through the wrappers and boxes scattered by the dumpster. It was just me and Vodka Straight.

"I need to know about what you do," I said. "Murder."

Muffled laughter echoed out from the closed hatch. She beat her fist against the trunk lid. "I know podcasts are cheap, but is this supposed to be a recording booth? Test, test. One, two," she taunted. 'How's that sound?"

I slammed back harder. "I mean it!" I yelled.

"Fuck you!" she screeched. "And I mean it too. Fuck! You! You've got me locked in a trunk with a broken release latch. I give you what you want and then you turn this thing into an incinerator with me inside of it. Eat shit."

I tried to laugh, but it staggered out in a pained wheeze. I was drenched in sweat, but shivering all the same. Trying to hold my head up was too much effort, so I let it slump against the trunk. "How did you start? Ten years old, you said. Was that part true?"

I waited for an answer, fighting the urge to close my eyes. Just for a minute.

"You want me to open up first?" I muttered. "Okay. Fine. I've spent... twelve years, my entire adult life, looking for someone I knew. Somebody... somebody who does what you do. But I never saw this part of her, and I'm just trying to *understand* it." I looked at the blood on my hands. The memory of Vodka Straight's screaming clawed inside of my ears. I tried to picture what it would feel like to actually kill her and the unprompted, visceral disgust that roiled through me made me choke. I tried to imagine *enjoying it* and failed. I simply couldn't fathom it.

"Why do you kill?" I pleaded to her. "Have you ever thought about it? Why!? What about cutting somebody to pieces makes you want to keep doing it? Don't you have anything else? What's your favorite show? Your favorite book?"

My head lolled to the side, leaving streaks of cold sweat on the trunk. I was so tired. And I felt like I was talking to an empty confessional.

"What about love?" I murmured. "Can you love?"

"...This is about the blonde, isn't it?"

The haze of blood loss clouding my thoughts was suddenly and violently swept out to sea. I practically crawled on top of the trunk. "What blonde? What do you know?"

"Word gets around if somebody's talented. If you're talking about who I think you are, she's been on a death tour all across the country." The voice in the trunk let out a throaty chuckle. "Even for us, that one's a real fucking monstrosity."

"Do you know where she is?" I asked. "Can you find her?"

"Open the trunk," she said. "Open the trunk and I'll tell you everything you need to know."

I wish I could say I hesitated. I wish I could say I saw through the obvious ruse.

I didn't. And I can't blame the blood loss. It was just Beverly. Always Beverly.

I opened the trunk and a spray of anti-freeze hit me right in the eyes. Vodka had found the spare bottle I kept in the trunk. The viscous spatter hit me right in the eyes and I screamed and reared back, groping at my eyes as the burning fluid worked between my clenched eyelids.

A mad weight hit me in the hips next and dragged me down. I landed on my back with that writhing mass still clinging to me. Hot, greasy fingers scrambled up my body and wrapped around my throat. I was totally blind. Alone in the darkness with those hands squeezing tighter and a voice hissing in my ear.

"I told you I would tell you everything you need to know. And I meant it."

She lifted my head off the ground and slammed it back down. Light in the darkness, exploding flashes as my head bounced off the pavement.

"Are you taking notes?" She slammed my head down again. Skin split. Something hot and wet ran down my neck. "Whoever you were trying to find? This was always how it was going to end. This is our love."

My heart was spasming out of control in my ears, but not so loud I didn't hear her laugh.

"Probably, anyway. I've never met her."

I lifted my own hands. Not to reach Vodka Straight, but myself. I groped my own face until I felt the smear of anti-freeze on my fingers. And then I went for Vodka Straight, groping in the darkness until I felt the ridges of her brow. I smeared the anti-freeze everywhere I could get my hands on, fumbling desperately for her eyes.

What I felt instead was the wetness of her lips and the slippery length of her tongue, but I went with it. I shoved my chemical-covered fingers down into her throat.

The hands around my throat loosened. The taunting voice in the darkness turned into revolted retching. I bucked hard, throwing my whole body into it and thrusting hard like there was a rocket in my ass. Vodka Straight rolled and I tumbled blindly after her. Her nails gouged my arm. I grabbed a handful of soft flesh, breast flesh, and twisted it as hard as I could. She bit my shoulder. I hit her in the side of the head with the bottom of my fist. We rolled and twisted and writhed, scraping and struggling for control.

Somehow, I wound up on top. Still blind, I dropped my fist and hit nothing but asphalt. Pain burned a fuse through my arm but I had no time to notice it. I tried again. This time, my fist came down like a runaway boulder and smashed against something like a honeydew melon. It cracked. Hot juice smeared my knuckles.

I kept going. Panting and sobbing. Hitting her again and again. Sometimes I felt hard resistance. Other times I hit something that squished inwards beneath my fist. I hit and sobbed and hit some more until the thrashing thing below me stopped moving.

I kept going. I didn't want to, but I learned that once you started this kind of thing it got very hard to stop.

No matter how badly you wanted to.

CHAPTER 16

———————————|———————————

I lived because of Tik Tokers.

A bunch of kids looking to do some parkour in the industrial ruins found me in the parking lot, bled white as a paper towel. And they found what was left of Vodka Straight mashed on the ground next to me.

Her real name was Betsy Rose. DNA evidence would later connect her to thirteen deaths in four states. Thanks to that little detail, there was very little interest in trying to parse what I was doing with her in the first place. It was easy to convince them that I was just another would be victim who got lucky.

The multiple stab wounds didn't hurt either.

I mean, obviously they did. You get what I'm saying.

I was heavily medicated for about two days. Apparently, the first thing I told the doctors was that I guess I had a type, but they assumed that was just the drugs talking.

I remembered none of this myself. It was cheerfully relayed to me by the gentleman in the next bed over. He was in very good spirits for someone stabbed in the stomach by a stripper with a broken martini glass.

I had over 200 stitches. Chemical burns from the anti-freeze had left me legally blind in one eye. Somebody gifted me with a pamphlet on adjusting to life with a missing finger.

And I finally had some clarity about how I'd spent the last twelve fucking years of my life.

When I woke up in the hospital, they had me pumped full of pain killers to numb all the damage that Vodka Straight had done to me.

The pain that Beverly had caused me was buried too. Not by drugs, but what I'd learned fighting to escape somebody who was just like the person Beverly really was.

I'd been chasing a shark, I finally realized. Beverly wasn't an angel. She was a monster who would as soon kill me as talk to me.

But she didn't though.

Oh, for Christ's sake, enough! It was time. What I finally understood was that my love for Beverly was like a pool. Ever since I first met her as a dumb fuck little fourteen-year-old, I had been in that pool up to my neck. Sometimes the water in that pool was frigid, the years I spent waiting for her to even look at me twice. For a brief, blissful period, it was gloriously warm and perfect. Maybe I could have stayed there forever.

But it hadn't worked that way. The water had turned into boiling, scalding blood, and like a fucking moron I'd sank down even deeper. I'd sank into the blood all the way over my head, and I'd nearly drowned.

No more. It was time. What I'd been doing was absurd and pathetic. And it nearly got me killed. It was time. I was going to get medically cleared and I was going to go home. I was going to talk to my parents for the first time in twelve years. I was going to learn who I could be outside of this pool.

My epiphany lasted all of about fifteen minutes. That was how long I got to breathe the air of a sane person before Eddie Harrington, my roommate, turned on the Nascar highlights. "I haven't missed a Yella Wood 500 in fifteen years," he volunteered. "'Course, I never been stabbed at the Rock Bottom before either."

I barely heard him. In between shots of cars turning left, they showed some B-roll of fans tailgating. Lots of sunglasses, cheering, and plenty of drinking.

I sat up straight. My pulse skyrocketed. My heart monitor suddenly started going crazy.

I didn't hear it. I didn't hear the nurses who ran into the room, convinced I was having a heart attack. I was halfway out of bed, ripping stitches and trailing blood behind me as I lunged for Eddie.

His eyes bulged, but with his bed next to the window he had no chance to get away from me.

"Get off! Nurse! Get him offa me! GET HIM OFF!"

"Where is that!" I screamed at him. "Where is that track!?"

Two nurses pulled me back. A third stuck another sedative into my ass.

As the effects took hold, my head cleared enough that I realized I could have simply waited for the track name to appear on the screen.

It did soon enough. Talladega Speedway.

Talladega Speedway was where I saw Beverly Kilbourne again for the first time in twelve years.

It was only a split second, her face briefly facing the camera before she turned partially away and pulled from a beer. Twelve years older than the last time I'd seen her, but I had no doubt.

It was her.

It was her!

The drugs made it a little easier for me to plan my next steps coherently. Drugs, go figure.

Talladega meant... some state. I'd have to look it up. She might have been visiting from out of state, but the split second I'd seen her was seared into my memory. Every detail. Including the people with her. One of them, a man, I noted with a stab of jealousy, wore a t-shirt that said Lansdale High School Boosters. That was a start.

Find a state. Get together a list of towns. And then look at real estate. Beverly's hair shone like melted gold. She was healthy, gorgeous, sitting at a packed event. She had at least some money.

I had to get out of the hospital. I had to finalize whatever I had to with the cops.

Then, I was going to the Lansdale area and I was going to start at the richest house and work my way down.

———|———

And I expected to work my way down. I thought it would take weeks to find even a hint of Beverly. Maybe even months.

I never thought in a thousand years that I would walk up to a sprawling estate, the first house I tried, and find Beverly.

There. Right there in the driveway. Saying, "Help, y'all?" as if she was Alabama born and bred.

Beverly Kilbourne.

My love.

CHAPTER 17

BEVERLY

"Beverly."

He kept saying it.

"Beverly. Beverly. Oh my God, Beverly."

I couldn't say anything. I couldn't *think* anything. He was the headlights and I was the deer.

Anthony. Jesus Christ, *Anthony.* Looking fifty instead of thirty. Woefully thin, hair brittle and already falling out. Christ, was he missing a finger? But his eyes so completely filled with joy. Practically brimming over with love for me.

All of a sudden, I was back in a Beverly Hills pool house. Anthony was naked and wonderfully, exquisitely inside of me, but it was his eyes that truly stabbed into me. His eyes that saw me in a way I'd never been seen before. It wasn't just desire, his desire was satisfied. Anthony had me and he looked at me like he never wanted to leave me. Never. And the thing about somebody looking at you like that was… you believed them. You believed that you were something rare and valuable. You wanted to bask in that feeling for the rest of your life.

He was looking at me the same way now. Lurching towards me like I was the holy grail at the end of a long quest. All these years later, and my head slipped down below the waters of that gaze. My entire body drifted away. In that moment, I was his for the taking. Go ahead, let me be his grail. Come to me, Anthony. Come to me now.

A mosquito bite saved both of our lives.

Moments before I could drown in Anthony's arms, I felt the burning incision of a mosquito bite at the base of my neck. There's no mosquito on earth like an Alabama mosquito, and that sting grounded me back in space and time. Green Mountain, not Beverly Hills. Thirty years old, not eighteen. This wasn't a pool house. This was Paxton Manor. And Anthony wasn't the headlights. He was the deer, and he was standing outside of a house full of hunters and calling out my real name for the whole world to hear.

For his *daughter* to hear.

"I can't believe I really found you, Beverly. You have no idea–"

I clamped my hand hard over his mouth. The same hand I impaled to keep myself from stabbing him in the eye. Could he feel the hard ridge of scar tissue pressed against his lips?

No time for that now. "Stop talking," I hissed. I kept my hand tight over his mouth, I fixed my eyes onto his.

"There is a bar three counties over," I told him. " It's called Campbell's Cabin. I will meet you there tonight at 9 PM. Nod if you understand me."

He did. No hesitation. No dimming of the mad light in his eyes.

"Go," I told him. "Now. Do not say another word." I threw him hard back towards the driveway, praying that he got the point.

He listened, thank God. He stumbled down the front steps back to his car. A rusted piece of shit with the passenger door flapping open as he reversed back up the driveway and wheezed back towards the road, nothing but a cloud of dust to mark his presence.

I remembered the El Camino he had in high school. He kept it immaculate.

"Anthony," I mumbled. "What the hell happened to you?"

As if I didn't know.

The door opened then. Reese poked her head out. "Was somebody knocking?"

I forced myself to shake my head dismissively. "Just a bible thumper."

Reese pouted. "And you didn't invite him in to discuss Ecclesiastes Chapter 3, Verse 3? Boo."

I shot her a look. Not quite a scowl. "Cat's home."

Ecclesiastes 3:3 was a family joke. *A time to kill.*

Reese's smile withered as she got a better look at me. "Pam, are you okay? You're shaking."

Well, that was a ridiculous thing for her to say. Why would I be shaking? I was fine. I had to be fine. *"I'm fine,"* I tried to say, just to prove it, but nothing came out of my mouth but empty air.

"Pam?" Reese asked. She spoke out loud, with actual words and everything. Show off.

But that was fine. I could use words too. Watch. *"I'm fine,"* I didn't say.

Reese's face contorted with worry, and then it contorted even more as my vision doubled, tripled, and then devolved into a bunch of blurry abstract paintings. I swayed on my feet. I might have fallen over if she hadn't grabbed my wrist. "Oh shit," Reese said. "Jen! Jen, get over here!"

She led me forward and I went along. It wasn't really walking though, more like a bunch of little falls strung together. Fall. Catch. Fall. Catch. It looked like we were going into the house, but it was hard to tell. Everything was so fuzzy around the edges, like trying to watch a video online when the connection kept dropping.

"Come on, Pam. Into the AC," she urged. Then, louder. "JEN, HELP ME!'

We stopped walking and this time I didn't catch myself. I just fell. I landed on something soft and sank into it. This was better. Much better. My head flopped backwards and, what do you know, something soft there too.

There was a rumble of feet. Another blurry figure and a new voice.

"Oh my God! Reese, what happened!?"

"I don't know. There's something wrong with her."

A rush of blood hit my head. My hand clutched at the armrest of the chair then. I sat up straight as the world sharpened into high definition. The way I needed it to be so I could clearly see Reese. Reese, who had said that there was something wrong with me.

"No," I snarled. I tried to lunge up, but the two of them were already there, hands on my shoulders trying to gently force me back down. "Pam, don't try to get up," Jen coaxed. "Just take it easy." Neither of them realized how angry I was. They were both just trying to make sure I was okay.

I said it again. "No. There's nothing wrong with me. I'm fine."

I was. I was fine. Pamela was fine. Pamela was in her house. Pamela was with her sisters.

Reese and Jen weren't convinced. "Okay, sure," Reese said. "You're totally fine. You're great. But I also think you're maybe having a heat stroke so let's just stay here, ok?" Her hand was still on my shoulder. To emphasize her point, she squeezed and my thin t-shirt actually *squelched* with sweat. "Jen's going to get you some water, okay? Just stay here until she does."

"Lemonade, okay?" I smiled at her, like my heart wasn't currently hammering my ribs to dust. "How about a lemonade?"

They both laughed then, the sound of it taking down the temperature in the room about fifteen degrees. "Whatever you want," Jen said.

She went to the kitchen while Reese continued to hover anxiously over me.

"I'm *fine*," I told her, hoping that at least one of us believed it. "You were right. Just a little too much sun."

"This is why I only go out at night," Reese observed.

I laughed. A real laugh.

"Are you really okay?" she pressed.

"I am," I assured her. "All good."

"Just take it easy," Jen added as she returned with my lemonade. I drank gratefully. It was exactly what I needed. Fresh and cold. Just tart enough to put some bite in my brain.

"I will," I promised her. "I actually think I'm going to go out by myself tonight. Just relax and look at the water somewhere."

"That's a good idea," Reese said.

It didn't strike either of them as weird. Pamela often went out by herself. Pamela would love to sit at a bar and have a drink or two.

Pamela might even have the strength to solve the Anthony dilemma for good. Something Beverly was never able to do.

"Holy fuck, LUKE!" Jen cried. She gaped at the doorway in pure horror.

I straightened up immediately as Jen called out his name. I couldn't let Luke see me off balance. Especially not if he'd killed some defenseless thing in the woods and was dragging the bloody carcass home to show off to the rest of us.

I didn't need to worry about any of that. Luke stood bare-chested in the doorway, looking as pale as a pig with its throat cut. I say "stood," but that was too generous. It was more like he was clinging desperately to the door frame just to stay upright. He swayed woozily. His one hand was on the doorway, but the other hung low by his hip in a gunslinger's stance.

Not that a gunslinger could do much damage with a hand wrapped in a blood-soaked t-shirt like Luke's was.

"Reese, call an ambulance!" Jen yelled. She was already uncoiling towards her brother.

"No need for that, dear."

The voice hit pause on the world. Reese froze. Jen stopped mid-uncoil. Nobody moved a muscle, even as Luke pitched forward, landing on his hands and knees and then sinking to his elbows. They just watched, totally immobile, as their brother crumpled to the ground with the ruin of his left hand, leaving a bloody smear on the hardwood as it sprawled in front of him.

Mama Charlize stepped in out of the hot sun's glare. Her sturdy bulk lumbered into the exact space previously occupied by her son. Her dress, pristine the last time I saw her, was now speckled with red splotches of her Luke's blood.

"Don't worry your pretty little mind, Reese's Cup. Your brother, bless his heart, was just careless working on the airboat this morning. Cost him three fingers on his throwing hand, so it did."

On the floor, Luke groaned.

"Can't unspill that milk now, of course. But Momma was there to patch him up and make sure things didn't get any worse." She fingered one of the many bloody patches dotting her floral dress. "Messy business, but it was taken care of in the end. Now, be good girls and help your brother up to his room. I've still got some painkillers from my knee surgery in the bathroom closet and if there's anything else he needs, make sure he gets it."

Mama Charlize's placid gaze met mine, still as the lake on a windless day. I could only guess how much was churning behind that poker face.

Probably about as much as there was lurking behind mine.

"Treat him good now," she cautioned the sisters. "That's what family's for, isn't it?" she asked me. "To take care of each other."

Jen and Reese knelt down. Luke probably weighed as much as both of them together, but the girls were built out of pipes and wire. They got him up.

"Come on, Luke. Move your feet," Jen coaxed. "We've got you."

"Pamela, dear," Charlize said, as if her son wasn't leaving a bloody trail between us as he was shuffled away. "I overheard you saying you might go out tonight. I think a little time to yourself sounds like a wonderful idea. All mommas need a breather once in a while, and I'd say you're long overdue." She smiled. There was a fleck of dark blood on one of her yellowed teeth. "And don't worry about Catherine while you're gone, I'll watch every hair on her little head."

I nodded, not trusting myself to speak without spilling out every suddenly living memory of Anthony I'd buried for twelve years.

I was going out to have some time to myself. That was all. I was just going out for some fresh air. I repeated it again and again. Mindful that Auntie was mounted up there on the wall, judging me with her polished brown eyes that saw all and knew all.

Liar, she told me.

Liar.

Pretender.

Fraud.

———————|———————

Campbell's Cabin got its name from someone who was either a genius or the worst person on earth.

It wasn't a cabin. The building had actually begun its life as a long, squat warehouse for a defunct fertilizer company before the current owners, Sam and Ted Campbell, bought it and converted it into a bar.

Then, a day before the grand opening of what was supposed to be called Campbell's Cans and Drafts, a drunk taxi driver had plowed his cab through one of the cheap tin walls and pulverized the bar to splinters. Rather than delay the opening, Sam and Ted proceeded as planned, but changed the name from Campbell's Cans and Drafts to Campbell's Cabin.

Cab-in. Get it?

The original cab was still there, converted into a bar top covered in twenty years of drink rings. The bar had become something of an institution for people who liked loud music and cheap drinks. A good place for people who didn't want to wake up with any memories of the night before.

And, therefore, a good place for people who didn't want to be recognized.

A good place not to be seen at all, in fact.

I hung back at the edge of the gravel parking lot. I'd taken Owen's big pickup truck and it blended in seamlessly with a dozen more just like it. This far from the door, I was wrapped comfortably in shadows, barely even touched by the neon lights in the windows.

Anthony wasn't supposed to be here for another two hours, but I wasn't taking any chances. There was only one entrance into Campbell's, and I had a clear view of it. The moment Anthony arrived, I'd know.

What exactly does that mean, Beverly? What are you planning to do to him?

I shook my head until that pesky voice was brushed off like an errant mosquito. I didn't know what I was going to do. I didn't have a plan. I just had a life that worked. A life I wasn't looking to screw up because an old boyfriend had crawled out of the woodwork. I wasn't a kid anymore. I hadn't seen Anthony in twelve years. I was going to do what I had to do. End of story.

Knuckles cracked against glass right next to my ear. I whipped around in my seat and instinctively raised the butcher knife out of my lap.

Anthony didn't flinch at the sight of the blade. He just gestured for me to roll down the window.

Filled with the same ethereal unreality that had possessed me ever since he showed up, I obliged. Just a crack.

"I learned a thing or two about parking lots from my last date with a serial killer," he said. "You ready to come out?"

…A lot to unpack there, but it was the most mundane part that jumped out at me.

"This isn't a date," I told him.

"Right. It's just a beer."

He walked towards the bar, not bothering to see if I followed.

CHAPTER 18

ANTHONY

I heard a door slam, followed by her footsteps crunching in the gravel behind me. After all this time, now she was the one following me.

It wasn't love I felt at the thought of her trailing behind me. It should have been. Love was what I felt when I'd found her earlier in the day. The pure, lightning bolt from the sky love that I used to feel when our lockers were next to each other and I made it just in time to see her sweeping down the hallway with that wreath of golden hair draped around her head. That feeling, the hardy permanence of it, had carried me the last twelve years. I just assumed it would still be with me.

Instead, I found myself thinking of one of the stories they told us in religious ed before my parents got tired of having one more thing to schedule every week. The story of Moses who had led the Hebrews to the Promised Land, but who had been forbidden to enter himself.

I listened to her feet dragging through the gravel behind me, and it was satisfaction I felt. Not love.

We grabbed a corner table in the back, far from the stage where a trio of part time musicians were slaughtering a Drive-by Truckers cover. A pitcher of bright yellow beer and two plastic cups sat between us. Beverly hadn't touched hers, but I'd already drained two cups in the five minutes we'd been sitting there in silence. She kept trying not to stare. Her eyes would settle on me for the briefest second and then flit away again just as quickly. She was a frog in a pan of boiling oil. No place to settle down.

"I know what you're going to say," I began, breaking the awkward silence. "I still kept my figure from high school."

Hardy har har. I was a skinny kid, but I ate just fine. I wasn't snorting Adderall or abusing myself – I was just thin. But that was then. I could only guess what I looked like right now. Probably like a meth addict going on 72 hours without sleep. A hollow thing with sunken eyes and gaunt skin stretched almost transparent over rickety bones.

I was what she made me.

"This is a mistake, Anthony," she said.

I took another pull of beer. "It's good to hear you say that," I said with caustic calm. "I mean, I figured there was some kind of mix up when you butchered all of our friends on prom night and disappeared without a word. Still, it's nice to know for sure that you didn't deliberately stand me up. That kind of embarrassment could really screw somebody up."

"How did you figure it out?" she asked.

I laughed humorlessly. "After the prom that wasn't, college didn't really work out for me." She flinched at that, but I ignored it and kept talking. I traced my finger along the rim of my plastic cup. "Instead, I went looking for you. What I found was your mother in the trunk where you left her. That was just a few months after you disappeared. I could have called the cops on you then, Beverly. How far do you think you would have gotten with every police station in the country looking for you?"

There was a flash of anger in her eyes then. "What?" she challenged. "Am I supposed to say thank you? I would have figured it out. I didn't ask for your help, Anthony. I don't owe you anything."

Her anger spread to me, like sparks flying in a wildfire. Fresh fury kindled deep in my own chest. I spilled beer over the table as I sloppily refilled my glass. "I'm pretty sure you do owe me, actually. You left me on prom night to find my best friend's head in a fucking bag!"

Beverly slammed the table. "Your head was supposed to be in there too." She didn't even hold her fingers apart. Her thumb and index finger were pressed together until the flesh turned white. "That's how close you were, Anthony."

"So, I'm the one who should be thankful then?" I hissed.

"I let you *go!*" Beverly said. Her eyes actually shimmered in the dim light of the bar. "I couldn't do it, Anthony. Not to you"

"You loved me too much to cut my head off? You really want praise for that?"

"I thought that it was love," Beverly said. "And maybe that's what it felt like. But I was a kid. We both were. We didn't know the first thing about love."

"I did," I snapped back. "I loved you."

She shook her head. Christ, she had the audacity to look like she felt *bad* for me.

"We dated for four months, Anthony. We were going to go to college on separate sides of the country. Maybe I would be the first one to take too long to text back, or maybe it would be you. Maybe I'd cancel a weekend visit and maybe that wouldn't bother you because some girl had invited you to a party. Eventually, the little kid love we felt for each other would have dried up. You would have figured that out too eventually, but you never had that chance because of what I did to you." She shrugged. "I'm sorry. Maybe I really should have killed you. Maybe that would have been easier."

"Oh, do *NOT* pretend that you're the emotionally mature one here!" I yelled. It was a good thing the music was so loud. Even the most diligent eavesdropper couldn't pick out a word between us. We looked like any other drunk couple arguing about whether over-the-pants counted as cheating. "You're depraved," I raged at her. "You really are. You cut people to pieces like they're fucking meat, and you do it because you like it. There's nothing wrong with you. Nobody diddled you at cheer camp or locked you in a closet after school. You're just a fucking monster."

"That's fucking right!" Beverly screamed back. "I knew who I was, and I didn't turn into some sorority twat just because that's what was expected of me. Judge me all that you want, but I made the life I wanted. What did you do?"

What did I do? I thought incredulously. *WHAT DID I DO?!*

"I chased the life I wanted too, Beverly! I wanted *you!*"

I dropped out of school. I abandoned my family. I lived on cheese sandwiches and dressed out of Salvation Army boxes. I was sliced up like deli meat and I lost a finger. I did all of that to be with you and you never once thought about what happened to me.

I ran both hands through my hair and slumped down in my chair. "Fuck, I spent so much time trying to find you. I thought you would be happy, but you don't care about me. You never did."

The screaming was done. The music was louder than ever, but it couldn't drown out the silence between us that followed my final statement. Beverly reached out with mechanical precision and cooly took a single sip from her beer.

"There, now we've had a beer," Beverly said. She spoke barely above a whisper, but I had no problems hearing her. "You're mad at me. I'm mad at you. So now we can both put the high school shit behind us and get on with our lives. Goodbye, Anthony."

She got up.

I didn't follow.

CHAPTER 19

———————¦———————

Of course, I fucking did.

———————¦———————

"Beverly!" I shouted.

I caught her in the parking lot. She'd made it at that far while I stewed at the table, swearing that I wouldn't go after her.

Fuck her. She had her life and she was happy with it. She hadn't spent the last twelve years obsessing over me. Wishing I was with her. Thinking about what it was like to lay on a bed side by side, our foreheads pressed together. How, sometimes, if she breathed just right, I would feel the warm current of her exhale across my upper lip. She was happy. She was sleeping in the fucking house from Gone with the Wind and having a jolly good time. My quest was done. I'd found her. I could do whatever I wanted now.

…I got up.

———————¦———————

She heard me, but she kept marching towards her shiny pickup at the back of the lot. "Leave it alone, Anthony!" she called over her shoulder.

"I killed someone!" I screamed, my voice echoing out into the trees surrounding the tiny bar.

That got her to stop at least. I jogged closer, the two of us standing there, surrounded by pickup trucks and tiny, beat-up compacts. I stood there facing her back, panting from even that much exertion. Waiting for her.

At last, she turned back around. She spun on her heels, so goddamn liquid smooth. Her blue eyes, dark as the Pacific in the parking lot's dim light, measured me carefully. Trying to gauge how truthful I was being.

In response, I raised my hand for her to see. The one with the missing finger.

"I went looking for you," I said. "I found someone else instead. And I beat her to death with my bare hands. The way it felt was..." I broke off as my mouth twisted in a wretched grimace at the memory. It probably looked like it was for dramatic effect, but it was honest as could be. I couldn't think about what I did, how Vodka Straight thrashed beneath me like a fish spasming at the bottom of a boat, without wanting to puke.

"It's not that way for me, Anthony," she said.

"Then what way is it?" I pressed. "It's done between us. You're right. But you didn't have to leave like you did. You didn't need to kill your parents. You didn't need to kill your best friends."

"Anthony –"

I plowed over her, ripping out words as fast as my heart pounded in my chest. "But you did kill them. You wanted to. You just couldn't leave without eating the last fucking cookies in the box. So, killing for you must be the best feeling in the fucking world. Am I right? What does that feel like? What about it made you do what you did? I tried it, Beverly. I killed, and I still don't understand. I need to, Beverly. Please, give me that much. Please!"

Beverly didn't answer me with words at first. She just poured closer, moving through the gravel like liquid smoke, not making a sound, until she was right in front of me. She grabbed my hand, the one missing a finger, and inspected it carefully.

"How did she do it?" She asked.

"She was waiting for me in the back of my car," I said. I turned around and lifted my shirt, letting her see the scars there. "She stabbed me before I even knew what was happening."

I turned back around, and Beverly was smiling.

"I love that trick," she said. "I go for the neck myself. Sideways. When you have to stab through the seat like that you lose too many inches on penetration. It's probably the only reason you're still alive."

You'd think I wouldn't be surprised. I already knew what she was. But hearing it coming out of her mouth, appraising my wounds like she was critiquing a piece of art, was something else. The difference between reading about lions on Wikipedia and finding yourself in the cage with a lioness.

"What do you want to hear from me, Anthony? Guilt? Do you want me to tell you that it was hard to massacre them all like I did? It wasn't. It's what I'm built for." She sighed then. "But that doesn't mean I enjoyed it."

She sauntered closer. She was in reach now. I smelled the hint of beer on her breath. The light was dim out here, but Beverly glowed brighter still as her hands came up and gently cradled the back of my head. I let her do it, docile as a newborn baby deer. I had no choice. The twin blue suns of her eyes had me trapped inexorably in their gravity.

"I didn't hate them, but I hated what they did to me," she said. "My parents. My friends... You. All of you had me in a box. A box that got smaller every day I stayed inside it."

Her fingers cupping my scalp suddenly slipped lower. They were around my throat now, her thumbs under my jaw and her fingers pressed against the sides of my neck. Slender, but so strong. Coils of copper cinching shut.

"I am a killer, Anthony. Not a cheerleader. Not a daughter. Not a friend. The smaller that box got, the less room there was for me. I couldn't share anymore, I had to get out. And the only way out was through all of you."

I didn't resist, even as blinking gnats of darkness started to cluster at the corner of my vision. I heard them buzzing as Beverly squeezed harder.

"Do you remember my speech at graduation, Anthony? "Make your essential self your only self. No matter the cost.' Well, I meant it. The cost was my mother. My father. My friends. I paid it, and I'm glad that I did."

She let my neck go. Fresh blood flooded back into the dry riverbed of my brain. My darkening vision brightened, and it was Beverly in front of me. Chin high. Eyes defiant.

"That's what murder means to me," she said. "More than their lives. More than being with you. Does that answer your question?"

In response, I put my hands around her neck.

"I do remember your speech," I said.

I kissed her.

No matter the cost.

CHAPTER 20

BEVERLY

He kissed me.

His hands came around the back of my head and up into my hair. His tongue in my mouth tasted like cheap taquitos, and his unkempt stubble crawled across my cheeks. He pressed the entirety of his body against mine and it felt like kissing a skeleton.

I caught his jaw. I pinched until I heard bone creak, forced his head as far back away from me as my arm would allow, and I held him there. Anthony didn't try to fight me, but his whole body thrummed with energy like a live powerline. I felt it tingling down my wrist, through my arm, stopping all the way at-

I yanked Anthony back to me with the force of an incoming comet. I tilted his head back – *Anthony's head. Anthony's skin against my fingers* – and this time, I kissed him.

That's too easy. I didn't just kiss him back. I tried to taste the very core of him. I tried to make up for twelve missing years in ten seconds of my lips against his.

Anthony caught up quickly. His mouth moved to match my furious pace. He pulled my hips tight against his and I responded by rolling against his thigh. "You should have killed me," he whispered in the gaps as our mouths mashed together. "You should have known I'd never stop looking for you."

I bit his ear, and then lathered the teeth marks with a slow sweep of my tongue. "Do you have any idea how fucked up that sounds?"

Anthony kissed down my neck in a molten trail of small bites and nips, exactly where I needed him to be. It was always like this between us. Almost rehearsed in how easy it was to make each other boil. "Good thing I love a monster then," he said.

I threw him away from me with the disgust of someone flinging away a dead rat. Anthony staggered and landed face first in the muddy tread marks left behind by some truck.

"Don't," I warned him. Everything came back to me. The humidity. The music from the bar. My life. I backed away from him like there was a bomb strapped to my chest. "You don't love me. You can't."

"Yes, I do," Anthony said. He was getting his knees under him in the mud. A boxer getting up for another round.

"Maybe you did back then, fine. But that was a lot of life ago."

He forced himself back up and tried to reach out for me. "Beverly."

Pamela.

"Anthony, I'm married," I told him.

Anthony didn't flinch. "…Yes, I can see how that could complicate things."

"Oh my God, I'm serious!"

"Beverly, does infidelity really seem like a deal breaker? Really?"

"It's not your marriage! My life is good, Anthony. I'm happy. You can't just roll in here like a fucking nuke and ruin it."

"I get it, Beverly. I know this is a mess." He took a slow step closer. "It is," he repeated. "It's a mess. It's an overturned septic truck of a mess. You're happy. I believe you when you say it, but if you want this to be done between us, I need to hear you say that you don't want to be with me."

"Have you not been fucking listening?" I said.

"You said your life is good. That's not the same thing. Two things can be good. Tell me that you don't want to be with me. Say it and I'll believe you."

I don't want to be with you.

I don't want to be with you, Anthony.

Go away, Anthony.

Anthony, you need to leave.

I pictured myself saying it a dozen different ways, but not a single one of them could make it past my lips. I expected a smug grin, but Anthony almost looked apologetic. "I can't leave Beverly," he whispered. "I can't make you do anything. This is your choice, I know that. But I can't leave if you haven't made it. Not until you say you don't want me."

"Or until I say I do want you?" I replied. "That's the other part of this, right? You want me to walk away from everything for you."

He shrugged. "It wouldn't suck."

"You really think that's going to happen, Anthony?" I asked.

That grin. That slow, wry grin I loved so much. "I've got no idea. I never had a clue, Beverly. All I ever wanted from you was a chance. You gave me one once, and nothing went bad between you and me. You wanted other things for your life. You had your reasons... but I don't care about any of that. I mean it."

I shook my head. "You've got no idea what you're talking about."

Anthony held up his hand with the missing finger. "I've got more than a layman's understanding. Listen, this is all fast. I get it. It's fast for me too." He let out a jittery laugh. "I didn't really believe that I'd walk right into you at the first house I tried. I thought I'd have time to figure out what to say, or how to say it. This... *this.* It's too much right now. I get it. Let's slow down. But can you think about it?"

"Think about *what?*" I asked. As if I wasn't still thinking about the kiss. Or the hot ash still smoldering in my belly.

Stop it.

"Think about seeing me again," he pressed. "Or just talking to me some more. Can we talk?"

He let it hang between us. I stood there opposite him, feeling like a complete fucking mess. I wished we were still inside. I needed a whiskey.

"I know what I want, Beverly. But whatever happens next is going to be up to you. I hope it's me, but I know that I can't control you."

He wanted to kiss me again. I felt his need thicker than the humidity. But he was filthy with mud now, so he kept his distance, smart enough to know not to get his mess on me any more than I already had.

I knew how I should answer. That my life was complete. That I had everything I needed. That Anthony ought to leave right now and forget any of this happened.

"...We can talk," I relented. "That's it. I'm not promising anything, Anthony."

He wiped some mud off his face. "It wouldn't be my first shot in the dark with you."

I didn't warn him that it might be his last.

I should have. He had no clue how dangerous the Paxtons could be.

But I saw the smile on his face, and I couldn't make myself do it.

I couldn't hurt him like that again.

CHAPTER 21

———————

It was going to be a beautiful day.

I knew it before I even opened my eyes. A summer storm had been drowning the whole county for the last three days. Roads were flooded. The sump pump in the basement had hummed nonstop until I dreamed of dentists' torturing me to death with a drill. If we weren't already murderers, seven people cooped up together for half a week might have done the trick.

On the fourth day, I could hear the Yellowhammers singing outside while I lingered in that dark awareness between sleep and wakefulness. Three short, high trills and one long, low note. Again and again, announcing that the clouds had fallen silent and the sun had returned.

I opened my eyes and felt vindicated at the gentle yellow light coming through the high window. I stretched for Owen and wasn't surprised to feel nothing but cooling sheets. Sunday mornings were his alone time. He was probably out in the barn, lifting hay bales over his head and banging out pull ups on the rafter. We'd see him right around breakfast time, squeezing in next to me at the table just as the eggs were coming off the griddle, sweat laminating the muscle shirt to his broad shoulders.

I stretched, feeling a stubborn kink in my back finally crack loose. From downstairs, the raspy murmur of Jen's voice and Cat's laugh drifting up. I got a move on before all of the good pastries were gone.

"Hey, look who it is!" Reese teased as I came down. I rolled my eyes. My morning tardiness and Mama Charlize's displeasure was a long running gag at this point. Today, if Mama had any comments, she kept them to herself. She felt the same excitement as the rest of us, even if she didn't show it. The day held too much promise for petty sniping.

Inadvertently confirming my point, Luke called over to me from the gas range. "Pam, over easy or scrambled?"

"Scrambled." I grabbed a lemon tart and sat down towards the end of the table. Cat on one side of me, the other seat open. "Hey, kid," I said.

A few minutes later, Luke set a plate down in front of me without so much as a whisper of the ceramic touching the table. No scowl. No passive aggressive comment. No lingering leer for either me or Cat. He just set a plate down for me and an identical one down in the empty seat beside me.

On cue, the back door swung open and Owen sauntered inside with a coat of sweat like a horse that had just finished running the Kentucky Derby. I was wrong about one thing though; he hadn't even bothered with the muscle shirt.

"Hey, beautiful." He kissed me just behind the ear before setting down beside me. "Cat," he nodded before scooping up a forkful of eggs.

"You ever notice how he never bids us a good morning?" Jen asked to nobody in particular.

"That's true, Jen." Reese looked at her brother over the rim of her black glasses. "Do you not want us to have a good morning, Owen?"

Owen mugged at them. "Of course I don't," he said. As if it were the most obvious thing in the world. Then he laughed as Reese threw a biscuit at him, snatching it easily out of the air and taking a hearty bite.

"Enough of that," Mama Charlize cautioned. "Or I'll cancel this whole trip right now." So she said, but we all saw the smirk trying to weasel its way out between those dark red lips. Luke hacked a cough into his clenched fist. A cough that sounded suspiciously like, "Bullshit!"

Mama Charlize methodically spooned up a mouthful of grits and pointedly avoided looking at her son.

They could have gone on like this all morning, but nobody had the patience for it. We were going antiquing today, and everyone was eager to get on the road as quickly as possible. It was a family tradition, almost as cherished as gutting a youth group.

Breakfast broke and we went back to our rooms for some presentable clothes. For me, that just meant shimmying into a romper and tucking my hair into a pony tail. Owen, needing to shower after his workout, would need an extra fifteen minutes.

With little else to do, I browsed through some mindless celebrity gossip on my phone as I waited. Jackie Galindo and Tracee Trance were having a baby. Paul Sheldon had died. Some new docu-series was coming out about the Lambert family. It was grocery store tabloid shit, but it beat scrolling through my social media and seeing another half dozen memes from Reese about Senator Fields and his jihad to save America.

Yes, that was the only thing keeping me away from social media right now. Just an aversion to my sister-in-law's propaganda bullshit. Nothing more.

Certainly not the red notification at the top corner of the screen. The message waiting for a response.

I heard the water in the bathroom die to a trickle. I gratefully set down my phone and rose to my knees on the bed as Owen came out with a towel wrapped around his hips. I pouted at the sight of the covering and he chuckled. "Rain check, babe. Don't wanna keep everyone waiting."

I shook my head ruefully, but he was right. Pam couldn't be selfish like that.

She was part of the family.

CHAPTER 22

———— ———

Antique Sunday.

The second Sunday of every month. That was the tradition. Rain or shine, but it was always so much better with the sun shining. That was why we'd all been in such good spirits at breakfast. It was impossible not to step out onto the porch, the air fresh and steam-cleaned, the sun dappling through the trees, and not realize it was going to be a perfect day.

The good mood carried over as we got onto the road. Luke, the sisters, and Mama Charlize in Luke's pickup. Me and Kat with Owen in his Mustang. We didn't have a destination in mind, but you don't have to drive far in Alabama to find things from another era. We headed west down cracked county roads, following the trees as they got bigger and older until we saw a sign for "Antiques." The single word was written on a propped up wooden plank with an arrow pointing down a dirt road.

"Paydirt," Owen grinned, easing down the fork.

The dirt road led to a barn that was already an antique itself. The paint had faded to bare wood, and the only animals I saw were a quartet of mournful crows loitering on a length of wooden fencing. The old man parked outside the barn was an antique too. Twelve pounds of flesh like beef jerky, wrapped in flannel and jeans on a 90-degree day, but not a single bead of sweat left to wring out of him.

"Afternoon, folks," he called out cheerfully as the group of us disembarked. Even his voice sounded dusty.

"Afternoon'," Jen called back, just as sweetly. "You open?"

"Til about one," he allowed. "Martinsville qualifier starts then and I'll be closin' up. You're welcome to look around until then."

"We'll be gone by then too," Luke chuckled. The bandages on his hand were clean and white, and he didn't have a care in the world.

The old man had about a dozen tables in and around the barn, and about an equal number of wooden shelves crammed with bric a brac. There was precious little in the way of organization – 1950s college textbooks next to a Sharper Image blender. A stack of DVDs on top of a tractor seat with no tractor attached to it. But there was gold in them there hills, you just had to have the patience to sort around for what you wanted.

It was only a matter of time before we started to sift some gems out of the wreckage. Mama Charlize zeroed in on a shelf of antique pink glassware. Reese snagged a batch of vinyl records from the 90s.

But it was Owen who found the real score. He caught my eye from outside the barn and mouthed, "Jackpot." I abandoned the collection of vintage Raymond Chandler pulps I'd been perusing and swung in his direction. The rest of the family followed soon after. Everything else that had caught our attention was completely forgotten.

Owen had found weapons.

This was one of my favorite parts of living in the country. Close your eyes and pick an old farmhouse trying to scratch a profit out from seventy years of dumpster diving. Every single one of them had blades. This was a particularly good stash, too. No cheap flea market daggers with dragon-shaped handles that broke in half the first time they hit tough meat. These were authentic knives, axes, and saws from the turn of the last century. Tried and true working blades. A meat cleaver. A long, slim watermelon knife. A butcher knife from when that actually meant something literal. The wooden handles were faded and rough, but still sturdy. The iron blades were clouded, but well-maintained. Not a speck of rust on any of them.

And not a single one cost more than five dollars.

"They've even got some straight razors," Owen said. He tested the hinge on a pearl-handled razor, stained yellow by the decades. I reached up and playfully scratched the stubble under his chin. "I like you like this."

He grinned. "I guess I'll just have to use it on someone else's face then." He leaned down to kiss me and I met him eagerly, pressing back for just a little longer than necessary. It was good. His hard body pressed against my chest. The warmth of the sun shining down on us. His lips against mine.

I knew he couldn't, but I couldn't help but wonder if he could still taste Anthony on me? It had been a week since I'd seen him at the bar, and I'd brushed my teeth three times a day ever since, but was there something fundamental that couldn't be washed away. Did betrayal have a taste of its own?

I was being stupid. Of course it didn't. Owen pulled away from me and all I saw was the same satisfied smile I saw every time we came up for air.

I matched his smile, hating the way I felt. Walking around like I was wrapped in a layer of insulation. Putting on a show and laying it on so damn thick that I couldn't properly enjoy the things I wanted to do.

It had been decades since I felt this way, but I recognized it the same way someone with a long illness knows when they're out of remission and the condition is back again.

I am Beverly. I'm head cheerleader. I am a murderer. I like to go out drinking with my friends. I like smashing people's heads like a bag of Doritos.

I am Pamela. I am married. I'm making plans to see my old high school boyfriend again. I'm happy with my husband. I've kissed another man. I have a family that loves me. I want to kiss Anthony again.

None of it came to the surface. I had plenty of practice keeping part of myself hidden, and I loathed how easily I was able to pick up the habit again.

But I had to. I had no choice.

You see, I knew the story of Owen's father.

"Does everybody have what they want?" Mama Charlize asked. At her call, the siblings started gathering up their purchases. Owen took the straight razor and he also lifted the watermelon knife from the assortment on the table. The razor was for him, but the long blade with the tapered end was not. Owen didn't need to ask, he knew what I liked. Long, slim, and sharp.

Just like Anthony.

"Come on," Mama chided. "Bring them here." This was part of the ritual. Whatever you picked– blades, vintage records. Luke had a vintage Plymouth Fury hood ornament, it was Mama Charlize who did the negotiating. Haggling for pennies as if she wasn't sitting on seven figures.

"Excuse me, sir?"

That was Cat. She was by the shopkeeper already, barely taller than the third button on the tall, lanky man's shirt.

"I noticed some Silky Canella growing over by the fence. Would it be alright if I put some in a pot?"

The old man's face cracked open in a wide smile. Cat had that effect on people. He glanced to the rest of us, arms full of potential sales, and said, "I reckon we could throw in a few flowers."

"You'll be throwing in a lot more than flowers!" Charlize put in. "I promise you that."

I left them to it. I joined Cat over by the wooden fence. She had a trowel in one hand and a plastic bucket in the other. She never went anywhere without them.

"Where is this gonna go?" I asked.

"The east slope," she said. She barely looked at me, too intent in digging a clean circle around the roots. "Next to the Milkweed."

"Really? I thought it would look nice next to those… you know, the blue ones with the red tips."

She looked up now. Long suffering patience.

"Mom, those are shade plants. Silky Canella needs full sun."

They were all just flowers to me. Colors, dirt, and water. Anthony would have known. The minute she showed an interest in horticulture, he would have learned everything he could. What species was this?

How much water does that one need? He had the ability to learn that kind of thing. More important, he would have had the devotion.

He would have been a very good dad.

I slipped away from Cat. Quickly. There was suddenly too much heat. Too much pollen in my eyes. I went back towards the others. Mama Charlize had a set of two knives and a PJ Harvey album set to one side, the already agreed upon pile, and was now banging a meat cleaver against the table.

"It wobbles!" she insisted. "I have been a butcher since I could walk and I know a wobbly cleaver when I'm swingin' one! I won't pay full price for it. No, sir. Not in a year of Sundays!"

I grabbed Owen by the arm and pulled him off to the side.

"Is everything okay?" he asked.

Oh dear, couldn't have him saying that. I tightened up the corners of my smile. It wasn't hard at all. Just flipping a switch.

"Allergies," I told him.

"Bad?" he asked.

I shook my head. "I'll be fine. I was just thinking, did you see that clearing off the road on the way in?"

"The one with the worn tire trails in the grass? The one overlooking the river?"

Of course he'd seen it too. And he'd been thinking the same thing I had.

Make out spot.

"Maybe Cat goes home with your family and we stay out a little bit, just the two of us. What do you think?"

He pulled me in close. "I think let's paint the town red."

The rest of the family went along when we told them. Cat with a shrug, Jen and Reese with knowing grins, Luke with his first scowl of the day.

None of it mattered. What mattered was they left with my daughter and Owen and I found a roadside stand selling boiled peanuts. We shared a sack of them in the car for dinner, and then we shared a pint of whiskey while we waited for the sun to go down. The windows in the Mustang were open, but we didn't have the AC on. The dark night air was much better, the heat of it making our backs stick to the leather and the sweet scent of our own perspiration growing heavier by the second.

It wasn't long after dark that another car pulled up. A wheezing jeep with cloudy headlights that painted the trees in murky yellow light.

The lights didn't stay on long. The jeep had barely shifted into park before we saw the two shadowy silhouettes inside meet in a tangle of black ink like a Rorshach blot. Clearly, very little time for formalities here.

That suited Owen and I just fine. We wordlessly slipped out of the Mustang, leaving the doors open so there wouldn't be any noise of them closing again. The grass was still damp from all the rain, muffling any sound from our footsteps as we sauntered closer to the gently rocking Jeep. We held hands most of the way, but as we got closer, we drifted apart, angling off to opposite sides of the vehicle. Closing them off from both ends.

The Jeep was an open top. Very considerate of them. I scrambled up onto the hood and over the windshield. They may have caught a brief glimpse of me, a shadowy tarantula crawling up over the glass, and then I was over the cage and dropping down like the Holy Spirit to break up their lustful embrace.

Up close, I could see them better. They were a young couple. Seventeen at the most. The girl was blonde. The boy had glasses.

Owen came in through the unlocked passenger door. He grabbed the girl by that long blonde hair and yanked her close to his chest. He clamped a hand over her mouth and jammed an icepick in her eye. He left the pick sticking out of her eye socket, grabbed her by the scalp and chin, and shattered her neck for good measure.

I landed in the boy's lap. My legs straddling his waist and wedged between his chest and the steering wheel. Tight, but I made it work.

He was afraid. Everything unfolded in mere seconds, but he must have been a smart kid. Smart enough to quickly understand what was happening, but not fast enough to stop it. I had the watermelon knife with me. Charlize had gotten the old man to sharpen it before we parted ways, and it was agile and beautiful to control. I swept the blade across his neck and the flesh parted like wrapping paper. Hot blood sprayed in my face and poured down his chest, pooling in the foot wells in a three-inch downpour. You couldn't put your feet down without ruining your socks.

Luckily, the river was right there for rinsing, and it was a nice enough night to go barefoot.

We left the bodies where they fell and found a small motel for ourselves. Dirty sheets. A broken air conditioner. Thin walls.

"It's our honeymoon all over again," Owen whispered, sinking his teeth into my neck before pushing me face first onto the bed.

I remembered too, and we fucked with the same urgency now that we did then. Sliding across sweat-slick skin. His fist pulling my hair until the roots screamed. My own teeth, sharper than his, leaving half a dozen red and purple circles across his chest and arms.

We didn't choose to stop. At a certain point we just couldn't keep going and he collapsed against my chest. Panting, I cradled his head close and threw one leg over his hips. My arms felt limp as old celery sticks, but I pulled him up to kiss him one more time. Sloppy, void of technique, and absolutely perfect.

"Tell it to me again," I said to him. "I need to hear it. What are we?"

"Monsters, beautiful," he panted. "We're monsters."

Satisfied, I let him slump back down. Owen rolled off and turned away from me. I didn't take it personally, he always said it was impossible for him to sleep while touching me. "Way too many incentives to stay awake," he'd said. A few moments later, all I heard was the rhythmic rise and fall of his sleeping breath.

I waited a few moments, to make sure he was sleeping, and then I rolled over the other way.

I took my phone off the nightstand and went to Facebook. The red notification was still waiting there for me in the top corner. This time, I opened it up.

The link took me to the group page for the Robert Englund Memorial Class of 2015. The post from Arnie Klinton was right there at the top of the discussion section: "Can't wait for the meet up at the Clam House next Saturday at 8. Going to be epic."

Arnie Klinton. That was the name Anthony and I had agreed on before we parted ways in the parking lot. There was lots of confusion in the comments.

"What?"

"?"

"I don't see an event for this. Where's 'the Clam House?'"

"I think you're in the wrong group."

I started typing. Except it wasn't really me. It was Ellen Crampton typing back. Ellen, not Pamela. Not Beverly.

This is what we'd been doing for a week, fake profiles talking in the comment sections. Arnie tagging me in a rare video of The Five performing live. Ellen responding with a laugh emoji at some stupid meme he knew I would like.

Remembering each other. Fumbling our way forward in cloaks, always fearful of daggers. The occasional furtive private message that I deleted as soon as I read it.

All of it leading up to this. "The Clam House." That was the name of an airbnb listing Arnie had posted a couple days ago. This was his way of saying he'd booked the property. This coming Saturday night at 8. If I wanted to meet him, that was the time and the place.

I glanced to the side, watching Owen's bare flank rise and fall with his steady breath. Still a spot of dried blood behind his ear. Then I started to type.

"I'll see you there!"

…Monster that I was.

CHAPTER 23

We got back home just about lunch time. It wasn't a long drive, maybe an hour at most, but we got off to a late start after a long delay in the shower.

I was quiet on the drive home, but that was normal. I liked to be quiet in the car, content to just disassociate and watch the fence posts pass by. Owen never complained. He was just as content to rest his hand on my knee and let Outlaw Country fill the silence. He probably just assumed I was basking in the moment. Enjoying another day of sunny weather and a life free from want. A life where I was accepted and understood.

Usually, he would be right but, today, I had the dead on my mind. My friend Alicia, still the most brutally honest, sincere person I'd ever met. She'd said something to me the night before I killed her, and the ghost of her words had been echoing inside my head ever since Anthony came back into my life."

"Beverly Angela Kilbourne. You are a fucking shark. You know who you are in a way most people never will."

I remember her getting into my face, close enough that I could smell the cheap vodka on her breath.

"Look me in the eye," she'd challenged me. *"Look me in the eye right now and tell me you don't already know what it is that you want to do."*

Maybe I did when I was eighteen. Christ, the road seemed so clear then. I knew who I was and I knew what I wanted. There was a price to be paid, sure, but beyond that the road looked a mile wide and smooth as paper. I had everything I wanted right in front of me and goddamnit I took it.

But then you start down that road and something happens, so you have to make a detour. And then something else happens after that. And then something else. And something else. Potholes. Broken axels. Rain so heavy the windshields couldn't sweep it away fast enough. You take a left at this fork, and then a right at that one. Suddenly, it's twelve years and twelve thousand miles later and you're somewhere you never expected to be.

That was the truth. The girl coming out of high school hadn't planned for any of this. The man beside me wasn't part of the plan. Neither was the country landscape whizzing by the window, not a skyscraper to be seen. Most certainly, a chance to join the cast of *Teen Moms* hadn't been in the cards.

I watched the Alabama pines walk past the car window. I could smell the crisp freshness, even through the glass.

It wasn't what I expected, but that didn't make it a bad life. It didn't mean I was unhappy.

But if my life was so good, then why was I planning to meet Anthony? Something had to be missing, right?

I had hoped last night would smother this. I thought it would be a reminder of what I'd built for myself here. And Owen had done his part. I was nestled in the passenger seat, still bathed in the warm memory of dead bodies and his live one. The bone-deep warmth was like carrying around my own personal bath.

Then why did I still want to see Anthony so badly? Even now, the urge was there, like a splinter under my fingernail.

Except that was wrong. A splinter hurts. It's painful. You want it gone as soon as possible. And I didn't want Anthony gone, no matter how badly I wished I did.

I remembered something else from that night with Alicia. I remember making love with Anthony for the first time, and how I felt afterwards.

Afraid.

Afraid that something was happening to me that I couldn't control.

I felt it again now, and desperately tried to be the shark my best friend believed I was. Clear. Unambiguous. Certain.

"Unbelievable."

I sat up in the seat, trying not to look guilty and loathing myself for even thinking it. What had he seen in my face?

But Owen wasn't looking at me. He was staring down the driveway.

"You seeing what I'm seeing?"

While I'd been trying to strangle my desires for my ex-boyfriend, the entire drive home had evaporated away. We were back at Paxton Manor.

And no, I didn't believe what I was seeing.

Cat was there, digging a large hole in one of the flower beds.

And she wasn't alone.

There was a *boy* with her. The two of them were kneeling together, stuffing some massive ball of roots into a hole and laughing together over some shared amusement.

They both looked up as the car pulled in. The boy immediately looking guilty, as if he'd been caught looking at something on the computer after midnight.

He didn't need to worry. I could tell immediately that he was harmless. He was a diminutive child, shorter than the lanky Cat, with a pleasant little crooked smile and hair a little longer than most of the middle school boys around.

"Hey, Cat!" I called as we got out. Owen tailed slightly behind me. I didn't need to look to see him smothering a grin.

"Hey, mom," she called back. The boy made himself stand up straighter. "Good afternoon, Mrs. Paxton," he said.

"Mom, this is Junji," Cat said. "He's new at school."

"And you've already put the poor boy to work?" Owen joked.

Junji blushed. "My mom's a landscape designer. I'm kind of her apprentice."

Cat brushed a bright red flower on the tropical plant they just buried. "He brought this Hibiscus with him!"

Junji flushed even darker. His skin was brighter than the red flower. "You said you liked red."

"Like mother, like daughter," Owen whispered.

I elbowed him. "It's very nice. Thank you, Junji."

I wasn't lying. It was a gorgeous four-foot flowering tree with lush green leaves and a dozen massive red flowers. I'd bankrolled enough of Cat's projects to know it was probably expensive.

I also knew what it meant when a boy with flowers was squirming in his skin the way Junji was.

Cat – sweet, blissfully ignorant Cat, clearly had no clue. A fact that seemed to delight Owen to no end.

"Staying for lunch, Jun? I was thinking about firing up the grill."

"Can he!?" Cat asked.

"Sure," I allowed. 'That okay with you, Junji?"

Not trusting himself to speak, the boy only bobbed his head up and down with great sincerity.

"Just remember to – "

"Wash up first," Cat finished. "I know, Mom."

"Of course you do. We'll call when it's ready."

"See you later, kiddo," Owen said.

We walked back towards the house. Owen started humming the wedding processional as soon as we were out of earshot.

I scowled at him. Owen laughed, but I didn't join in.

Weddings didn't seem so funny to me at the moment.

CHAPTER 24

———|———

The Saturday I was supposed to meet Anthony ambushed me. It creeped up behind me, drove a knife into my guts, and left me to bleeding to death in the dirt.

I knew it was coming of course. I learned the days of the week in kindergarten just like everybody else. I was aware of Saturday's inexorable march to the now. I watched it kill Monday and decapitate Tuesday. I watched it stack the rest of the week in a bloody pile. I knew how close I was to seeing Anthony again, and my heart pounded like a Sunday School teacher locked in the trunk of a car every time I thought about it. Fear. Excitement. Dread. Desire.

All of it. None of it.

I nearly called it off twice. I nearly tried to move it up once. Every day that passed, the greater the disruption. Like the hum growing in the air ahead of a coming thunderstorm.

Yet, somehow, I still never believed Saturday would actually come. Not until I woke up with Owen sleeping with his head against my bare chest, and the reality of Saturday looming over my bed with an axe and a sinister grin.

It was here.

It was time.

"Pamela? Pam?"

Snapping fingers in front of my face. I shook the static out from between my ears. I wasn't in bed. It wasn't the morning, it was already 5 o'clock-

So Late.

-And I was out shopping at Tily's with Jen and Reese. While I was planning to spend my night maybe cheating on their brother, the two of them had tickets to a single's mixer in Huntsville and they wanted to look cute.

Tonight. Saturday.

Murder was the sisters' real goal of course, but they were putting in the effort anyway. "You never know," Reese was fond of saying.

"I know something's getting wet tonight, and I don't care much if it's me or a knife," was Jen's take.

"Pam!" Reese again, shouting now to drag me back to reality. "You with us?" she asked.

I focused on the sisters. They'd gone for a matching gimmick. Both of them were wearing white summer dresses. Tight around their high, firm busts, but loose and flowing around the thighs. Reese had gone with a red floral print. Jen had blue.

"Big surprise with the red, Ree," Jen cracked. "I guess Senator Fields would never forgive you if you wore blue."

Reese rolled her eyes. "Pam, please provide me with an opinion that's actually useful."

I forced myself to be present. "You guys look great," I said. "But I'm not sure if there's enough in the way of concealment."

"Don't worry," Reese said. "A Mediterranean restaurant is hosting the event."

Ah, so plenty of skewers on hand. No need to bring in your own killing tools.

"Say no more," I said. "Bag them up."

Reese seemed satisfied, but Jen wasn't. She pouted and struck a pose in front of me, looking like she belonged on the calendar page for April. "That's it?" she asked. "Come on, Pam. What's your deal?"

"Jen," Reese warned.

"No," Jen said. "We've tiptoed around this ever since the camping trip."

She grabbed my wrist. Before I knew what was happening, she was dragging me in between clothing racks to the back of the boutique. Where the dressing rooms were. Reese trailed behind us like a worried shadow, making it into the dressing room just before Jen slammed the door.

Tily's was one of the premier boutiques in the state. The dressing rooms were solid-walled, floor to ceiling enclosures. It was just us inside. Reese, Jen, and my own rigid-faced reflection staring back at me from the mirror. My own eyes were the worst. The false calm staring back at me looked like the face of a stranger.

Jen turned the lock and then turned on me. "I was waiting to see if you said something, or if this cleared up on its own, but it's not. Something's been wrong with you for days, Pam. You've got to talk to us."

"If you want to," Reese added.

"No," Jen snapped. "She doesn't get a choice. No bullshit, Pam. What the hell's going on with you?"

I could have lied to them. They were the sisters I never had, but that was nothing new. The people I cared about never knew who I really was. I thought I'd gotten past that, but apparently it was like riding a bike so what difference was one more time?

It was my reflection I couldn't deal with. The ugly tightness in my brow and the clenched set of my jaw staring back at me was bad enough. I didn't want to watch the lie pour out of my lips. I didn't want to do it anymore, damnit. Maybe I should get it over with and just fucking say it.

"Reese and Jen, I've been texting with my old high school boyfriend for the last week. It's not anything your brother did wrong, Owen's still so perfect that it's like I grew him in a fucking lab, but I can't help it. I saw Anthony again and I can't stop thinking about him. You remember when I got Poison Ivy my first month here? I thought that shit was a bad cartoon gag, 'Haha, you can't stop scratching,' but I wasn't laughing for long once I got it. My skin was scalded, splotchy red and bubbling with hard little welts. Calling what it does to you an itch is like calling glass in your gums mildly uncomfortable. I couldn't

think, I couldn't sleep. But a Poison Ivy rash turns scratching into an addiction. All I could do was lay there and think about how fucking good it would feel to take a piece of sandpaper to my skin and scratch, scratch, SCRATCH until I hit bone.

That's what it feels like with Anthony. I'm supposed to meet him tonight. He's already messaged me the address. It's sitting in my inbox on the fake Facebook profile I made so Owen wouldn't find it. I've got this plan but it's not really a plan. I don't know who to choose. I don't know if I should bring condoms. I don't know what to do, you guys. I DON'T KNOW WHAT TO FUCKING DO.

"It's Luke, isn't it?" Reese asked. "You're still worried about him and Cat."

I let some of the tension out of my shoulders. "Yes," I said. It wasn't the thing keeping me awake every night, but I still caught his eye lingering on Cat too long before wiping at his mouth with the hand missing fingers. I let the truth of it be the excuse to let my face abandon the half smile I'd carried around all afternoon.

Reese grabbed my hand. "I know Cat ain't like us, but that don't matter. You're family. And that makes her family."

"Luke's family too," I pressed. "He's her son."

"All that mean's is he's got no excuse," Jen said. "That river only runs one way around here. There ain't gonna be no blowback, Luke sniffed around where he shouldn't and he got his wrist slapped for it. End of story."

"You don't cross family," Reese finished.

That would have set me at ease... before Anthony. Before I had crossed the family.

There was one more question. I hadn't asked it in all the years I'd been here, but I had to ask it now.

I hesitated. "This may be too personal..."

Jen cut me off. "It's not, Pam. That's what we're trying to explain to you."

"...Your dad."

The temperature in the dressing room dropped about twenty degrees. I pushed on.

"Owen told me a story. Years ago. Is it..."

"It's true," Reese said firmly.

"River only runs one way," Jen said with chilling finality.

"It was a woman from church," Owen told me.

We were still in New York then, but we'd been talking about Alabama. Meeting his family. How it would all work. Owen was drinking as he talked. The first glass of bourbon was already gone.

"That's how momma found out. Her conscience was getting the better of her so she came 'round to Paxton. To confess her sins. Momma was... not forgiving."

He refilled the glass. Steady pour. The only shaking came from the ice at the bottom of the glass as the liquor rushed over it.

"Momma handled the other woman herself. Did it right there in the kitchen. But she left the mess. Daddy came home, and there was momma. And there was the mess. You know my family now, and daddy was the same as the rest of us, he'd seen a mess in the kitchen before. But he knew right away that this was different. Momma had left enough knowable pieces to make sure of that.

'Friend of yours stopped by, Fredrick,' she said. 'She told me the most fascinating story. What say we talk about it while you get a bucket and start cleaning this up?'

"Now, my momma. Once she knows she's got you, she can sit like a Copperhead and just watch you for hours. You know and she knows that she could bite you at any second, but she's gonna wait for her moment. That moment's coming no matter what. You know it but, until it comes, you do what she says anyway because you're too damn scared of what'll happen if you don't.

"The cleaning things were under the sink, so that's where Daddy goes. And that's where Reese already was. You haven't met my sister Reese, but she's a slim little thing now and she was downright shrimpy

when she was eight. No problem at all fitting in under the kitchen sink; Daddy opens the cabinet and there's his little Reese's Piece with the cap already off the bottle of drain cleaner... You ever hear anyone scream with a face full of drain cleaner, Pam?"

I allowed that I had. Owen poured another drink. I reached out and poured one for myself.

"Then you know it was already over. He staggers away towards this big island we've got in the middle of the kitchen. My other sister, Jen. She's a hellcat but she's quiet when she wants to be. She got up on the counter with a tee ball bat. But she hits him kind of low, see? Smashes his shoulder and not his head."

Another glass gone.

"She wanted us all to have a hand in it. Family. My brother and me, we were last. Daddy was down on the tile, writhing like a fish that can't breathe. The chemical burns made it look like his eyes were covered in sunburnt worms. His one shoulder was hanging down by his shirt pocket. He's moaning, but he's not begging. He understands. Even then, he understands that there's no other way this can go."

Fourth glass.

I've got a hatchet. I'm not confident with a full axe yet. Luke isn't either, but he's got one anyway. You wanna know about the two of us? There you go. He gets to be careless because I know to be smart."

Fifth glass.

"Sometimes I wonder if he knows who hit him first, me or Luke. Luke's swing with that Mark McGwire axe was choppy, he just took off an ugly chunk of flesh without going in deep. But, me? I was straight and true. I chopped down on Daddy deep and true, and the bubbling blood out of his mouth told me so."

He sighs then. Sixth glass.

"I suppose it doesn't matter in the end who did what. What matters is that it was done the way it was supposed to be done, and then we took what was left of both of them and sank it down by the boat dock. He was fond of that spot."

Ice cubes clinked at the bottom of the glass. He didn't pour another one.

Looking at him then, I wasn't sure what he wanted me to think. It wasn't pride I saw in his firm, unblinking gaze, but it wasn't shame either.

"You said you wanted to come home with me," Owen said. "I want that too. But I want to be clear on what that means. I'm sure about you. Are you sure about me?"

I cocked my head at him from my stool on the other side of the small bar in his apartment. "Is that your way of asking me to marry you?" I asked.

"Not that we'll actually have the benefit of clergy. Kinda hard when the bride doesn't have a birth certificate. But... yeah. Will you marry me, Pamela?"

———————|———————

I listened to their story. Maybe the timing wasn't great, but I was smiling at Jen and Reese now. For real.

"I'm going to be straight with you… everything is fine. I mean it."

"For real?" Jen pressed. "Don't lie to us."

"Yeah. I'm not lying. Everything's fine."

"You want to come with us then?" Jen asked.

"She can't, remember?" Reese said. "She's got a date with that shop teacher from Bantr. The nice one she's going to take to that great little shithole motel with the sinkhole behind the property."

I shook my head. "Nah, I'm not feeling that anymore. I'm just gonna hang around Paxton tonight."

"By yourself?" Reese asked. "Mama's at Mahjan and Luke and Owen are going fishing."

Jen scoffed. "They're going to drink their weight in beer, and then pull up Youtube and try to guess which yoga video instructors also have OnlyFans."

"Home by myself sounds just right," I said. "Besides, Cat will be there."

"Then forget what I said," Jen grinned. "Don't leave that girl unsupervised with the boyfriend." '

Reese just tried one more time. "You're sure?" she asked.

I nodded. "Yeah, I'm sure."

———————|———————

We went our separate ways from the boutique. Jen and Reese went to paint the town red. And I went home.

My Home.

Are you sure, Pam?

I was. Maybe not as sure as I was that night in New York, but it was easier to be sure when you were twenty-five. Not as easy as eighteen, eighteen was easiest, but twenty-five was still a damn sight easier than thirty. It was harder not to think about what-ifs at thirty. Somewhere along the way, you stop trusting your gut and every decision becomes a three-hour power point. Everything seemed to take so much damn longer, but if you were lucky, you made up for it by being smarter. It may have taken me too long to put it all together but, in the end, my life was good. Very good. The right thing to do was keep it that way instead of chasing some idiotic phantom.

That's what I would tell Anthony. He asked me to think about it, and I had. That's what I'd done, and he was going to have to accept my choice. I'd call him once I got back to my room and tell him it was done. I just hoped that he would understand and stay away. I didn't want to have to tell Luke that there was a bible thumper knocking at the door tonight.

That's how it would end between us. No real resolution. No future. The past would stay the past and the present would stay the present. And that was just fine.

It felt appropriate that the sun was setting as I pulled into the driveway. I had to call Anthony, but I had a few hours before I was supposed to meet him. First, I had to put away what I got at Tily's, and then a cold beer on the porch sounded like a nice treat.

Stalling, a small voice whispered. But I ignored it. I wasn't stalling. I was just going to enjoy the life I'd built, starting with showing Cat this cute top I'd bought her.

I didn't see her in the flower beds. Not the ones along the driveway and not the big one by the house. A quick glance out to the fields didn't turn up anything either. The most likely place after that would be the barn, but I suddenly found myself thinking of Jen and her little joke about Cat and Junji. It couldn't be time for that yet though, could it?

OK, it had already been that time for me. But Cat was… Cat.

Still, I made sure to drag my feet through the gravel, making plenty of noise as I approached the barn where she kept her fertilizer and garden tools.

"Cat!?" I called for good measure as I reached the door and slowly pushed it open. "You guys in here?'

She was. The falling sun was perfectly aligned with the open doors of the barn loft, casting Cat in a bath of melted orange petals, wider and wider as the lens of the barn door dilated open.

She looks like a tiger, was my first thought. Her face burning orange, broken up by the darker stripes of blood streaked across her face.

There was so much more blood. It dripped from the spade, still clutched loosely in one hand. It spread in a pool around Junji's smashed open skull. His eyes were still open too, staring blankly back at the sun. No harm in it now.

Cat looked up at me. The stunned look on her face was similar to how I'd imagined she'd look if I caught her kissing him.

Kissing. Not standing over his split open skull with a bloody shovel.

"He said he wanted to play swords," she told me in a dazed voice.

CHAPTER 25

———————— | ————————

When Cat was three, I bought her a gerbil.

And a hammer.

I was curious what would happen. Three was old enough. I knew by then that I was planning to keep her, and if that was the case then I wanted to know what she was made of. The lights didn't really turn on for me until I was older, but I didn't have anybody to guide me. Nobody to show me what I was meant to do.

Cat did.

She was never an expressive child, but she was sharp. Sharp as a knife since she could walk. I came home with a large brown paper bag in one hand, and a cardboard box with a few holes punched in it under my arm. That was enough for Cat.

"Mommy, didyoo get me a pet?" she asked with the characteristic slowness of somebody still new to forming sentences. Not smiling. Earnest. Even then. At that age they're all just so much person stuffed into such a small space, and it overflows out of their eyes. Cat's eyes were focused on the box with careful interest.

"It's an animal," I allowed, which wasn't exactly the same thing. I crouched down in front of her, opened the box, and deposited the little brown and white ball of fluff on the floor. I watched her pick it up. Again, no smile. No little kid giggling. She inspected the animal with the careful scrutiny of a Westminster dog judge. The gerbil's nose twitched companionably in return.

"He's soft," she finally decided.

"Very," I agreed. "And he's all yours. You can do whatever you want with him."

Without saying anything else, I reached into the bag and felt for the cold rubber handle of small hammer I'd picked up. A little two pound nothing that you'd keep in an apartment for hanging pictures.

But hard, oh so beautifully fucking hard.

I set that hammer down in front of Cat, right in the same place I'd put down the gerbil.

Cat's big brown eyes looked to the hammer. To me. To the gerbil.

Back to the hammer.

I was perfectly still. No influence. No suggestions. Just waiting to see what she wanted to do. But I wondered what was going on between those sandy brown pigtails. Did the hammer sing to her the way it did to me? Did she feel the metal humming in her molars? Did she ache to sully that polished chrome finish the same way that I did?

"...Mommy, where's he supposed to live?" she finally asked.

I sighed. "Come here, Cat."

I reached back into the bag for the small cage I'd bought as well, just in case things turned out this way.

That gerbil was still alive in Cat's bedroom.

Junji was dead. Smashed. Pieces of his skull littered the barn floor as if someone had dropped a clutch of chicken eggs and shattered the shells everywhere.

And Cat wasn't in a mood for careful scrutiny. Cat was rushing towards me, letting the shovel fall with an ugly thud and throwing herself into my arms. I felt the twin heat of blood and her rapidly panting breath pressed against my chest.

"I swear, Mom," she babbled. "I didn't plan this. I didn't *want* this. I thought maybe we would kiss. But then Junji got nervous and wanted to play this stupid game instead. And we did, but I felt weird and confused and I *hit* him! And then he started bleeding and I hit him again!"

She clutched my arms until her nails drew blood. Beyond the shuddering crown of her skull, Junji's head was twisted so his blank eyes stared right at me. They were dusty, empty things. No questions in those fogged crystal balls. No recriminations. It was the bloody gorge in the center of his skull that spoke to me. The gorge still bright and glistening from the flood of blood that had swept through it.

What are you going to do, Pam? The gorge asked. *What are you going to do?*

"Cat, get in the car," I said.

She just burrowed deeper into my chest. "I'm sorry, mom. I don't why I did it. I don't know!"

I grabbed her by the shoulders and wrenched her back. Her nails dragged a half dozen bloody scratches into my arms as I disengaged her, but that didn't matter.

"Cat," I hissed through clenched teeth. "Stop crying. Get in the car. I don't have time to tell you again."

"He's dead, mom!" Cat wailed. The house was supposed to be empty, but I wasn't chancing anything. Even if it was, Cat was screaming loud enough for Luke and Owen to hear all the way out in the damn river. My arm uncoiled fast as a spark, clamping around her jaw and pinching her mouth shut.

"We are leaving. Do what I tell you."

She did. One last glance at Junji sprawled on the floor, taking a wide route to avoid walking through the blood, but she let me lead her out of the barn.

I didn't look back. Not at Junji, and not at the neat little plans I had made for my life just a few minutes ago.

———————

I pulled out onto the main road in a spray of red dirt. Nobody coming in either direction. I pushed hard on the accelerator. If a cop tried to pull me over, then that was their bad luck.

Cat lurched for the door. I reached over to grab her, thinking she was trying to jump out of the car at 80 miles an hour, but she was groping for the window control. She got the glass about halfway down before she couldn't wait any longer. She pressed her mouth to the slitted opening and I watched a fan of vomit splatter against the glass. When there was nothing left to choke up, Cat flopped violently back into the seat. She wiped her mouth and arched her entire body up, eyes clenched tight as some indescribable pain ripped through her. "Oh my God!" she screamed in the narrow confines of the truck. She dug her hands into her hair, leaving long streaks of Junji's blood in her wake, and screamed again. And again. The sound burrowed deep into my own skull. If she kept going like this, I'd be deaf by the time we got there.

And then, just as quickly, she stopped. She slumped forward in the seat, elbows on her knees and her head in her hands. When she looked up at me, Junji's blood was a red popsicle smear across her entire face.

"I'm a monster," she said.

No, you're not, I thought.

And I ought to know.

The highway entrance was coming up, I slowed down just enough to keep us from flipping into a ditch, and then sped back up as we got onto the interstate.

We couldn't be late.

CHAPTER 26

ANTHONY

I caught myself humming the love theme from *Lofts* as I walked out onto the deck with a beer in my hand. I certainly didn't want to be drunk when Beverly got here, but a little toast by myself while I waited wouldn't kill anyone.

I'd emptied out my meager bank account to cover a night in an... above average airbnb, but it was worth it. The house was clean, in good repair, and sitting all by itself at the edge of a pond. There was an elevated deck with a view of the water, and the outside chairs came with cushions. The only thing missing was Beverly, and she was probably already on the way by now.

That's where I was as the twilight finally sank into full darkness. Even without Beverly here, it was still wonderful. There was none of the mania that I'd known for the last decade. No little rat's teeth gnawing between my ears, urging me to one more internet search, one more story of pain and death that maybe hinted at the woman I loved. I had an open beer, a sky full of stars, and nothing to do but sit and listen to the reeds swaying off in the darkness.

This is the most relaxed I've been since I was eighteen years old, I realized. Christ, what a sad thing to think, but it was the truth.

I glanced at my watch, but only out of curiosity. I wasn't even worried about Beverly. It was 7:52 but I believed, all the way down to the bedrock of my soul, that she would be here at 8 o'clock. Just like we agreed. She was coming.

I meant it when I said I would accept whatever she decided. I knew things could get messy for her, and I didn't want to minimize that, but I was prepared to do whatever I had to for her if she did choose me. And it might have been wishful thinking, but I think she felt it too. She felt the same thing I did when we kissed. There was unfinished business between us. One night wouldn't decide everything, but it was a start.

I toasted the full moon, hanging high overhead. "To a chance."

On cue, I heard tires crunching through gravel. Perfectly on time. I felt a flooding sensation of assuredness sweep through me. For the first time, things were working out between us exactly as they were supposed to. No twists, no surprises.

I got up out of the chair, my joints popping with an amiable crack as I stood. The elevated deck was positioned over the driveway like a lookout tower. I had a clear view of the truck coming up the driveway. The same one Beverly had taken to the bar the last time we met. I stayed there on the deck, watching her pull in. I considered rushing down the steps to meet her, but the beauty of tonight was that we could take our time.

Beverly got out of the truck. I caught a quick glimpse of her face, quick but plenty long enough to make my heart stutter-step, and then she was shadows again, backlit by the headlights as she cut across the front of the truck and went to the passenger side.

"Find the place okay?" I called out.

Beverly didn't answer. She opened the passenger door and stood there for a moment, longer than she'd need to be there if she was just grabbing a bag of groceries and a bottle of wine.

"Beverly!" I shouted. Louder this time. Less cool. "Are you okay?"

Still no answer from the shadows by the truck. That's when I felt the first skittering legs of anxiety crawling up my back once again. Something wasn't right.

The slamming door cracked in the still night. Beverly came across the front of the truck again and she wasn't alone. There was another silhouette hanging off of her, cast into shadow by the LEDs as they staggered towards the house. Somebody at least a head shorter than Beverly and stick-thin.

And hurt. Hurt very badly. That much was immediately obvious. Whoever they were, Beverly was practically carrying them forward.

"Anthony!" Beverly called. My God, the panic in her voice. "Help me!"

I flew down the long steps, no concerns about the dark night, no worries about maybe breaking my neck.

Beverly needed me.

I could see the two of them more clearly as they got closer and the lights from the house fell onto their faces. I saw Beverly, looking as close to losing control as I'd ever seen her, and I could see the person with her now. A girl of eleven or twelve, barely able to stand on her feet. She was drenched in blood, totally soaked in it, and that should have been the thing to command my attention.

But all I could do was look at her face.

Her eyes. The color of her hair.

"Mom, who is this?" the girl asked.

Mom.

I tripped down the final step and landed on my ass with paralyzing force. Not that I could be anymore numb than I already was.

"Oh my God," I breathed. I didn't feel any pain from the fall. What I felt was sensation like a redwood tree sprouting in my chest. Like something massive was relentlessly growing inside of me. Something so huge it needed to push out everything else there was so it had enough room to exist. "Oh my God," I repeated. "Oh my God. Oh, my fucking God. Oh my-"

"I know," Beverly said. They had made it to the stairs. Beverly guided the girl—

Our daughter.

-To the railing and let her cling to it like a buoy in the middle of a hurricane. She was beautiful. Even like this, my Christ, she was so fucking beautiful. And tall. And she had my hair. My eyes.

"I know," Beverly repeated. "I didn't know how to tell you before and now there's no time."

"B-Beverly –" I stammered.

"*No!*" She hauled me up to my feet like she was plucking a dandelion out of the dirt. "There isn't time! You've got to get her away from here as fast as you can."

Whatever was wrong with the girl –

OUR DAUGHTER.

What Beverly said certainly wasn't helping. The kid lurched forward and now the three of us were in an ugly tangle. "Please don't send me away, mom. I know I'm a monster, but I don't wanna leave you. Please let me stay, mom. Pleasemom. Pleasemom."

"*STOP,*" Beverly hissed. *"Both of you!"* She focused on me again. Her blue eyes glowed like propane fire with deadly urgency. "I thought she was like you, and she is, but she's like me too. She can't stay here, and you're the only one I can trust to take care of her." She stuffed something into my hand. The crinkle of money. "Take her away from here. Get her as far away as possible."

"No!" I yelled. "Not after I just found you. I'm here. You're here. Whatever this is…"

Whatever covered our daughter in blood.

"We should figure it out together."

"No, we can't!" Beverly screeched. "*This* is how we figure it out, Anthony. Her name is Cat, do you hear me? Catherine. She likes horticulture and she's a picky eater. She's the future we made." She slammed a finger into my chest and then pointed back at herself. 'We're the past. Together or apart, we are the past. We don't matter. But we started something." She grabbed the girl and flung her towards me. The reaction was automatic. I locked my arms around her and held her close. Her heart beat was thunder against my chest.

I'll die for you. The thought birthed itself into my head, immediately and fully grown. No second guesses. No uncertainty. *I'll die for you in an instant.*

"Mom," the girl pleaded again. Cat. Catherine. She tried to squirm away from me, but I held her close. "Mom, please don't leave me."

No screaming now. Beverly cupped Catherine's bloody face. She didn't wipe away the tears running down the girl's pale cheeks, but she didn't flinch away from them either. "I'm not leaving you, Cat. You're leaving me."

"I WON'T!"

"You're going to go with your father," she continued. "He's going to take care of you now."

The words struck the girl like a hammer, momentarily wiping away the hysterics. She gaped at her mother, and then slowly swiveled to me for confirmation. Even through her distress, she stared at me with a kind of blunt evaluation. Sizing me up.

I wanted to shrug. Shrink in. I was a screwup. Unstable. A wreck.

But I did my best to pull my shoulders back. "It's going to be okay," I told her. I tried my best to mean it.

"Better than okay," Beverly said. "What happened tonight was a bad dream, Cat. That's all. You're going to wake up tomorrow with your dad and you're going to be whoever you want to be." Her lip didn't quiver. Her eyes were clear and firm. God, she was so beautiful. Beautiful because she was older. Stronger. She knew exactly what she needed to do, and she didn't hesitate.

"You could come with us," I said. I had to try one more time.

Beverly only shook her head. "It's not going to be that way."

She gently reached out again for Catherine. Took hold of her daughter for what was probably the last time. "But it's all going to work out," she promised.

A voice called out in response. "Funny, I was just thinking the exact same thing."

It wasn't my voice speaking.

It wasn't Cat's.

It wasn't Beverly's.

CHAPTER 27

BEVERLY

I heard Owen's voice and my blood ran cold. Part of me tried to convince myself that I hadn't really heard him. Because for Owen to be here would be a calamity. Therefore, it wasn't true. It couldn't be.

I whipped my head around anyway, trying to see where the taunting voice had come from, but I was on the wrong side of the powerful truck headlights. Trying to see into the woods behind the aching glare was like trying to stare through a spotlight. He could be anywhere behind the tree line.

Plus, you were distracted by Catherine. And Anthony. And your precious goodbye. Stupid little drama queen. You're all dead now.

No time for that now. I could hear the crunch of gravel getting closer.

The calamity was here.

Owen came strolling up through the curtain of the headlights. Blue jeans and an open chambray shirt over a white t-shirt. Were it not for the sledgehammer dangling from one hand, he might have been coming over to say hello at a barbecue.

"I think you hit the nail on the head, Pam. Everything is gonna turn out goddamn fantastic. I knew it the second I saw the mess that Cat left in the barn. I guess she's just a late boomer after all." He smiled at Cat. The same smile he favored her with when he suggested we stop for ice cream. "This is what we always wanted for you, kid. No more sneaking around behind your back. No more pretending to be at

Nascar every time we want to go out into the woods and cut off some heads. You're one of us now."

I put myself between him and Cat. No weapons. No comforting weight in my back pocket. We were close enough that I had to crane my neck all the way back to look up at my husband's face, but he didn't even seem to notice me.

"I'm just happy everything's out in the open," he continued. "The lying really bothered me, you know. Didn't I always say that, Pam? 'I hate lying to Cat.' I said it all the time." He laughed, showing off teeth as neat and hard as a row of bricks. "What a relief to put all of that behind us." Owen let the sledgehammer hang lower. The head was the size and shape of an artillery shell. He was looking right at me now. "No more lies," he said. "No more secrets. Just us." Owen punctuated each word with that hammer head crunching in the gravel.

"One."

"Big."

"Happy."

Family."

From behind me, I felt Cat clinging so close she was practically crawling up my spine. Her breath, hot and frantic, paced in my ear.

Scared. So scared.

Owen looked past me to Anthony. "I don't think we've been introduced. I'm Owen. You must be the guy from the Facebook group." Casually, he added to me: "Family phone, hon. I told Momma we didn't need the spy software, but I guess she showed me a thing or two... Or maybe you was the one doin' the showin'."

Say something, Beverly. You have to say something.

Nothing came. Not an idea. Not an explanation. Not a lie. Nothing. All the plates I'd been spinning had fallen and shattered. I couldn't think. I couldn't see anything except for Owen looming over me. With his hammer. It was over. I had nothing to say.

Until I saw the back of Anthony's head as he cut in between me and Owen.

BEVERLY KILLS AGAIN | 165

"Don't!" I screamed.

Anthony ignored me. He put himself toe to toe with Owen. Half my husband's size, swimming in a threadbare sweatshirt and jeans with holes in the knees. The hammer was redundant. Owen could pop his head like a champagne cork with his bare hands. And Owen knew it, I saw his bloodthirsty urge to hurt something pacing behind the toothy bars of his shit-eating grin.

"If I may, sir," Anthony began calmly, "I don't think you have the entire picture here. Yes, Pamela and I have been talking. And yeah, there used to be something between us and we were supposed to meet tonight. But that's just half of it. The part you missed is… she came here to tell me that I'm out of line." Anthony held his hands out. *Win some, lose some.* "She picked you. You're her future, and I'm a memory. That's what she came here to tell me."

He held his hand out for a shake. "I respect the lady's choice, sir. And I take my hat off to you. You're a lucky man."

Anthony's hand hung in the space between them, untaken. Owen merely hefted the hammer and balanced it back up on his shoulder. A man standing before a nail.

"…Not buying any of this, are you, pal?" Anthony asked with amazing cheer in his voice.

The answer flew out of the darkness and buried itself in Anthony's shoulder. Nothing there one second. The next, Anthony staggering against me with an arrow sticking out of his flesh and a donut of blood forming on his shirt.

"Seems a little suspect to me," Reese said. She materialized out from the light, already notching another arrow into the bow.

I was making noises as I clutched at Anthony and tried to slow his collapse to the ground. High-pitched, yelping bursts that made my throat ache and my heart thunder until I thought it would burst out of my ears. I recognized the sound from a hundred victims writhing with their guts around their knees or a tent stake driven into their eye socket. The sounds of mortally wounded meat that knew their time was up and they had nothing to do about it but yip and shriek their final moments away like a dying coyote.

I had just never heard those noises from my own mouth before.

I wish that was all there was to hear, nothing but my own ruined shrieks waiting for the end. But there were worse sounds still, and even now my ears were sharp enough to pick them up.

The sound of footsteps on the patio behind us. And the sound of reeds bending and water sloshing from the pond.

It shouldn't have surprised me. I knew the story of Owen's father.

One.

Big.

Happy.

Family.

Jen came down the porch steps, rattling the wooden spindles with a meat hook as she descended. Luke was easy to spot now that I heard him. He was wearing his hunting ghillie suit, this massive creature of synthetic vine and moss shambling out of the shallows with a mud-soaked axe in his thick mitts. Most terrible of all, he pulled back his ghillie hood so I could see his camouflage-painted face twisted in a gloating sneer.

Mama Charlize came last, as I knew she would. She stood beside her son. No weapons in her hands, only a look of tremendous, terminal disappointment.

They were all here.

One.

Big.

Happy.

Family.

CHAPTER 28

ANTHONY

Funny how pain works. The arrow was in my shoulder, but it was my legs that felt it. I dropped backwards, no chair to land on, only Beverly scrambling to hold onto me as I kept slipping… slipping…

And then I was flat on my back, remembering how I felt about fifteen minutes ago. Relaxed. Assured. Confident that everything would work out. Just waiting for the woman that I loved.

The last time I'd felt that way had been the night of the senior prom. I'd thought about that before, a hundred years ago when I had a cold beer and nothing could go wrong. If I'd been thinking a little more clearly, I might have remembered that that was also the same night Beverly left me and murdered my best friend.

Funny how these things work out.

Beverly's hands hovered over the shaft in my shoulder, warring with the instinct to try and pull it out, but I guess that in her experience that only made it worse. I saw the storm in her beautiful blue eyes. I saw her trying not to drown.

And I saw them gather around me, just past Beverly's shoulder. Her husband with the sledgehammer. The swamp man with the axe and the girls with the hook and the arrow. The old Karen with no weapons except for her cold eyes. I didn't know who they were, but the particulars didn't really matter. I knew why they were here.

"Anthony," she whispered. She wasn't crying. Not gonna lie, I kinda wish she was. But she held me, and her eyes stayed fixed on mine. She was there with me. Solid as stone. She would have been with me to the end if I would let her.

But I couldn't do that. "Pam." my voice was a shaved half of a whisper, but I still used the same name the other guy called her, just in case anybody was listening. "We don't matter. We're not the future."

"Stop it, Anthony."

I shook my head. "It's already stopped, Pam. Done. Over... but it's not bad."

"Pam," the guy with the hammer called out. "Come on now. Cat needs you."

"He's right," I said. I squeezed her hand. Her fingers against mine was about the only thing I could still feel. I knew she needed to walk away. I wanted her to walk away... but one more second. Just one more second with her face.

She gave it to me. She didn't kiss me, and I understood why not. I was grateful for what I got.

"Anything that happens now is just achievement points."

That was what a kid in high school once said to his only friend. A kid in love with a girl who barely knew his name. That kid had just wanted to take his shot, just so he could know what would happen instead of wondering for the rest of his life. Well, he had his answer now.

Kind of a mixed bag overall, just being honest.

But I'd gotten my chance. That's what I held onto as Beverly finally stood up and stepped back away from me.

And the others stepped forward.

CHAPTER 29

———————¦———————

BEVERLY.

"Pam. Come on now. Cat needs you."

He was right. I knew it. Anthony knew it, too.

"He's right," Anthony breathed. His voice thin as a scrim of algae on the water.

But he was still strong. I saw the hard glint in his eyes. His death was moments away but, whatever he was feeling, he kept a tight lid on it for the sake of me and Cat. He was there on his back, not screaming, not pleading. His shoulders were shaking, but I knew he would have stopped that if he could. He was trying to take care of us.

I couldn't do any less.

I didn't kiss him. I didn't brush the sweaty hair away from his forehead. I just stood up, forcing myself to stay steady. My knees didn't knock together. My lips didn't tremble. I held my head high and looked straight ahead as I went back to my daughter.

Cat was shaking. Her eyes kept darting from place to place, no idea where to settle. Owen's hammer. Aunt Reese's bow with a fresh arrow notched to the string. The bleeding father she never knew. Aunt Jen's curved hook.

I closed her eyes and pulled her tight to my chest. "Try to sing something," I murmured to her. "Sing it in your head if you can't talk." And then I met Owen's gaze. I made my voice stay as steady as my eyes.

"Get it over with," I told him.

None of them made a move. They stay in their circular formation around us, like a pack of hyenas, so I said it again.

Or, not said it. Screamed it. Shrieked it to make the leaves shake in the trees.

"Get it over with, Owen! Do what you're going to do!"

There was another moment's inaction from the frozen statues around me. Long enough for the echo of my scream to die away.

Then, finally, my husband flipped the sledgehammer around in his hands. I'd seen him perform that spin dozens of times, limbering up with anticipation of the violence to come, but this was different. He slowly rotated the football-sized hammerhead in a long arc. It seemed heavier than usual for him.

Finally, he sighed and gripped the hammer at shoulder height.

"Bring him here, Jen."

"Happily," she said.

She put the hook in Anthony's other shoulder. He didn't scream, but I heard the hiss of pained breath as the metal point broke flesh and a fresh blood pool spread across the other side of his shirt. Jen dragged him forward, the sound of Anthony's heels in the gravel gnashing in my head until my eyeballs throbbed.

She dropped him at Owen's feet. Anthony coughed and rolled over onto his side. Towards me. Our eyes met one more time. He looked peaceful.

"Eyes front, motherfucker," Luke snarled. He reared back and kicked Anthony in the jaw.

I thought the gravel was excruciating. The sound of Anthony's jaw breaking like a stomped candy apple was a thousand times worse. I lost Anthony's gaze as the kick brutally rolled him away from me and onto his stomach. But never fear, I could still see the blood and shattered teeth pooling underneath him, and I got to see Luke regarding me with vicious glee as he steadied his seven-fingered grasp on the axe. He planted a boot on Anthony's sprawled wrist, holding it in place as he raised the axe head until it blocked out the moon.

"None of that," Mama Charlize said. "He'll go into shock and won't feel a thing after. You already got your lick in. Just be a good brother now and pick him up."

Luke almost disobeyed. I could feel how badly he wanted to. I felt it thrumming in my veins.

"Mind me now, Luke."

"Fuck!" Luke screamed. He slammed the axe blade-first into the driveway where it stayed upright, humming and thrumming, and then he knelt down like a good boy and hauled Anthony up by the armpits. Luke carried him forward, hefting Anthony along as easily as a tacklebox. His feet didn't even touch the ground.

He brought Anthony over to the truck and slammed him face first into the hood. Cat winced at the hollow thud of it. She burrowed deeper against me. I held her tight. Useless comfort that it was.

Luke had one hand, broad as a hawk's wing, flat between Anthony's shoulder. Holding him in place.

"All yours, bro," he said. "Make him pay." Luke's teeth were pulled back in a savage grin. He wasn't the only one. Jen and Reese, Mama. The whole hungry pack of them had crowded in with eager eyes that glinted like chips of black ice. They all wanted to see but — ever mindful of who this was for — they made sure to leave a space for me to keep watching.

I didn't want to, but I forced myself to look. I owed Anthony that much.

I wish I could say I saw his face one last time. That I could have met his eyes in his final moments. I didn't have much to offer in the way of comfort, but at least I could make sure he was seen at the end. That he was known. That it was real between us.

But they had him facing the other way. All I saw of him at the end was the back of his head. Shaggy. Greasy. Overdue for a haircut.

The scar on my hand burned. The one I gave myself on prom night when I wasn't able to kill him. Because I loved him too much to do it.

Owen, coming forward now. Owen, raising the sledgehammer up against the dark sky.

He didn't drag it out. He brought the hammer up, and then he brought it down as hard as he possibly could. There's no other way to say it. Owen brought the hammer down as hard as he possibly could, and Anthony's head shattered to nothing. He simply ceased to exist from the neck up. There one minute, the next just blood, bone chips, and brain matter flying in a wide halo. Luke and Owen were splattered. A good misting dusted the rest of the family.

Cat and I were a little further out. A solitary chunk of skull bounced against my cheek. A tooth landed in Cat's hair.

I didn't scream.

I didn't cry.

I waited to see what would happen next.

The Paxtons didn't linger long over their kill. They were already pivoting towards us before Anthony's body was finished sliding off the hood of the car. The pack of them in a horizontal line with blood on their faces. Blood on their clothes. Their weapons like bared fangs.

No point in running. Not when Reese already had an arrow notched and waiting. Not when Luke loved a good chase.

With a hand that barely felt like mine, I brushed the tooth out of Cat's hair and let my hand linger against her cheek. It might have looked like a comforting motion.

In a way, it was.

I was about to die. That was how the story went.

But Cat…

They're going to kill her.

Maybe. Maybe not.

They're going to torture her to death and make you watch. Break her neck now.

Not yet.

For fuck's sake, you didn't have the stomach to do right by

Anthony and look how that worked out. Are you a monster or not? Kill her quick before they do it slow.

They know about Junji. Maybe they think she can be taught.

I'm sure Luke wants to teach her lots of things. DO IT NOW.

I held off. Cat's breath was hot against my neck. Her tears hotter against my face. Her blood hottest in my hands. At some point, I'd dug my nails through the skin of her cheek and it was burning my palms.

I wanted her to live. Even if that meant being raised by the Paxtons, I wanted her to have a chance.

The family sauntered closer. Owen in the lead. Mama Charlize puffing along with her cane to keep pace.

They wouldn't kill Cat after me. That was the way I had it figured. The point of all this was to punish me, so it didn't make much sense for them to kill Cat if I was already dead. So, I waited to see what Owen would do. He still had the big hammer. If he swung it at me, fine. Lights out. If he so much as looked Cat first... Owen was stronger than me. I knew that.

But I was faster. He wouldn't beat me to the kill.

The moment came. The family formed around us in a half circle. Owen in the center. The sledgehammer dripping with blood and mashed hair. He was so close now, I could smell the iron stench of Anthony's blood.

Owen loomed over me. His nostrils flared. The anger coming off of him was hot enough to boil water. He spun the hammer in that warm-up circle.

Cat sobbed against my neck. Low, choking cries. I squeezed her chin tighter, ready to yank her neck like an engine starter and shatter her spine. I was coiled as tight as Reese's bow string, hoping he would kill me, ready to kill Cat. I waited for the tell. For the shift in his eyes, the rise of the hammer. Something. Anything.

The head of the hammer sagged down into the gravel.

"Get in the truck, Pam," Owen said.

He didn't wait to see if I followed. He turned around, the

sledgehammer dragging through the gravel behind him, and he went back towards his truck idling in the driveway.

I stayed where I was. As still and motionless as if the hammer had actually hit me. Which must have been what happened. The hammer had hit me. I was dead. This was all some Owl's Creek Bridge bullshit —

"Pam!" Owen yelled. He was all the way by the driver's side door now. "Get in the truck. Jen and Reese will take Cat."

On cue, their hands were there. Scrabbling between me and Cat, prying her away from me. Cat fought. She twisted and tried to slip back towards me. "No!" she yelled. "I want to stay with my mom! I want to stay with my mom! Let me go! Mom! MOM!"

"Go with them, Cat," I said. "It's just Aunt Reese and Aunt Jen. They're going to take you home."

I hope.

They pulled my daughter away with the grace and care of prison guards removing a detainee, dragging her off to wherever their vehicles were hidden. Luke and Mama Charlize followed, both of them looking at anything except me. Luke made a point of kicking Anthony's feet as he passed by.

They left.

And I went and got into the truck with my husband.

CHAPTER 30

———|———

BEVERLY. JUST BEVERLY.

At first, the only thing I could look at was the dent in the hood.

Anthony's head made that, I thought. I found myself repeating it over and over again. Anthony's head made that. Anthony's head was there. Right in that spot. But not anymore. Now there was just a dent the size of a dinner plate. A plate covered in raw meat and blood.

Highway speeds had taken care of the worst of the gore – whipped and dried the viscera into a smear of crusty gore across the hood of the truck. Plenty on the windshield as well. Owen had to keep hitting the wipers, leaving long, dark streaks across the glass. There could be trouble if a cop happened to pull us over, but not too much. We'd both killed cops before.

My eyes eventually drifted to the glowing blue lights of the odometer ticking by as we hummed along the interstate.

Five miles.

Ten miles.

Twenty.

Fifty.

Owen had the radio on. The actual radio. Not Sirius or Spotify, just genuine middle of the night country music radio. The mournful dregs of bad luck. Broken-down trucks. Dead dogs. Shitty bosses.

Unfaithful wives.

It went on. We should have been home twenty minutes ago, if home was where we were supposed to be going. I suspected at this point there was no destination. It was just me and Owen in the dark. We were going to drive like this forever. Maybe all the way to California.

"Do you understand how this was supposed to go?" he finally asked me.

I nodded.

"Say it," he demanded.

"...I think there were supposed to be two dents in that hood."

"Three dents," Owen snapped. He still wasn't looking at me. He was fixated on the road ahead. He was going faster. The engine snarled its sympathy. "Three dents is what my family wanted. So why not? Why didn't it happen that way?"

I looked at him. Knuckles clutching the steering wheel like he could strangle it to death. Tendons straining in his forearms like ten-thousand-volt lines. Anthony's blood on his face.

He took one hand off the steering wheel. Reached up and ripped the rearview mirror off the windshield. Smashed it to pieces against the console. The infotainment screen bled liquid crystal. The radio died in an agonized spasm of static.

"Why are you still alive, Pam?"

I hadn't flinched. Not even when a piece of flying broken glass from the mirror cut my cheek.

"...Because you love me," I said.

Owen shook his head. "My mom loved my dad. She still sank him to the bottom of the lake. We're not here because I love you, Pam. We're here because you love me." He pushed harder on the engine. The speedometer was clawing fast towards 90. He wiped Anthony's blood off of his own face. Held his red hand up for me to see. "You had a past, Pam. I knew that. You had a fucking kid. I thought all of that was settled, but if it wasn't then I wished you would have fucking talked to me instead of sneaking around behind my back."

"I didn't know what I wanted," I told him. "I needed to think."

"So, think out loud. With me."

"You wanted me to run it past you if I was thinking about leaving you?" I asked incredulously. "I see some flaws with that plan."

He smiled at me. There was blood and dark bits of flesh spattered on his teeth like gnats.

"You weren't going to leave me, Pam. I heard you talking to him. 'We're the past.' That's what you told him. 'We're the past.' But you and me, Pam? The thing between us? That's the future. That's what I want, and deep down you still want it too."

"That easy?" I asked.

He actually laughed. "Nothing easy about it. Nothing easy at all. My whole family wants to cut your fucking head off. They think I'm a pure-bred horse's ass for letting you breathe this long. But they don't know you like I do. You love me, Pamela. And we're going to get through this together."

It was my turn to laugh now. "Do I get any say in this?"

Owen slammed on the brakes. I wasn't wearing a seatbelt and I wasn't able to get my arm up fast enough to keep my head from slamming into the dashboard. Pain crackled in my forehead, but not so sharp that I didn't know what was going on. The truck screaming through the dust on the side of the road, shuddering as Owen fought to keep control. The thud as we hit the guardrail anyway, hard enough that we both rocked in our seats.

Owen grabbed me by the collar of my shirt and twisted me around so we were eye to eye. He yanked me close until I felt his hot breath churning across my skin.

The sudden stop had churned up our own private dust storm. The windows around us were an impenetrable dark cloud. It was just me, Owen, and the boiling holocaust of fury inside of him.

"I asked you if you were sure about me," Owen seethed. "That was your say. And if I thought for a second that you didn't mean it then I would have stayed in New York. Maybe you forgot, but it was your idea to come out here!"

The clutching claw let go of my collar then, and it was Owen's hand that gently caressed the side of my face. His thumb brushed my ear the way it had a thousand times before.

"But I still believe you, Pamela," he said softly. "And I know that I meant it when I said I was sure about you."

He let go of my head and put the truck back into gear. We drove the rest of the way in silence… and this time we did go home.

———————

It was after two o'clock by the time we got back. The other cars were parked outside of Paxton manor, but that was the only sign of life. The windows were black. The house silent.

We walked side by side up the front steps. Owen opened the front door and stepped aside, letting me enter first. I crossed the stone floor into the entryway. Auntie was there on the wall, still up and waiting for me to come home at this ungodly hour.

"I'm going to sleep in our room," he said quietly. "You can join me. You can stay in the guest room. Whatever you want to do."

He crossed the room to the stairs, but lingered with his hand on the banister. He didn't turn to face me, but his face twisted over his shoulder.

"We're going to get through this, Pam. I may not be your favorite person right now, but I did this because I believe in us. You'll see that eventually."

He went up the stairs.

I did too, but just far enough that I could check on Cat.

She was there. In her room. Her body a small range of hills and valleys beneath the covers, gently rising and falling with each breath. Her back was to me, but I didn't need to check to know that she was awake.

"I'm home," I told her. Then I closed the door behind me.

I went back down to the kitchen. I poured a tall glass of orange juice and sat down at the big kitchen table. I sat there for a long time.

'I believe in us.' That's what Owen said. It could be as simple as that. I could go upstairs right now, and we could wake up together tomorrow. Things wouldn't be the way they were, that was impossible, but we could do the adult thing. We could move forward. Try to forget this. Rebuild.

Make each other happy.

It was close to four AM when Jen came into the kitchen. She stopped briefly in her tracks at the sight of me, but evidently decided, fuck it, it was her house. Not mine. She came up to the table and crossed her arms expectantly.

"I'm thirsty," she declared, her voice frostier than anything she could have found in the fridge.

I still had my glass of orange juice. Barely touched. I slid the glass across the table. "By all means," I said.

Jen took a sip and then twisted her face in a disgusted grimace before flinging the full glass into my face.

"Tastes like whore," she said.

I didn't react. I just sat there. Orange juice, lukewarm and sticky sweet, ran down under the collar of my shirt. Pooling in all the miserable spots where things stick.

"I asked you what was wrong. At the dress shop, I knew something was wrong and I asked you to talk to me… and you fucking lied to my face."

Jen went to the fridge. I watched her open the door and lean inside, her upper body disappearing behind the panel of stainless steel.

"Just understand one thing, bitch," she said over the clatter of shuffling bottles. "My brother maybe spared you, but the rest of us haven't forgiven shit. The rest of my life, I'm going to spend it…"

I kicked the fridge door as hard as I could, catching Jen square in the ribs. The breath wheezed out of her lungs. The bottles clanged together in the shelves like Hyena pups fighting for milk.

The kick wasn't hard enough. I pulled the door all the way open and then flung it shut with all my body weight. Jen had slumped a little from the first shot to her ribs, and this time her head was perfectly aligned with the edge of the door. I slammed it hard and her head made a sound like the beautiful crackle of December ice shattering.

But no time to appreciate it now. Jen was too winded and stunned to scream, but that wouldn't last forever. I looked for the knife block, but it was too far to reach without walking to the other end of the counter. I reached for the nearest drawer instead, willing to settle for anything that would do the job.

In the time it took me to get something, Jen had slumped down to the floor and rolled onto her back. Blood leaked from one ear in a drizzle of strawberry syrup. Her dazed eyes struggled to catch up with what was happening, a computer CPU trying to reboot.

Did she see me coming towards her? Did she know what was happening as I shuffled the sharp tip of the thermometer probe so it stuck out from between my knuckles like a spiked claw?

I don't know for sure, but I can hope.

I straddled Jen's chest, punched the sharp point of the meat thermometer down through the blue pool of her eye, and kept pushing until the tip was deep in her brain and the temperature gauge showed a solid 98.6.

She didn't scream as I killed her. A couple thumps of her heels against the tile, and then nothing. Silence.

I got a real knife then, a butcher knife, and waited in the shadows behind the main entrance to the kitchen. Jen's murder had been quiet, but not totally silent. The bedrooms were all further up, on separate floors, but the old house echoed. I waited, holding my breath. Straining for the sound of footsteps and counting my heartbeats to keep time.

By the time Jen's body temperature had cooled down to the high 80s, I figured I was safe. Nobody was coming.

I still had to move quickly but — if I was lucky — I could get everything I needed before anyone else woke up. Cash from the emergency fund in the library. A set of keys from the hook by the door.

And Cat.

But first, I dipped two fingers into the well of Jen's punctured eye and came away with the tips dripping in blood. I left my final message on the face of the fridge.

"MY NAME IS BEVERLY."

CHAPTER 31

————————|————————

I cursed as I hit the brakes and shifted the protesting gear shift back into reverse yet again. I backed up, tried my best to straighten out the car's massive ass so I could line the hood up with the parking spot, and pulled in again. I breathed out through my nose as the sedan finally made it into the parking lot without scraping the vehicles on either side of it.

Mostly. I'd pulled in so close to my neighbor on the left that there was no way I could open the door enough to get one leg out, never mind the rest of me.

"Fuck!" I yelled, nobody in the cabin to hear it but me. I hated this car. It was an ancient boat of a Lincoln with a janky transmission and brakes that screeched like a tortured co-ed. I hated it so fucking much, but I needed to ditch Owen's truck as soon as possible and it was the first thing I saw. An ugly, maroon relic from the days of Chris MacNeil movies with a "FOR SALE" sign in the windshield. It was sitting in the driveway of a rundown little house that we passed just as the sun was coming up. Luckily for me, the owner was awake and just getting ready for work.

Unluckily for him, he wasn't going to make it to work that day.

To hell with it, I shuffled across the bench seat with the bag of fast food hugged against my chest and went out through the passenger side.

Finally clear and standing outside of the car, I did a cursory sweep of the parking lot without really knowing what I was looking for. The Paxtons, obviously. Maybe a rental car that stood out for some reason. I was going on instinct here, trying to imagine what I would do in their position, but I had never done this before. Never gone into hiding from my own kind. Never been the prey.

I made two sweeps around the parking lot and called it good enough. All I saw was a guy with a beer belly sheperding two kids under seven into the lobby.

A teenage girl trailed behind them, her nose buried in her phone.

————————

I entered the motel room. Like I did in the parking lot, I swept it carefully from corner to corner and came up with nothing. No sign of Reese's summer sandals sticking out from under the curtain. None of Luke's ever-present swamp musk in the air. Twin beds. Desk. TV. Mini-fridge. Some people might have gone for a shithole hourly motel, but we weren't hiding from the cops. I wanted a place with lights in the parking lot and a desk clerk that you couldn't bribe with a $50 bill and a bag of weed. Someplace that called the cops when people with knives showed up in the parking lot. A solid, dependable, standard Holiday Inn room.

Everything was exactly the way I left it, including my daughter lying flat on her back in the bed. Cat had not shifted from that position since we checked in.

I crossed the room and set the Baja Burger bag down on the TV stand. "12-piece nugget and fries," I said. "Ranch and Barbecue sauce, as always."

No response from the coma patient on the bed. She stared up at the ceiling. Sometimes she blinked, but you had to look closely to catch her. I sighed and sat down on the other bed with my own burger and ripped into it. "What's the plan, Cat?" I asked. "Are you going to starve?"

I expected more of the silent treatment, and I was technically correct. Her lips moved, but no sound came out along with it. I cocked my ear towards her silent question. "What was that?"

Still lying flat, Cat's head rolled towards me. Her eyes bulged from her pale, hollowed out face. Her white lips moved slowly, enunciating every syllable.

"I said... who are you? Was it true what Owen said? Have you been keeping this from me? You just... kill people? Is that why you didn't freak out when you saw what I did in the barn?"

"Don't worry about that now, Cat."

"Don't *worry about it?*" She said, not quiet now. Not quiet at all. She sat up straight. "It's all I've been able to think about! What's the truth? Are you some kind of psychopath? Is that why things were so messed up when I was little?"

"Cat-"

She rocked back suddenly. I watched her eyes and saw a lifetime of little incidents suddenly take on new meaning. Every time I'd left her alone at five years old. Every time I came home and had to wash my hands before giving her a hug. Every trip to "the races" with the Paxtons. All of it suddenly revealed in a light she never wanted to examine. "Oh my God," she gasped. "You've been lying to me my whole fucking life." Gas had sparked inside of her, burning rapidly out of control. "Did you... *do something* to me? Is that why I killed Junji?"

I tried again. "Cat, listen to me."

"GET OUT!" she screamed. "Get out! Get out! Get out! Get out of this room! Leave me alone!"

I let my burger fall. I lunged across the space between the beds and clamped my hand over her mouth, cutting off her scorching eruption. "Keep screaming like that and you'll get your wish. Someone will call the cops and you'll spend the rest of your life locked away because you beat some little boy's brains out with a shovel."

I let her go. Cat scurried back against the headboard, watching me warily. Her whole body thrummed with terror. Terror of herself. Terror at me.

"I am protecting you," I said. "I am the only person looking out for you. *And I am feeding you.*"

I threw the bag of food onto her bed and then retreated to my own. My burger was a lost cause, scattered in pieces across the floor. It didn't matter, I'd had enough.

Tentatively, Cat reached out. Paper crinkled as she took out the package of chicken nuggets and opened it with careful neatness.

"...We can share," she offered.

"You eat," I said.

That was all for a while. Long enough for Cat to stop shaking like a child at a January bus stop without her jacket. I got myself a glass of water and then I sat at the foot of her bed. We used to sit like this when she was small, her tiny head and freshly cleaned hair sticking out from under the blankets. I would sit at the foot of her little bed and tell her it was time to go to sleep. No story time though. That wasn't part of what we did.

But it was tonight.

"I'll answer any questions you have, Cat."

She swallowed and regarded me with deep thoughtfulness. "Is it really true?" she finally asked.

I nodded. "It is."

"I mean, Owen and the others. Did they make you? Were they forcing you? Or threatening you?"

"No, Cat. It started long before I met Owen. Before I had you."

"...Why?"

"For the same reason you like to plant, I suppose," I said. "There's no explanation for it, Cat. It just is."

Her jaw worked like she was physically trying to chew it over. When her mouth was clear, she asked, "And what about the rest? The man that Owen... was he really my dad?"

I took a deep breath. I thought about the scar on my hand from prom night. It had been throbbing ever since Anthony died. I'd been able to ignore it for most of the day, but it ached all the way to my elbow now. But what was I supposed to do? Curl up with that pain and let it keep me warm?

"His name was Anthony," I said. "We went to high school together. In California, not New York. That was another lie, kiddo."

"How did you meet?" She was sitting up now. Curiosity pulling her in despite everything else that had happened.

I smiled. It made my arm hurt worse, but there was nothing to do but live with it. Carry it.

"We actually met the first day, but I didn't pay him any attention. I was a cheerleader…"

"A cheerleader!?" Cat gasped.

"And he was just a dorky piece of the scenery. But then, senior year we were in the school play together. He was just supposed to be acting as my boyfriend, but then one thing led to another."

"And led to me?"

A massive burst of laughter caught me by surprise. The kind of laughter that clears away the aching behind your eyes. "Yes," I said. "Something like that. He was quiet, but very funny once you got to know him. And very smart."

"So, what happened?"

I took her hand. "Catherine. Ever since you were born, more than anything else, I have tried to make sure that you had the freedom to do whatever you wanted with your life. The most important thing to me has always been that you know that you can be whoever you choose to be, no matter whether or not anybody else approves. The only thing you should care about is knowing, every day, that your life is exactly what you want it to be. For me, that meant murder."

Cat tried to recoil from me. I seized on her hand and held it tighter. "It's what I am, Cat. I am a killer. That's what I wanted to be, and I did the things I needed to do to make it happen. I killed your grandparents. I killed my best friends. I made my choices… but I couldn't choose to hurt your dad. But I got him killed anyway, and I need to deal with that. And what I need from you is to do exactly what I say until that's done."

Cat swallowed. "But I can choose not to listen, right?"

I threw my hands up. "I guess you can. But I'm asking you to listen to me so I can get us through this. Can you do that?"

Cat looked at me for a long time. She looked at me with a clarity that I never wanted to see. My daughter looked and saw the entirety of who I was. Her dark eyes turned over that reality.

"…I'm going to sleep," she said.

It was only six o'clock at night, but I didn't question it. She'd had a long twenty-four hours.

I stayed awake. I had a few hours of research to do on the cheap phone I'd picked up at T-Mobile.

I needed to know where Reese's boss, The Senator, was going to be this week.

CHAPTER 32

———————————¦———————————

I'd never wanted to kill anyone.

It wasn't like that for me. I never had a hit list. I wasn't some school shooter looking to stack bodies because I didn't fit in and people were mean to me. I wasn't born angry or radicalized by the internet. I wasn't just looking for understanding or for somebody to reach out to me.

I was just in love with the act of killing. Cutting. Slicing. Severing. Blades, hammers, axes. Decapitations. Eviscerations. No color was brighter than fresh blood. No sound sweeter than the final scream. My heart never beat faster than when it was stopping somebody else's. It's just how I was wired. It was never personal. Personal is for psychos.

Watching Anthony die didn't make me crazy. I didn't lose my shit when his brains landed in my hair. I didn't run through the halls of Paxton Manor and try to massacre everyone all in the same night. I was here, pushing a shopping cart through an S-Mart, and nobody shied away from me or recoiled from some perceptible stink of madness coming off of me. I wasn't walking around with my blood boiling and replaying the moment of Anthony's death in my head over and over again. I was just another millennial perusing the garden supplies with her blonde hair in a messy bun.

But it wasn't vegetables I would be burying. I didn't feel insane, but I did feel The Need.

My entire life, The Need was the force that always drove me, the antennae attuned to whatever mattered most. I never questioned The Need.

The Need told me that I had to kill them all.

I added a couple things to the cart. A shovel. A pick-axe. I was starting over again from scratch, no more going to the barn and picking up my favorite machete with the duct tape around the handle. I needed to load up. I could get everything I wanted here if I wanted to, but it didn't feel right. The squeaky, polished floors. The overhead LEDs with their scalding white light. It was fine for some things...

But not everything.

"Help you?" the big man with the long beard asked.

I leaned on the counter and peered through dirty glass. "I need something dependable," I said.

"Dependable for what? Utility? Whittling?"

"Hunting," I said. As if I needed to say it. As if anybody came into this tiny shop with wood paneling and shotguns on the walls if they weren't looking to kill something. The shopkeeper behind the counter wore sunglasses, but there was no hiding the sly grin that crinkled his long, gray beard. He reached underneath the counter.

"Well, you've got two schools of thought." He set a pair of blades down on top of the glass counter. "This one here is a RC58. 420 HC steel. Full tang into the handle for a nice, sturdy body. Nylon, contoured grip. Most advanced knife on the market for my money."

It was hard to argue. Four and a half inches of hard blade with a dusky black carbon finish. I picked it up and admired the lightness of it. Practically a killing feather.

"And the other?" I asked.

"A Woodsboro Bowie knife. Not as strong, but thinner at the tip with that nice, tapered curve. Good for precise work. Deboning, tight punctures. That sort of thing. A little more versatility. And the traditional wooden handle is a nice touch."

I saw what he was saying. This second knife was a classic, right down to the gleaming blade of chrome steel. It looked like something

Davey Crockett carried around on the Frontier.

I thought it over. "Which would you prefer?"

Again, that beard rippled with amusement. "Depends on what you're hunting. It'd be a sin to send a pretty picture like you out there without proper framing."

I leaned in over the glass and looked theatrically over my shoulder, making sure we were alone in the tiny hunting shop. "Can you keep a secret?" I asked.

"Kept the best chili recipe in five counties to myself for forty years now," he promised.

I leaned in closer still. My reflection filled his sunglasses. My own face staring back at me. I didn't look crazy. I looked hungry.

"I'm hunting wolves," I said. "A whole pack of them."

If the shopkeeper had any ethical judgements, he kept it to himself. The only thing he cared about was the pair of blades he'd laid out for me. Old and new. His tongue probed thoughtfully inside of one cheek. Finally, he nudged the Bowie knife a little closer. My own hard eyes stared back at me in the polished steel.

"Wolves sound like classical work to me. I'd say stick with the classic," he said.

I looked more carefully at the blades set out on the dusty glass.

"...Give me both of them," I said.

The shopkeeper was happy to oblige. Happier still when he saw me pull a roll of cash from my pocket instead of a credit card. I noticed that my payment went right into his pocket instead of the cash register.

"I don't mean to engage in any type of unfair generalities, ma'am, but I hope you don't mind me saying that I hope you're being cautious. Wolf hunting ain't careless business. You gotta respect what you're dealing with, or you may find yourself on the wrong side of the food chain."

I allowed a smile of my own. "I'm bringing extra knives, aren't I?" I asked.

He didn't return my smile this time.

"All things being equal," he said, "I hope you don't plan on getting that close."

Of course, that wasn't an option for me.

I had every intention of getting as close as I could.

CHAPTER 33

I played chess with Anthony a few times back in high school.

"You should come with me to chess club," he said. "Let those MENSA dweebs see that the real brains are out there shaking pom poms and twirling their skirts."

He wasn't just trying to bullshit me out of my shorts. I was never able to actually beat him, but I understood the rules and I could see the traps he was setting for me on the board. I was good enough to prolong a game, make him work to put me away, but I was never able to execute an efficient offense of my own. Anthony thought I just needed practice, but the truth was that the game wasn't stimulating enough. Chess pieces didn't bleed. Chess pieces didn't scream or beg for mercy before you tipped them over.

The last time we played, I told him that you had to take a piece of clothing off every time you lost a piece. That game was a lot more fun. Quicker too.

That was the last game of Chess I would play for twelve years. I'd pushed the game completely out of my mind. Murder wasn't chess. It was about the moment. Improvisation. Taking what was in front of you.

This game with the Paxtons was chess. I made the first move by killing Jen. And I made my intentions fairly clear: I was out there. And I wasn't done. The rational thing for the Paxtons to do in this position would be to go to ground. Stay in the mansion and watch each other's back. That would be a stalemate, but it would be in a stalemate in their favor. They had the money and they had strength in numbers. They could spend weeks getting Postmate groceries, sleeping in shifts, and waiting for me to get antsy and make a mistake.

But that wasn't the Paxton way. They showed up for Sunday

services, but the social calendar was their real bible. They were the honored guests at every party. They sat on committees and knew every store owner by their first name. To hole up like the title family in some Southern Gothic novel was simply unthinkable. Especially not if they were cowering in fear of their slutty, Yankee daughter-in-law.

They weren't going to hide. They weren't going to live in fear... and I was going to make them pay for it.

It wasn't all sunshine and roses. I wouldn't be able to pounce freely like I did with Jen. They knew I was coming now, and the element of surprise couldn't just be assumed. I had to carefully choose the right moment to attack. I couldn't afford to be antsy and impulsive.

Patience. Patience was key.

No matter how many speeches I needed to endure.

I could hear him clearly, even all the way here at the rear of the parking lot. "*This is a family state!*" the voice boomed out of the PA system. "*Maybe that's out of style these days. Maybe deviancy and critical race theory are what's hip right now! But let me tell you, here in Alabama, WE ARE PROUD TO BE OUT OF STYLE!*"

I could hear the crowd roar too. They reliably went off like hungry dogs in a kennel every time Senator Fields dangled some red meat in front of them. I sighed and turned the radio up a little louder. The Senator had been going on like this for an hour. In a race where he was ahead in the polls by twenty points.

It was the county fair. I couldn't see the stage from the VIP parking lot, but I could picture it easily enough. The Senator was a beefy former shrimp farmer with yellow teeth and combed back wolf-grey hair. And he walked the stage like one too, prowling back and forth and snapping his teeth at every imagined inequity coming for the good people of Alabama.

There were probably a thousand people crammed shoulder to shoulder to hear him speak. Luke and Owen would be in the crowd too. Not that they cared about politics, but because little sister Reese wouldn't miss the Senator's speech and nobody from the Paxton family was going anywhere alone anymore. Not with me still out there.

I was almost sorry I couldn't see their faces. I was sitting in an air-conditioned car, munching on Sour Patch Kids, and they were out there on red alert. Sitting in the crowded stands up some guy's armpit, stewing in sweat and body odor, nothing to do but listen to the same talking points repeated over and over again. Groomers, gun-grabbers, media elites… groomers again. My eyelids were starting to get heavy. I couldn't sleep, too easy to miss the end of the speech… but maybe dozing was ok.

Yeah, just a quick… light…

We were playing flip cup.

Me. Lyndsay. Alicia. Music blasted so loud the speakers crackled with distortion. There were bodies all around me. Live ones. Teenagers grinding on each other and passing joints back and forth.

"Are you ready, Beverly?!" Alicia was right next to me, but she had to scream to make herself heard over the tectonic shake of the bass.

No, I wasn't ready. I wasn't ready at all. But I was here again, crammed into some little asshole's Beverly Hills mansion, and this is what we did. We played flip cup. I dutifully sidled up to the table alongside my best friends and faced off against a quartet of the same thick-skulled jocks and preening Abercrombie boys I'd been so happy to get away from.

But four was too many. There were only three of us. I said as much to Lyndsay and Alicia.

"Did you have a brain aneurysm for breakfast, Beverly?" Alicia asked. "Our lead off drinker is ready to go."

I swung my head towards the head of the table, and there was Cat. Baby Cat. Her chin was level with the table, her forehead even with the top of the red solo cup.

I shook my head. "No, she's way too little," I said. But Alicia and Lyndsay just squeezed me in a double-sided hug. "Come on, Bev," Lyndsay chided. "She knows what to do. She's a natural."

"No," I insisted. "She's not ready."

"Look's ready to me," Alicia said. In agreement, Cat's little peach pit fists pounded the tabletop.

"You don't know her," I said. "This isn't who she is."

Lyndsay cracked open a beer and filled the cups on our side. "She's her mother's daughter though, right?"

"Not just mine!" I screamed. The party seemed louder still. I screeched my throat raw to be heard. "Not just mine!"

"Oh, enough of this shit," Alicia said. She and Lyndsay fell into their places. "It's her call and the kid wants to play. Everybody ready!"

I saw that it didn't matter what I said. The boys were ready. The girls were ready.

Cat was ready.

Alicia started the countdown. "3...2..."

The snap of the door opening brought me back to my senses. I was here. I was in the car. People were ambling along past the window, making their way back to their cars.

The fair was over. Senator Fields was getting back into his car. I watched him slide his hefty bulk across the leather seat, leaving the seat closest to the door open.

Reese occupied it a second later. She settled into the limo with much more ease, not even making a wrinkle into her smart little business skirt.

"Sir," she gushed. "The first social media impressions are in. Trending on Twitter. Fifty Thousand likes on Facebook. Plenty of activity on Truth Social. Your visibility is through the roof."

"That's all well and good, Ms. Paxton. But between the two of us I hardly think I'm the one that that ought to be visible."

Reese flushed, but pressed on. "I think this positions us for the governor's mansion, sir, but we can't afford to let the momentum slip. I've got some other venues lined up that I think we really need to consider."

"That sounds top shelf, Reese. But you know I need a steak and a bourbon before I can even start making sense of these charts of yours. Driver, can you take us to Gunner's?"

I pulled the chauffer's cap down lower over my eyes and shifted the limo into gear.

"Right away, sir."

CHAPTER 34

————¦————

Senator Fields had security, of course. All politicians do. But there are levels to these things. Two guys following a State Senator around are basically just cashing a check for showing up. They tend to get sleepy.

And they weren't about to get any more awake, I'll tell you that much.

The Senator and Reese weren't on the ball either. Neither of them thought to look back and notice that the security car wasn't behind them. And, sure, maybe I looked a fair amount like the blonde chauffer with her neck slashed in the trunk, but a closer inspection would show we weren't exactly twins either. Senator Fields didn't strike me as particularly observant, but Reese was living under the shadow of a dead sister. She should have been paying more attention to her surroundings, not the latest hashtags.

Sleepy.

The two of them continued on, blathering about demographics and TV news hits. It wasn't until I peeled off on some godforsaken exit off 280 that Fields finally caught wind of what was happening.

"Hold on, Sheila. This isn't the right exit. You're supposed to be taking us to Kellyton. You're all turned around, darlin."

The Senator may have caught on first, but Reese had the knowledge to know what was really happening.

"Hey!" she screamed. "You! Turn around! Let me see your face!"

Movement in the rearview mirror. Reese clamoring towards the divider between the back of the limo and the front. I pitched the wheel hard left, and then back right. Reese staggered off balance with a warbled cry. "Jesus Christ, what's going on!?" Senator Fields shouted.

Reese was quick getting back her balance, but it was time enough for me to raise the opaque glass divider between the two compartments. The panel slid up seconds before Reese's fist slammed hard against it. "LET ME IN YOU PIECE OF SHIT!" Reese screeched. "TAKE DOWN THIS GLASS AND LET'S SEE WHO BLEEDS MORE!"

"Damnit, Reese! What the hell is going on?" The Senator was just as loud as he'd been at the rally. Just as outraged too, but I already heard the thin string of fear thrumming beneath his bellow. This was no stage now. He'd be trying the doors soon, if he hadn't already done so, but the child locks were the first thing I'd engaged. The windows too. They were stuck.

"What's the plan, Pam?" Reese challenged. "Are you gonna kill a fucking Senator?"

State Senator, I corrected mentally. I pushed the pedal a little harder, and the Limo growled in response.

"What!?" Field's voice again. I couldn't see him with the divider up, but I could hear the fear in his voice. "I'm calling the police," he said, trying to shout it loud enough to mask the tremor beneath the bellow. "Do you hear me up there!? I'm calling the cops!"

I heard scuffling from the backseat. Then, "Reese, give me my phone!"

Good luck with that, Senator. No chance Reese Paxton was about to let the police get involved. I started to bounce up and down in my seat as the paved road transitioned to hard-packed dirt. The trees overhead grew thicker, a tunnel of foliage blocking the stars and the moon. No streetlights. No curbs on the side of the road. Nothing existed beyond the range of the Limo's LEDs. We were a lone dart shooting through empty blackness.

Blackness was fine by me. I knew where I was going. Lake Hodder. Lovely little spot. Tranquil. Isolated. Very deep.

In a perfect world, Reese and the Senator would die quietly in the lake. But, deep down where all lies were revealed, I secretly hoped that Reese would find a way to come crawling and coughing out of the water. I had a pickaxe that I would *love* to stick in her ear.

"Reese, what are you doing!?"

I twisted backwards instinctively. Not that I could see anything through the opaque glass, but the tone of Field's voice set off a warning bell. He wasn't just afraid. He was affronted. Indignant.

"Damnit, Reese. Knock that shit off! Stay here!"

Stay? Where the fuck is she going? The doors and windows are locked. I would have heard it if she'd broken glass.

"I'm sorry, Senator," she said. And my pulse doubled. I recognized Reese's tone. Not afraid, but a little eager. Almost giddy.

She killed with that tone.

"I'm sorry," she repeated, "But you're the one always talking about family values."

Senator Fields didn't answer. Senator Fields gurgled. There was a rattling that might have been his hands in their final death spasms.

But I didn't hear any doors opening. No windows breaking. "What the fuck?" I muttered. I checked the console, making sure the windows were locked. The little window button with an "X" through it was set. But just above it…

I didn't do the fucking skylight!

I slammed on the brakes. The long chassis of the limo protested. It lost traction in the dirt and skewed diagonally across the road before groaning to a stop. I was out before the car even stopped moving. I threw open the driver's side door and stripped off the stupid hat and jacket. I ran to the back of the limo and yanked the door open.

Fields was there, sprawled into the corner of the limo in a twisted pile from the sudden stop. The corkscrew sticking out of his throat was still there too. Blood dribbled out onto the carpet, mixing with scotch from a broken bottle.

But his body was alone. Reese was gone. The open skylight gaped at me like a laughing, open mouth.

I whipped around, half-expecting to see her almost on top of me, but there was nothing to see except black trees.

If she had jumped off the top of a limo going 60 miles an hour, she would have broken a leg for sure. I would have been able to see her writhing in the dirt behind the car.

It must have been the trees. She'd reached up for a low hanging branch and held on tight as the car rolled out from under her.

And now she could be anywhere. The headlights were about as much use as a match in the mouth of an alligator. The shadowy hulks of old trees around me crowded close together on all sides. No chance of seeing anything hiding behind them.

Or anyone.

I found a refugee from the liquor cabinet that had survived unscathed and removed the bottle from underneath the senator's bulk. Vodka. I took a small swig.

"Don't suppose you'd want to come out for one last drink before we finish this?" I called out.

Silence from the woods. "Okay then," I said, heading back to the driver's side. "That's fine. I've got something else to share with you." The pickaxe was still waiting for me in the passenger seat. A black, fiberglass handle with a yellow rubber grip and a mean, curved head like a steer's horn. I was going to get to use it after all.

"Get used to the darkness, Reese," I muttered. "You're going to be seeing a lot of it."

I killed the headlights. We were both in the darkness now.

I stepped off the path as smoothly as I could. Into the underbrush, but not too far. Just enough to get out of plain sight. I could be quiet, but I wasn't magic. There was no way to move perfectly silently through the underbrush in the pitch dark. Every move I made was a dropped hint leading Reese to me. I knew it, and she knew it. Ripples in the dark. But it cut both ways, Reese couldn't move on me without revealing where she might be.

That was the game.

I had the pick axe. I wasn't naive enough to think that Reese wouldn't be armed. There was a compact folding knife that she kept for just such an occasion. Either one of us could kill the other at any time, it was just a question of who was going to screw up first.

Branches cracked somewhere in the pitch-black.

The first move. Reese changing position? Or just throwing a rock for me to chase after?

I waited right where I was.

Time passed. Could have been a minute. Could have been an hour.

Another sound, more subtle this time. More likely Reese than rock.

I was perfectly happy to remain where I was.

More time. I counted cricket chirps.

This time, I moved. Just a small slide backwards, closest to the nearest tree. I tried to stay silent, but there was still the gentle rustle of dead leaves.

It wasn't long until Reese creaked through the brush again. Probably Reese. So hard to discern between what was true stealth and what I was supposed to hear. But if it was her, then she was getting closer.

She was patient by nature, Reese. Careful. Methodical. Perfectly willing for just the right opportunity to make her move. It was easy to picture her out there in the dark — sweaty blouse clinging to her skin. Her perfect veneer of professionalism frazzled and smeared by her escape from the limo. The knife in her tiny, clenched fist. And yet, totally unbothered by all of it. She would wait all night if needed to for the perfect moment.

I slammed the pickaxe hard against a nearby tree. The sound echoed out through the dark woods.

"I'm right here, Reese! Let's finish this!"

No response of course. She wasn't dumb. If she knew where I was, she could creep closer to my voice and pick her time. It was still pitch black in the woods. I couldn't see her. I had no idea where she was. But it was possible she was already right on top of me. Reese with her eyes narrowed and her prey, me, right in her sights. The perfect target, and I had no idea even as Reese stalked closer, ready to-

I waited another second, and then I pushed the alarm button on the key fob. The limo suddenly came to life in a blast of flashing lights and a screeching horn loud enough to send the birds flying out of their nests.

I was expecting it. I was ready for the murdered silence and the sudden assault of flashing light spoiling the darkness.

Reese wasn't. I clearly saw her jump in the strobing white and yellow lights. Saw her head whip involuntarily towards the car and raise her small knife in one clenched fist.

I was already uncoiling. Sprinting towards her, seizing my moment. Blood racing in my head.

Now. Now. NOW!

I hit her hard in the side of the head with the butt of the pickaxe. Reese went down flat on her back, and I raised the pickaxe high to finish her off. I was fast, but Reese wasn't slow. She still got her bite in. She lunged up and buried her small blade deep into my shin. "BITCH!" she screamed.

It didn't matter. The pickaxe was already over my head. Already coming down on the soft target of her stomach.

What I did to her wasn't a disemboweling. Disemboweling was neat. I excavated a fucking trench into her torso. The blunt pickaxe point sunk deep into her flesh just above the pubic bone. Reese wailed as blood bubbled up like struck oil. I braced a foot against her shoulder and *pulled*, ripping a furrow of meat through her core until the metal hit her breastbone. I took my foot off her shoulder, but kept pulling on the pick. Dragging Reese's body through the dirt, a massive swath of blood trailing behind her like a red carpet.

I stopped when my back thumped against a tree trunk. I took the reprieve to sink back, letting the tree take the brunt of my weight. Reese was limp at my feet, her blank eyes reflecting the white LEDS and yellow hazards in alternating flashes. I groped for the key fob and shut off the alarm.

Even the crickets were silent then. The only sound was my ragged breathing, still trying to slow down from the exertion of dragging a hundred and ten pounds of sister-in-law through the dirt.

Reese's knife was still sticking out of my shin. I bent down and the pain in my leg bit back before I could even get my hand around the knife handle. *Not a good sign,* I thought grimly. Not good at all. I took some deep breaths, bracing myself to pull it out. *One... Two...*

And then, a *buzz* from Reese's pocket.

I yanked the knife out. Oh fuck. Oh fuck, yeah that hurt.

Reese's phone kept buzzing. Notification after notification coming in. Trying to ignore the Suffering Scouts making a campsite in my leg, I reached over and fished the phone out of Reese's ass pocket. It was locked, but a thumbprint off her dead hand took care of that.

I didn't read the last message yet. I started at the beginning.

"Its her shes in the limo"

Hm. Too panicked for punctuation. I was always curious how that would work.

Owen and Luke responded with what you'd expect. *"Where are you?" "Were coming." "Hang on."* Etcetera, etcetera.

It got a little interesting right around when she made her escape.

Reese: I'm out. She's mine.

Owen: Wait for us.

Luke: Stay right fucking there Reese we'll do it together.

It went on like that for a while. Pretty downhill by the end. "Answer us." "Where are you?" What's happening?"

I typed back.

Reese: It's alright, I ripped her fucking stomach out. Come now.

I didn't wait. I left them the phone.

And the mess.

CHAPTER 35

———|———

I made it back to the motel shortly after midnight. I entered as silently as possible in case Cat was asleep. Thankfully, she was sprawled out on her side in the sleep of the deeply unconscious. A good night's sleep wasn't going to wring all the awful shit of the last 48 hours out from her brain, but it certainly couldn't hurt. If nothing else, it was good to see her looking like a normal kid. Her brow wasn't twisted into some wretched contortion of anguish, and her breathing was calm and even, no moans or muffled screams to be heard as she slumbered.

Intent on keeping her that way, I moved as quietly as I could into the bathroom, even when every other step came down on a leg that felt like it was wrapped in barbed wire.

I managed to make it into the bathroom and set myself down on the toilet without screaming, but it was very a near thing. I hadn't looked at the wound in my shin yet, but I knew enough about pain. This was bad. This was very bad. But there was nothing else to do now but check out the damage. I unbuckled my pants and pushed them down to the floor. It felt like dragging powdered glass over the wound. The exertion of holding in the screams left me sweating before the jeans were finally on the floor.

I stretched my leg out to get a better look, marginally reassured by what I saw. It was a deep wound, the pain left no doubt about that, but at least it was clean. A vertical gash the size of a cat's eye pupil, just to the inside of my shin bone. Easy enough to bandage, but it was going to hurt even worse by the time the sun came up. That much I was sure of.

The bathroom door opened then. The lights came on, making me squint and turn my head to the side with a hiss.

Cat wasn't ready for me either. She skidded and nearly fell in her haste to scramble back over the threshold.

"I didn't know you were back," she said apologetically. "I didn't see anything in the hallway." She was wearing a long sleep shirt, and she straightened the hem nervously.

"I'll just be another minute if you need the bathroom," I said. "Sorry."

Cat stayed in the doorway. I caught her eye flicking down to my shin and the small pool of blood forming on the tiles.

Not much in the way of a first-aid kit, oversight on my part, but I scavenged around in my bag and found a few loose maxi-pads. I stuck one over the wound and held it in place.

"If you're here anyway, hand me that stupid little hotel shower cap by the sink."

Cat obeyed. The plastic cap made it around my shin and I barely managed to knot the two ends together around the back, holding the pad in place. It would do until I could get a first-aid kit tomorrow.

"…Can I have one of those?" Cat asked quietly.

At first, I thought she meant the shower cap, until it hit me what she was really looking for. "The pad?" I asked. "Why would you need…" The pain in my leg was suddenly swept away beneath a wave of shock.

"Oh."

"Do not make this weird, mom," Cat snapped. "You're a serial killer. I murdered the boy I had a crush on with a shovel. I met my dad, watched my stepdad murder him, and apparently, you've been lying to me my entire life. I have enough fucking problems. Give me a fucking pad."

Fair enough. I nodded towards my bag on the floor between us. "Help yourself."

Cat reached out meekly and grabbed one of the pads. The silence grew between us like fungus as she stood there and twisted it between her fingers. "Thanks," she muttered before finally pivoting back towards the bedroom.

"Stay for a second," I said. "The first time can be tricky."

I walked her through how to put the pad in place. "Change it when it starts to feel heavy. That means there's too much blood."

Blood. She winced at the word, but she nodded when I was done.

"Thanks, mom."

I nodded and tried to get up. Bad idea. I made it halfway up before my bad leg went off like there was demolition charge in my shin. I windmilled and dropped back down, hoping to land back on the toilet and not –

Cat grabbed my arm, steadying me in place. "Hang on," she told me.

The extra moment's reprieve was all I needed. I got an arm against the wall and managed to get fully on my feet.

"I'm alright now," I said.

Cat looked at me critically but relented. "You're sure?"

I nodded. "I'll give you a minute," I said. I hobbled out of the bathroom, using the sink and then the edge of the door for support. I could have made it all the way to the bed, but I lingered at the door for an extra moment. I debated leaving it alone, but I'd kept it to myself for long enough and I didn't know if I'd have another chance. The pain in my leg was a reminder. None of this was guaranteed to go my way. I might not come back next time.

I turned back to my daughter. She was there by the sink, no taller than the towel rack with her first menstrual pad twisted in her hands. The Alabama Highway Department shirt I'd bought at a rest stop hung down to just above her bony knees.

"Listen to me," I said to her. "Just so you understand…the first time I killed someone? I was about your age. It didn't make me feel the way you're feeling."

"But I still did it," she said. "I killed Junji."

"You did. And there's no taking that back. And I don't know why you did it, but I just want you to understand that there's no curse on you. You are not a monster. You are not going to freak out at the next full moon and do it again. There's nothing in your blood forcing you to be a killer. Okay, Cat? I want to be clear on this. There. Is. No. Such. Thing. Destiny is horse shit. *You* decide who you want to be. That's the only thing that matters."

"Did you ever think about stopping?" she asked me.

"I thought about it once," I said. "For a couple people's sake, but mostly for your dad. But never for me, do you understand that? Eventually, I realized that I had to choose between being someone who could be in their lives or being the person I truly was meant to be. I chose myself. Maybe that's selfish, but it wasn't a lie."

"What about Owen and the Paxton's? It sounds like they were everything you wanted?"

I nodded. "It does, doesn't it? If Anthony hadn't come back, we probably could have been happy there forever."

"Did you love my dad that much?" Cat asked.

"...I've got to get some sleep," I said. "Don't worry about waking me in the morning. Watch TV, get room service. Do whatever you want to do, just don't leave the room."

"How much longer are we going to be doing this, mom?"

I had an answer. "Three days."

"What happens after three days?"

"California," I told her. "You'll love it there. Some of the most beautiful flowers you'll ever see."

She wouldn't leave it alone. "What else, mom?" Cat pressed. "What are we staying here for?"

I nodded towards the pad. "Take care of you what you have to do," I said. "If you need any more help, let me know. And remember what I said about tomorrow. Just stay in the room, okay?"

I left my daughter to her business. My business was sleep, and the fervent hope that tomorrow I wouldn't wake up too stiff. I had a lot of moving around to do.

Three days. That was the timeline. Tomorrow was a day for

preparations. The third day would be the end of it.

Day two was Talladega.

CHAPTER 36

————┼————

I could have killed Reese.

I mean, obviously I already had, but I would have happily killed her again if I had the chance.

One knife. One fucking knife was all it took to make an already terrible day even worse. It was bad enough that my leg throbbed to the bone with every step. But it was also ninety degrees out and I couldn't wear shorts because I had one leg bandaged up like I fought in World War I. I mean, yes, leather pants got my ass across but, all things being equal, I would have preferred to go about my day without feeling like my legs were a pair of bratwursts cooking in the oven.

I took a sip of beer to try and distract myself from my myriad discomforts. When that didn't work, I took another.

The party I was at looked identical to the last three I'd floated through. Thirty people, sweating and scantily clad, crammed together in front of an RV. Their speaker system battling for dominance against twenty speaker systems in front of twenty neighboring RVs.

This one was putting up a good fight. The subwoofer made my beer shake like something out of Jurassic Park. The speakers were the size of coffin lids, but they weren't blaring party country. This was strictly an early 2010's Jams pop punk playlist. Low Shoulder, The Ain't Rights. They even played some Kincaids and it didn't make me wince inside. It was actually nice to hear Brucey Kincaid wail while a bunch of happy drunks threw ping pong balls at beer cups. I'd refused two offers to take a turn at the table, but my wrist was tingling in a way that made me want to take a crack at it. Maybe next game.

Those good feelings lasted until The Five came on, and then everything fell apart like fall leaves in a bonfire. The pleasant buzz of a few minutes ago was now bees in my ears. The warm mass of bodies felt like a funeral home oven. Too much. All of it, too goddamn much. I took my beer and retreated away from the party, gritting my teeth against the half dozen more I would need to fight through. Past keg stands, body shots, and more boobs for beads transactions than I could count. I tried to keep my gaze focused beyond the writhing mass of revelers. Beyond them, there was the smooth curve of the track and the silent rows of the bleachers. I tried to pretend I was there, and that the parties in the infield were nothing but a dull hum that blended in with the crickets and mosquitos. I tried to imagine I was there with a cold drink, sitting underneath the lit up banner that said, "THIS IS TALLADEGA."

In my imagination, it felt like there was somebody sitting next to me, but I couldn't make out their face.

I finally made it back to my trailer. Not really mine, technically. It belonged to three friends who hadn't asked enough questions when I told them I wanted to do terrible things to their bodies. They were currently stored in a storage area under the bed, soaking in a four-inch pool of terrible things.

I traded the beer for a shot of Fireball and flopped down on the bed. I unbuttoned my godforsaken leather pants and peeled them off, one sweaty inch at a time. Grateful for a little goddamn *air,* even if the material scoured my wounded shin like a fistful of rock salt.

This wasn't working. Trawling random parties and hoping to just stumble into Luke was like searching for a single beer in a dozen coolers.

But he was here. He was here somewhere. Luke Paxton hadn't missed a single Talladega 500 since he was in diapers, and the Paxtons didn't abandon their traditions, not even when they were being hunted.

And I could be wrong, but I don't think he had the rest of the family with him. Mama Charlize didn't move well enough, and Owen hated this thing. "The only racing I'm interested in is me against somebody screaming their head off," he once told me.

It was probably just friends around him. Norm friends. Friends who had no idea what monster was stalking him.

I found myself wishing I'd ever bothered to learn any of their names. I could have zeroed in on their social media feeds in a second and known exactly what skank-den party they were holed up in.

There was nothing else to do. Certainly too much pounding bass for any hope of sleep. I drank more Fireball from the bottle and opened up Instagram on one of the dead guy's phones. I scrolled through the Talladega hashtag, looking at parties and car exhibits, scanning the mass of faces for Luke's jaw and hulking figure.

Nothing. Nothing, nothing, nothing. I tried to ignore the blood building up in my ears. I couldn't let this drag on forever. It was my best chance to pick Luke off by himself. The three surviving Paxtons together were too much. There had to be some way to draw him out.

What I ought to do is just slit the throat of the jumbotron operator and put myself up on the big screen. "Here I am Luke, come and get me." That would send him running.

…I slowed my scroll.

I'd been so focused on myself. It finally occurred to me that there was more than one way to send Luke running.

A couple minutes later, I had the three phones of the dearly departed up and open. I was into all of their accounts – Twitter, Instagram, the works:

Quint Motors at Talladega? Bulging Eyes emoji.

#QuintMotors about to get into the race! #HearditHere

Quint Motors says big announcement at Talladega Boulevard tomorrow at noon!

It was a good start, but there was more to do. (Ugh. Pants.)

I went back out to the parties. I batted my eyes and asked drunks if I could borrow their phones. I said I was texting a friend, but I was actually posting tweets. By midnight, the rumor had become self-sustaining and was spreading without my help. Quint Motors, Luke's favorite airboat manufacturer, was either debuting a racecar motor or unveiling a car sponsorship. The details were hazy, but the gist was the same. If you were a Quint Motors fan, you needed to be on the Main Boulevard at noon tomorrow to find out.

It was complete horseshit. There was no event planned. I made the whole thing up out of thin air.

But Luke would have to show up to find out.

And I would be waiting.

———————

I was still waiting.

It was almost one o'clock. People had showed up. Old men with bushy beards and Quint Motors hats. Squirrely guys with ponytails who looked around and muttered, "Fucking Facebook," before sauntering off.

But no Luke. Damnit, maybe he hadn't come after all.

I paused expectantly.

...*I said, universe, "MAYBE HE HADN'T COME AFTER ALL."*

I waited another five minutes.

…Shit.

"Excuse me," somebody said from the corner of my vision. "Is this where the Quint Motors things is happening?'

"No," I said curtly.

"Ah, shit," he groused. "I was really counting on that."

There was a nibble of the familiar in his voice. I turned and examined him a little more closely. I'd seen plenty of guys with sunglasses and sandy hair poking out from under a trucker hat, but my impression of him seemed a little more familiar than just this weekend.

The feeling seemed to be mutual. I was wearing my own pair of aviators, and my hair was tucked tight under a ball cap, but he seemed to be evaluating me with the same nagging familiarity.

"Do we know each other?" he asked. "What's your name?"

"Beverly," I answered truthfully.

That just confused him more. "But have we met? Are you from Alabama? Perry County?"

It clicked then. Zac Bana. I'd met him at a crawfish boil at the manor.

He was a friend of Luke's.

My face didn't flicker, even as the blood started pumping in my veins like oil through a Quint Motors engine. 'I live in Texas now," I lied. He was wearing a U of A shirt, and I ran a finger across his chest. "But I'm Alabama class of 2016. Roll tide!"

I fudged the years a little to make myself seem a little younger. Zac obviously didn't' see an issue as he let out a short laugh. "Oh shit, that must be it. Did you go to the frat parties?"

"As much as I could without losing my 2.5 average."

Another laugh from my new old friend. "Yeah, that was my motto too. Listen, are you here with anyone? Friends?"

"A few girlfriends, but we kinda split for the day. They made some new friends, so I'm on my own."

Zac tilted his head, measuring me like a carpenter trying to judge if a plank would fit in a deck. "What about you?" he finally asked. "You looking to make friends?"

He preemptively held up his hand before I could speak, letting me see a glint of golden wedding band. "I don't mean me," he quickly added. "I'm with a buddy of mine. He's a guy I've known for twenty years, a really good dude, but he's been a real mess lately."

"What's that mean?" I said, drawing out the line. "Did he get indicted for something?"

"No, no. Nothing like that. Guy's never done anything worse than steal a keg from a frat house. And those Betas deserved that shit." He lowered his voice and leaned in close, encasing me in the beer mist hovering around him. "It's bad family shit. Tragic shit. But it's not his fault. This is supposed to be his favorite weekend of the year, but we had to *beg* him to come with us and all he's done is sit alone in the trailer the whole time. I just want him to have a good time. "

"It sounds like you should be on Adult Friend Finder," I deadpanned. Just enough bite to be critical, not enough to appear disgusted. It was an art.

"Shit. Sort of," he said with a charming lack of shame. "But I'm not saying there's any pressure. You don't have to do anything you're not into, but I'm asking you as a Christian, ma'am. Maybe just talk to him a little? He needs a wakeup call."

I pretended to think about it. "I'll talk to him, okay? But that's all I'm going to do."

I watched relief break over him like a water balloon on a hot day. "That's all," he said. "That's all we want."

A lie. I could tell that without even needing him to take off his sunglasses.

But that was okay. It wasn't all I wanted either.

CHAPTER 37

———————

Zac brought me back to their spot, where a few more guys were gathered around a keg. All of them were slight variations on the same model. I recognized them all from various events around the manor, but I didn't see any glimmer in return. The volume of the parties all around us seemed to muffle as I entered the area. They were all drinking, but the vibe was more like a wake than a party.

Zac introduced me with the awkward gentleness of a divorced parent introducing his kid to a therapist. 'Guys, this is Beverly. I told her about Luke and she wants to meet him."

Oh, thank God it actually was Luke. I was pretty sure, but part of me was braced for an awkward interaction with some entirely different guy whose sister drowned in a lake or some shit.

The others mumbled awkward greetings to me from their keg-side vigil. I offered a thin smile in return and then nodded towards the RV behind them. The door was closed and the blinds were pulled down.

"In there?" I asked.

They nodded in a disjointed chorus.

"Better go introduce myself," I said.

———————

Making my way past the stench of stale beer and spilled whiskey was like pushing aside a physical curtain. Empty beer bottles rattled on the short steps as I climbed inside the RV. The lights were off, and the interior was drenched in shades of morbid grey. It was cramped inside, as even the nicest RVs were, but that didn't make it cheap. There were polished finishes on every surface. Leather seats. A flat screen TV mounted to one wall.

Also, more empty bottles scattered everywhere. Crumpled chip bags on the floor. A half-eaten pulled pork sandwich lay on the small table.

It was grief. The RV was a tomb of grief.

Movement rustled in the shadows at the darkest corner then, coming from the semi-enclosed "bedroom" at the back of the motorhome. Something stirred there in a knot of stinking sheets.

"I said let me fucking sleep!" Luke shouted.

"Sleep when you're dead," I called back softly.

The fitful figure in the tangled sheets went still... and then slowly sat up. I watched the shadowy body slowly lean forward until it was Luke's bleary face staring at me through the murky light. His artfully maintained stubble had degenerated into a scraggly beard. He rubbed his bloodshot eyes, as if he wasn't sure if I was really there or if I was just another nightmare come to torment him.

"Come on," I taunted. "You finally have a chance to make your move and you're just going to sit there?" I took off the sunglasses and hat, just to ensure there could be no doubt who I was. "Or maybe you'd rather just bunk up with your sisters like you did when you were a scared little kid?"

He knew it was me then, no question. And once we were re-introduced, Luke didn't waste any time. He flung himself up out of the bed and charged forward. Barefoot, shirtless, so tall that his head nearly scraped the roof of the RV. He barely fit through the narrow gangway as he barreled towards me like a 5.8 liter V-8 engine filled with fuel-injected hate.

There was no way of evading him in the saltine-box RV. No room to dodge to either side.

I didn't bother to try. Luke slammed into me and I brought the Woodsboro knife up and under into his guts. I pushed hard to the side, opening up a good-sized horizontal gash in his abdomen. A Big Gulp cup of his hot blood spattered both of our feet.

It didn't stop Luke from squeezing my biceps until the bones creaked. He lifted me up and slammed me against the wall. That nice flat screen I was admiring? It crumpled into ice chips as Luke smashed me through it. The entire RV rocked violently with the force. One of his hands went to my throat and pressed my larynx down until I gagged.

My knife hand was still free. I stabbed him twice more, driving the knife all the way in until my knuckles touched skin.

He didn't go down. He didn't stagger back. He didn't even whimper.

Oh Shit. Oh Shit Shit SHIT.

I stabbed higher, going for his eye, but Luke got his hand up first. The blade punched through his palm, pressing all the way down to the hilt and causing Luke about as much discomfort as a hangnail. He yanked his hand back, taking my knife with it, and then he lunged at me with his fucking teeth. I twisted at the last moment and he caught my shoulder instead of my neck. Precious little comfort as pain flared up and down my side like a cattle prod. I screamed as the warm blood came coursing down my chest.

Luke flung me against the opposite wall. I don't mean a toss or a throw, I mean he heaved me like I weighed nothing. My feet never touched the floor. I flew the length of the RV, slammed against the far wall, and dropped down in a heap among the rest of the trash. My head rumbled like Grand Central Station at rush hour.

I felt the floor shaking. Luke, stomping closer to finish me off. I had to get up, but it just wasn't happening. I couldn't even tell which way was up.

A weapon. You need a weapon. Come on.

I needed to see first. My vision was fucked with dancing spots. And what I could see was useless. Garbage. Food scraps. I got the briefest glimpse of Luke steaming towards me. Blood rained in a storm pattern behind him. A short loop of his intestines dangled from the gash I'd made in his abs. It looked like he was moving in slow motion, so why couldn't I get up? Why couldn't I-

Luke's foot stomped down on my head. Was it the floor creaking?

Or my skull?

He pushed harder. My ear mashed to the floor roared with my own rushing blood.

"You fucking bitch," Luke seethed. "How does that feel?"

My free hand groped across the floor, feeling desperately for something. Anything. Crunching chips. Slimy chicken wing bones.

The glass slope of a beer bottle.

I grasped the bottle and smashed it. I seized the first shard I could get my hands on, felt like the size of a Dorito, but it would have to work. I groped for the source of pressure against my skull. Luke's leg. I lashed out blindly, making short, shallow cuts with the shard of glass. Again. Again. Warm blood in my hair. It was a race, my skull threatening to shatter, or-

At last, a cut no different than any other, but this time Luke shrieked and tumbled forward. I saw the blood gushing from his leg and a gash like a fish's mouth at the back of his heel.

The Achilles tendon. I'd slashed it and Luke's ability to stand anywhere, never mind my head, was gone. He dropped to the floor, clutching the bloody gash.

I pounced on top of him, but Luke was ready. We rolled around on the floor, both of us snarling like wild dogs. He grabbed my wrist and twisted it until tendons screamed. I jammed my knee into his balls. I slashed at him with my nails. He tore a chunk of hair out of my scalp. My fumbling hand came into contact with something slimy and muscular, like a nightcrawler fresh out of the dirt. Luke's dangling length of intestines. I wrapped my hand around it and pulled, uncoiling another two feet of intestine from the gaping wound.

Luke scrabbled for his innards. To put them back inside his body, I thought, but I was very wrong. He took the rope of his intestines and looped the slimy length of them around my neck. I realized what he was trying to do, but it was already too late to stop him. Gritting his bloody teeth, Luke cinched the noose of his own bowels tight around my neck and pulled as tight as he could.

I gasped and sucked at air that wasn't there. He extended his arms back, pushing me away from the range where I could gouge his eyes. I clawed anyway, as if I could physically grab air to breathe, but there was nothing. Nothing but the crushing pain around my throat and the thunder of my heart. My hands followed the trail of his intestines, skimming over slippery, bloody innards until at last I felt the hard iron of his clenched hands. Desperately, I groped around his fingers, each massive digit as thick and hard as a railroad spike. I pried back at his fingers, expecting to feel like I was trying to wrest open a bear trap.

To my surprise, my fingers wormed easily into his clenched fists. I clawed at his fingers and immediately felt the first tremor of his grip threatening to give way.

My vision was growing fuzzy as my blood screamed for oxygen, but I fought through it to look at Luke. Really look at him. What I saw was vanilla ice cream skin with streaks of strawberry syrup. His eyes were still bright with hate, but I could see the hazy clouds gathering at the edges of his vision. As badly hurt as I was, so was he. I strained again against his fingers, and that first tremor of weakness expanded.

It was an endurance race now. Luke fought to keep the death noose around my neck. I'd killed his sisters. I'd broken his brother's heart. I'd chosen his brother instead of him. There was probably nobody on earth he hated more than me, and those smoldering embers kept him going when others would have died two pints of blood ago.

And yet, I still had more hate than he did.

I pulled again and this time his hand came free entirely. I untangled myself from the ropes of his innards and pushed his head down. Luke bucked, trying to throw me off, but I squeezed my thighs tight around his hips to deny him the leverage to buck me off. He thrashed with futile fury, moaning and roaring, but he was mine now.

And it was not just Anthony I thought about. It was Cat, too.

Panting, I leaned down on his forehead, pinning him in place. With my other hand, I scooped up a fistful of broken glass. "Eat it," I growled.

Luke spat blood at my face. "Fuck-"

I slammed the fistful of shards over his tongue. Down his throat.

"EAT IT!"

Luke's heels hammered thunder against the floor. The blood overflowed from his ruined mouth. A glass somebody overfilled with too much sangria. I kept my fist pressed in place, keeping him from spitting up anything solid. Teeth, glass. Let it all go down his throat. I put my other hand over his nostrils and squeezed. Let him grow gills or die.

I should have enjoyed this more than I did. This was my gift. My art. A lot of the things I believed when I was young turned out to be too simple for the real world, but I still sincerely believed that it was a privilege to know what you were born to do and to have the freedom to do it well.

But this wasn't about my gift. Not Luke and not the sisters. It was about doing what I had to do to thaw the block of ice that had been sitting in my chest ever since Anthony died.

I couldn't wait for Luke to be dead. I couldn't wait for this to be over.

It took a few more seconds. His gurgling moans slowed and then stopped. His eyelids slipped down to half-mast.

I rolled off his dead body and flopped down shoulder to shoulder with his corpse, the only difference between our sprawled bodies was the heaving of my chest as I fought for air. The adrenaline surge that had gotten me this far was gone. My muscles ached. Deep pain snarled my every bone in barbed wire. I lay in the wreckage of the trailer, panting and trying to bolt together enough inner workings to sit up.

There was a checkered shirt knotted around my waist. Purely a decorative piece, but I unwrapped it now and buttoned it up, covering the worst of the bloodstains on my tank top. I winced shrugging it over my shoulders and I winced at the workings of every button before finally giving up at tit-level. Good enough to hide the worst of the blood. I tried to stand up once and dropped back to my knees just as quickly.

"Come on," I coaxed. "Almost there."

No point in taking a deep breath, it hurt as much as everything else did. I just stood up.

And this time I stayed up.

I staggered out of the RV. At first, all I saw was sunspots after the gloom of the trailer. Once those cleared, I saw Luke's friends staring at me in wide-eyed awe. Different faces, but all with the same mixture of trepidation and deep respect. I took another unsteady step forward, trying not to sway and doing a lousy job of it.

Zac cleared his throat. "So, did you guys... did you... hit it off?"

I considered what I must look like to them. Swaying unsteadily. Button-down dirt not quite closed enough to hide the bite mark on my shoulder or the massive bruise already forming around it. I ran a hand through my hair and felt the chaotic, knotted mess of it.

I found my voice. "Yeah," I slurred. "We had a helluva time."

"You did? He enjoyed it?"

"...Let's just say whatever was bothering him before, I don't think he cares anymore."

Zac's grin was genuine. "That's awesome. What about you? You want a beer or something?"

"No. I... I need to find my friends."

"Are you sure?" he asked. "Maybe you should sit down for a minute."

I shook my head. Mistake. My vision shook side to side with it.

"Just do me one favor," I said. "Give Luke a few hours to sleep it off... I really gave it to him."

222 | Sean McDonough

CHAPTER 38

———————|———————

Cat sat straight up in bed as I came through the door. If I had any doubts about how bad I looked, she cleared that up in short order.

"MOM!"

Nonsense to pretend like I was fine, but I did it anyway. "Sit," I told her. "Nothing broken, just a lot of bruises."

And one wrist was swollen like a leg of lamb. And I nearly blacked out from the pain in my throat every time I took a breath. There was an explosion on the TV, and I winced as a dozen sympathetic booms went off between my ears. "Do you mind putting something else on?" I asked. "Something quieter."

Cat looked like she was about to say something. Thankfully, she kept it to herself and obediently channel surfed through the hotel's limited options.

"Not like streaming where you just take your pick, eh?" I joked. "This is how we made do when I was your age." I went to the mini-fridge and found the leftover remnants of a chicken tender dinner in a Styrofoam container. By the time I brought it back to the beds, Cat had settled on an old Turtleshell Pictures movie.

"Much better," I said. The movie was Lavender Twist and the Golden Hinoke. Tiny little forest elves running around a plant nursery. Shenanigans abound.

"You always loved this one," I told her.

Cat didn't answer. Her eyes stayed fixed insistently on a spot a few inches above the TV.

We stayed like that for a while. Nothing between us but the ongoing adventures of plant nursery elves while I fended off nausea and forced myself to get some food into my body. When I'd eaten as much as I could, I sat down at the edge of her bed. "Talk to me, okay? I don't feel like going to bed yet."

I couldn't let myself fall asleep is what it really was. I'm not sure how long you're supposed to stay awake after a concussion, but you probably need to stop seeing double first.

"What's going to happen, Mom?" she asked me.

"What do you mean? You've seen this movie a million times."

She flung the remote across the room. "I'm not joking, mom. Stop it!" she cried.

I sighed. "I told you already. One more day and we're done here."

"Yeah, and then what?" Cat challenged. Not to be denied. "Where are we going to live? What are we going to do? Am I supposed to just start at a new school somewhere while you work at a nail salon? Are we supposed to have new names? How does this work!?"

I sighed. "Go into my bag," I told her. My plan had been to put this off until I'd finished with the Paxtons, but in my current condition I didn't have the energy to lie.

The bag was right where I'd left it, dropped haphazardly by the door. I watched Cat cross the room. She was getting so tall.

"You want the envelope," I directed. I waited while she gingerly rummaged around, listening to the clatter of knives, before she finally emerged with the folded envelope with the greyhound logo on it. I waited for her to take out the single ticket, but started talking before she had time to get a word in.

"That's a ticket to Monrovia, California. Great growing climate. Lot of greenhouses there. You've got a great-aunt and uncle that live out there. At least, I assume they still live there. It looks like they do if Facebook is anything to go by. When you get there, find a police station and tell them your name is Catherine Kilbourne and they need to contact Audrey and Allen Kilbourne. There'll be some hoops to jump through, probably a blood test, but once the dust settles, they'll take you in. They're those kinds of people. It's a long bus ride, so make sure you have food. There's cash in the drawer by my bed."

"What do you mean, they'll take me in? For how long?"

"...For always, Cat. This is it. I've got to finish things with the Paxtons-"

"You can't! Look at you, mom!"

"I'm not going to die," I plowed on. Probably. "But I'm not going to be able to pick up the pieces of a life in the way that you need. This is how you move forward. You go to Monrovia, you find solid ground, and then you do whatever you want to do next. I mean that, Cat. Whatever you want to do. Don't ever let anyone make you think otherwise."

"Then why are you making me leave if I don't want to?!"

"Because that's my choice, Cat. I'm not taking you any further."

"Why not!?" She was crying now. Eyes shimmering in a way that made my headache worse. "Why do you have to do this?" she yelled. "Why can't you just stop with the Paxtons and why can't we-"

"BECAUSE I WON'T!" I roared. I lunged across the bed. Cat tried to shrink away but I grabbed her by both forearms. "Why," I mimicked. "Why, why, fucking why. You can spend the rest of your life paralyzed by that one word. 'Why' doesn't matter, Catherine. You *DO*. Do you understand me? You listen to your soul and you *DO*. I didn't ask why I kept you and I'm not asking why I have to kill them all. I am *DOING*. And that's what you will do. You will take that fucking ticket. You will go to California. You will murder, or garden, or do whatever you want to do, but you will find your path, Catherine. And you will walk it to the end."

By the time I finished, I was heaving for breath and so was Cat. She was sobbing, hysterically clawing for every breath just to cry it back out. There was no way that she could answer me, not in this condition, but I assumed I'd made my point.

I saw all of this clearly. My own vision had finally stopped doubling. Everything in front of me was crystal clear. The searing pain that had accompanied my every step had also settled down into background noise.

I didn't ask why. I picked my bag up off the floor and kept going.

I didn't look back at her. That part of my life was over.

The last of the Paxtons, Mama Charlize and Owen, were waiting for me.

CHAPTER 39

I made it into the elevator and down to the lobby without any problems. It wasn't until I stepped out through the main doors that the parking lot suddenly started spinning, as if somebody had given the earth a few extra spins. My feet threatened to spiral out from under me, and I was suddenly cold despite the hot Alabama night. Through my spinning vision, I managed to lock onto a bench by the front door. Step by shuffling step, I made my way to it and dropped in a graceless heap. I sat for a moment, forcing myself to breathe slow and deep until the lingering episode passed. *You're still recovering from the fight with Luke,* I repeated to myself, trying to ignore the erratic spasming of my heart against my ribcage. *You're not at full strength. You have to be smart.*

Yeah, that's all it was. Just pain. I could take it.

Stupidly, I glanced back up to our room overlooking the parking lot. The lights were still on, but of course they were. The bus didn't leave until 8 AM and Cat wasn't some little baby who needed to go to bed early. Why wouldn't she still be awake?

I realized that I hadn't told her where the bus station was, but she was a smart kid. She'd find it.

"You all right, ma'am?"

I suddenly noticed that I wasn't alone. A hotel worker, a young woman with dark hair and a belly hanging over her belt, was leaning on a broom and looking me up and down with a skeptical eye.

I nodded and sat up a little straighter. "Long day," I said. "You don't have to worry about me."

That was good enough. Apparently convinced that I wasn't about to have a heart attack or OD, the woman's tone turned immediately.

"Long day. Woo, I hear that!" she sympathized. She resumed her sweeping of the entryway. "Two more hours for me and then me and my sister are hitting the bar. Hopefully you're doing something fun tonight?"

I shook my head. "Just home to my husband."

It got better once I made it to the highway. I could step out of my skin and let the ghosts of memory pilot my muscles to our destination. My body knew the directions as surely as it knew the way from any point in Los Angeles back to Beverly Hills. Exit 12 off the interstate, a right on Route 14, drive until the fork in the road with the big pecan tree and hang left, then down through the tunnel of Dogwoods for about another fifteen minutes, and there it was.

The long country driveway to Paxton Manor.

I'd come back here drunk and deliciously delirious after too much sun. I'd come back here at three in the morning, wrapped in a still-warm coat of fresh blood. I'd come here perfectly content in so many different ways. Often with my husband's hand squeezing my thigh. The ghost of that sensation still tingled on my skin, still incredibly potent even after everything that had happened.

I had been happy here. There was no sense in pretending otherwise. I didn't ask for Anthony to find me. I hadn't wanted any of this to happen. Just like I hadn't wanted to kill my parents or my friends. Maybe happy wasn't enough. Not if you wanted to move forward.

I returned to my body, at the controls for real as I returned to the house for the final time. Me. My choice. I slowed to a stop on the main road, about a hundred yards from the turn into the driveway and killed the car. From here I was on foot, traveling light with nothing but the two knives and a length of sturdy nylon rope.

I made my way through the woods bordering the driveway. It was just a short walk from here to the house, but the trees were thick and overgrown to cut visibility to almost nothing. I would catch a glimpse of the house looming in the distance, then it would be obscured by underbrush for another twenty feet before I saw it again. That being said, the porch lights were on and I had no problem staying oriented.

I was eager to finish this, my blood ached for it, but I forced myself to move slow and steady. Luke may have been the only hunter in the family, but his traps were still in the garage, and I assumed they wouldn't be too hard to set up. Or maybe Owen had broken out Reese's compound bow with the night vision scope and saw me clear as day, just waiting for a clean path to let loose an arrow. I'd already ran down every weapon in the manor, making sure there were no possibilities I'd left out, I was confident that I could make my way safely to the manor.

Except I hadn't thought to worry about the outdoor speakers.

I could hear them as I got closer to the end of the tree line. The speakers were turned all the way up, and the sound of The Five filtered out through the tangle mass of branches and undergrowth.

"Today the new old world

Was the old world

Today the new old world."

I got closer, finally to where I could see the house in its entirety, and there he was. It was a scene I knew all too well, Owen sitting on the porch, sipping beer from a coozy. I wasn't close enough to read the lettering, but I was close enough to see the red and recognize his Roll Tide coozy for what it was. The porch lights were on, bathing his handsome face in a comfortable golden glow. He wore an olive button-down shirt, unbuttoned low enough to show the prominent curves of his pectorals.

There was no tension in his posture. He was sitting there as if he could comfortably never get up again, totally motionless except for the gentle back and forth of the rocking chair and the occasional crank of his arm as he took another sip of beer.

Just as the song started to wind down, Owen added the can to a long row of empties on the railing. In perfect synchronicity, he cracked open another beer just as the song started again.

How many times had he listened to it on repeat? How long, listening to that song over and over again while working steadily through a rack of beer? How many empty cans were littered on the floor around his feet?

How long, with his dead mother sitting in the rocking chair beside him?

CHAPTER 40

———————

"I knew you'd save us for last," Owen said.

He tracked me the moment I stepped out of the trees and the lights caught the dim edges of my outline. He switched off the speaker. He also switched the beer for the bottle of Blanton whiskey sitting beside the chair. "Mama because you hated her. And me because you loved me." He didn't bother with a glass, just swigged the whiskey straight from the bottle. "You did love me, didn't you?" he asked.

I didn't answer. My only focus was on Mama Charlize. Her normal, carefully coiffed hair had collapsed in a deadfall of lank, lifeless blonde hair. Death had taken the same care from her face. Her cheeks and chin hung slack and doughy. It matched the slump of her shoulders.

The knife handles were still in her chest. Twin towers of black surrounded by lakes of red. More blood had run down her body and seeped through the wicker seat of the chair, darkening the deck boards underneath her from pine to redwood.

Owen whistled softly as I reached the porch steps. "Two days ain't long, darlin'. You'd think I'd have remembered just how beautiful you are. Then again, some things just can't be remembered true. You try, you think that you do, but the reality just has too many details you can't replicate. You need the real thing." He shook his head and drank some more whiskey. Up close, he was almost as slumped over as his dead mother. His eyes were almost as lifeless.

"What is this, Owen?"

"You killed three of her children. How else was I supposed to keep you safe?"

I wanted to rage at him for that, but the whole sordid diorama was too dreamlike for it. The world around me felt like wet cement. Nothing had hardened enough to be real. You didn't rage at dreams. When I spoke, the words felt just as surreal. Smoke floating out into the night air.

"How do you think this ends?" I asked him.

He heaved a sigh. "Probably with you killing me."

He stood up and walked back into the manor, the whiskey bottle dangling by the waist of his jeans. Not stopping to see if I followed.

Of course, I did.

I wasn't afraid of dead bodies, but I gave Mama Charlize's unmoving hands as much of a wide berth as I could.

"He was the one that introduced me to The Five, you know," I said. "Anthony. He liked them first."

If I expected Owen to bite at that, he didn't oblige. He was a machine moving methodically through the house. At the kitchen Island, he poured the Blanton into two glasses with a chilled whiskey rock at the bottom of each one. "Was that his name? I never got it. A bit too occupied smashing his head open." He pushed one of the drinks across the counter towards me.

"What else did he teach you?" he asked.

So many things I could have answered. Music. Mini-golf. Sex that felt like more than just scratching an itch. What it meant to matter.

Owen gestured to the fridge. Somebody had scrubbed it, but the ghost of my final message was still there in the steel.

"I guess he knew your real name. Beverly, is it?"

I nodded.

He sipped at the whiskey, tasting my name. "It's pretty. I would have liked to have known it. Would that have been so bad, Beverly?"

"It wasn't about you," I said.

"It had to be on some level. You kept things from me. What is it? Did you think I wouldn't accept your past? I thought we had something good here, but was I wrong? Were you ever even really happy with me?"

My throat was getting tight, but I nodded and forced out the words. "I was, Owen."

"Then why?" he asked. "Why start this with him? Why escalate it after I gave you a second chance?"

"That's what you think?" I asked him. "I'm ungrateful? Listen to me, Owen. I am not yours to give anything to. Do you think I *wanted* your forgiveness? I made my own decision, and I was ready to accept the consequences."

"I would have smashed the consequences out of your skull and spilled them out on the gravel in front of your daughter!" he roared.

"Then that's what happens!" I screamed back. "I own my life, Owen. You want to know about my past? I killed my parents. I killed my best friends. I left Anthony even though I loved him. I did that. Me! I chose the life I wanted and I paid the cost." I stabbed a finger at him, sharper than any knife. "You wanted to take that from me! You didn't want to forgive me, you just wanted to own me. That's why you spared my life. So, you could have it for yourself!"

He looked flabbergasted. "Own? I don't want to own you, Pam – Beverly. I just didn't want to lose you. I wanted us to move forward together!"

"Then you should have talked to me!"

"You should have talked to me!" he screamed back. "You lied first! You snuck around behind me! The only thing I did was try to keep our marriage together!"

"But you didn't, Owen! You spied on me! You waited until I put a toe out of line so you could discipline me. You and your fucking family played games with me while *I* felt like a piece of shit because I was the one lying to you. That's why I killed them, Owen. You tried to decide who I was. Nobody does that except me."

Owen tilted his head. He examined me with a strange unfamiliarity, as if seeing me for the first time. "That's why you did all this?" he asked. "I thought this was about revenge because you loved that guy, but you're saying my whole family... you murdered all of them because I damaged your tin shit little ego?"

He laughed. He laughed long and hard, the sound of it shattering the quiet in the empty house like the first bird calls on a misty morning. It sounded tremendously liberating. When he found the breath to do it, he straightened and wiped a tear from the corner of his eye. "You didn't love him more than me," Owen said. "You can't love anyone. Not really. There was nothing I could have done differently." He shook his head, still chuckling to himself.

"Okay, momma. Go ahead."

I didn't even have time to turn around. The agony moved first. Hot pain going through my lower back, and then icy cold in the front as the slick, red-soaked harpoon point pierced out through the belly of my shirt.

A hand braced against my shoulder, and then there was a sound like a boot coming unstuck from the mud, except the only thing getting unstuck was the harpoon from my torso. I felt fresh heat as the metal shaft withdrew from my body, leaving a gaping hole in its wake that felt queerly like an empty stomach. I didn't even sink to my knees. I dropped all the way down, my face slammed into the stone tiles in a way that probably hurt like hell, but my whole body was suddenly in a haze of Novocain. I didn't feel much of anything.

I gasped for air. I tried to move, but all of my parts had suddenly gone in different directions, and nobody was answering my calls. I spat blood and tried again. And again. Finally, my hands decided to respond. I groped around with numb fingers and managed to place my palms against the stone. Something wet under my palms. Blood. My own. But I couldn't make myself realize what that meant. All my energy was focused on pushing up and trying to roll onto my back. It felt like trying to flip a Mack truck. But, slowly, surely, I creaked myself over until...

"Well, well," Mama Charlize said. "Look who managed to get on her back one last time."

She loomed over me, her doughy face finally baked solid and hard. She surveyed my bleeding body like I was a cockroach twitching out my last moments after a bootheel had burst my guts out. Her harpoon cane, slick with my blood, planted between her feet. She swayed. Not a lot, but even a small wobble in the ancient idol's footing was worth nothing.

But the waver didn't reach her face. Neither did any hint of pain from the knives still oozing blood from her torso.

She must have caught me looking. "I told you family was there to take care of each other," she said. "And if that means spilling a little bit of my own blood, that's fine by me." She lifted the harpoon and stuck the point under my chin. "When all's said and done, it's going to be a lot more of your blood on the floor than mine."

"That's enough, Mama" Owen said.

Charlize didn't look away from my eyes. "I know, honey. She's all yours."

Mama Charlize stepped back, but I heard more footsteps coming closer. The floor shook with the force of them. I couldn't turn my head to look, but I recognize those footfalls intimately. Hands cupped my face, and I had the phantom memory of those same hands cupping my face to kiss me until my insides quivered. Now, they squeezed until my teeth creaked and dragged me across the floor, leaving a trail of my blood behind me.

The Knife... I had it in my belt. I groped with one numb hand, trying to work my suddenly clumsy fingers around the handle.

Owen dropped me then, and erased any design I had on the knife with a sudden kick in the ribs. I heard my bones break. Heard it like uncooked pasta noodles breaking in half. "Nuh ah, darlin'," he tutted. He yanked the knife loose from my waistband and slid it across the floor. Found the other and did the same thing.

Then, his hands on my face again. Owen grabbed me by the skull and hauled me up as if I were a stray scrap of food off the floor. We were between the oven and the edge of the kitchen island. I had a moment's clarity as I rose up, enough to see the whiskey bottle on the edge of the table. I snatched the bottleneck up in one fluid motion and swung the heavy glass towards his face.

Owen was faster. One hand held me by the throat, the other caught my wrist before I could smash the bottle against his nose. All I managed to do was splash a liter of $200 whiskey down both of our shirts.

"You should have taken the drink when I offered." Owen said. He ripped the bottle from my hand and threw it across the room. "Too late now." He slammed my head down against the counter. Pain went off in an earthquake of blinding light. I felt some teeth come loose and rattle against my tongue in a bath of salty blood.

As badly as it hurt, I realized it could have been worse. He could have killed me. He could have brought over two hundred pounds of muscle behind that slam and broken my skull into pieces. He'd held back, and the thought kindled fresh dread in the pit of my stomach. If Owen restrained himself, it hadn't been out of kindness.

I knew he had something twisted in mind, but I didn't start to understand what until my vision cleared enough that I could see the surface my head was pressed against. I was wrong, it wasn't the rust-colored stone plane of the counter pressed against my face, it was the polished black obsidian of the electric stove range. Owen had me pressed against the stove. One of his arms, unyielding as a stone pillar, had my cheek pinned against the stovetop.

The other hand reached down, outside of my field of vision, and twisted something with a *clicking* noise.

Then, just at the fringe of my sight, the glass underneath my face started to glow red. The heat started to build.

I hissed. I clawed at his arm and wrist and tried to twist myself free out of his grasp.

None of it mattered. Nothing changed except the steadily rising temperature of the glass pressed against my face.

"Don't get soft again, Owen." I heard the savage satisfaction as Mama Charlize spoke. "You keep her right where she is. Let the bitch burn."

"I will, Mama," Owen promised. He leaned in so close that I felt hot breath all the way down my ear canal. "Until it's time to cook the other side," he said.

The heat kept climbing, past discomfort and to the point where there was no denying how badly it hurt. I gritted my teeth against it. I bit my lip until the skin split and the blood ran and sizzled against the hot burner.

Eventually, I screamed.

I screamed. I spasmed. I twisted and writhed and did whatever I could to recoil from the agony of the electric heat. I did all the things people do when they're being murdered slowly and sadistically.

Owen just pressed harder. He mashed my burning skin against the hot stove until the only thing I could smell was the stench of my own burning flesh.

I teetered on the edge of panic, it was so tempting to just writhe in unthinking pain until the blissful silence of death, but I forced myself back. I groped again for Owen, trying to squeeze his balls until they burst, but he was smart enough to angle his hips back so all I could grab onto was a damp shirt tail.

Damp.

My eyes would have widened if one of them wasn't burnt shut. I tightened my grasp on the wet chunk of shirt and pulled with all the strength I had left, ripping away a ragged chunk of fabric.

A ragged chunk of fabric soaked with whiskey.

I took the piece of shirt and brought it close to the hot stovetop. The whiskey-soaked cloth flared up instantly into a burning tail of flames.

"Owen, get away from her!" Mama Charlize yelled. She understood, and oh how delicious her terror sounded. "Get away from her right now!"

Too late. I flung the rag of fire over my shoulder and was rewarded with a dull *twhump* as the rest of Owen's whiskey-drenched shirt went up in a curtain of fire.

Owen cried out. The pressure of his grip disappeared as he tried to recoil away from the fire clawing at his chest.

I gritted my teeth and pulled hard and fast, ripping my bubbling, caked flesh away from the hot stove. Leaving a pancake sized square of flesh behind to burn to cinders. I stumbled the length of the kitchen and collapsed against the far cabinets. I was free from the stove, but my hot flesh was still oozing and sizzling. I could feel the sickly heat from my scorched face all the way down at my shoulders. I smelled it.

But there was no time to recover. Mama Charlize shrieked and steamed towards me, relentlessly coming forward with her bloody harpoon cane.

Get up. Finish this.

I pulled up the strings of my broken marionette body. Mama Charlize and I lurched towards each other, both of us leaking a trail of blood in our wakes. Both of us yelling out our fury as we collided.

Mama Charlize lifted the harpoon to skewer me, but she lifted it too early for her own good. Bloody and weary, she still needed the weapon as a cane, and she sprawled over her own feet without the extra support. She would have fallen to the floor if I hadn't been there to catch her. We mashed together, face to face. Her rancid breath hot in my face. I felt her squirming, trying to angle the harpoon into my guts, but I grabbed the shaft first and wrenched it out of her hands. I spun the hissing, scratching old woman around so I had her back. I pressed the harpoon under her neck.

"Get back, Owen!" I yelled. "Just stay the fuck on your side!"

Panting, Owen held his ground. While I'd been grappling with his mother, Owen had managed to rip his flaming shirt off without getting too badly burnt, but he must not have been careful enough with the flaming pieces. The curtains over the sink had caught fire and were burning merrily. The cabinets were wood and could join the party at any time, but Owen didn't try to extinguish the flames, guessing correctly that I would skewer his mother through the head and be on him in a second if he gave me the opportunity.

The house fire could wait. We had to finish killing each other first.

Owen stood, tensed like a bull ready to charge. Spit seeped from between his clenched teeth. Mama Charlize, slick with sweat, squirmed and tried to slither loose from my grasp, but I just tightened me grip around her chest and jabbed the point of the harpoon under her chin until blood started to run. The standoff wasn't a perfect solution, but it was a few minutes to get my breath. A few minutes to think of a plan.

In my clutches, Mama Charlize's frantic breathing steadied. "I told you I wasn't afraid to give my blood for my family," she said to me. To Owen, she said, "…I love you, baby boy."

"Mama, no!" Owen shouted.

Mama Charlize didn't hesitate. She ripped one of the knives out of her chest and rammed it into her own eye socket. I felt the death shudder pass through her as my human shield turned into nothing but a liability. I let her slip and held tighter to the harpoon. Leveled the point between me and my husband.

Owen hadn't uncoiled yet, but I saw the building fury in his clenched jaw as his mother's body slipped to the floor. The fire had spread over the counter, the cabinets were burning merrily now, but that didn't stop Owen. He reached through the flames and drew a butcher knife from the knife block.

Owen flipped the knife over in his hand, getting a feel for the blade. He didn't charge blindly at me, because he didn't have to. He was taller than me. Stronger. Just as deadly. Worst of all, he was healthy. He wasn't struggling not to slip in his own blood. He wasn't the one with one eye burned shut and half his face alive in scalding pain.

He came forward with slow, methodical steps. I stabbed at the air between us, a snake with a broken back, and Owen came to a stop just out of my range. He smirked at my attempt to keep him at bay. Just for shits and giggles, he twitched forward again and easily danced back away from my jabbing spearpoint. He could be patient. I couldn't. I was sucking for every breath. The harpoon in my hands felt like I was carrying around a steel girder.

"This is good," Owen said. "I'm glad you're going to die looking as ugly as you really are."

He wasn't lying. I could see my reflection in Owen's knife. One side of my face was melted candy. Half my hair had burnt down to the scalp. My eye was a tumor of blackened flesh.

I looked like a monster.

That was fine. I bared my teeth.

Owen feinted forward again. I stabbed at air with the harpoon, and this time he flicked out with the butcher knife and cut a gash across the back of my hand as I extended it out.

He's going to kill you, Mom. Cat's voice was in my head. *What's the point of this? Get out now.*

I panted for air and coughed back smoke. The fire was quickly getting out of control. The air between me and Owen shimmered with the oily blackness of it. Sweat mingled with the blood coating my body.

"Lie to me," he said. I drove the harpoon for his face. He batted it aside and cut out another chunk of my forearm. "Lie," he repeated. "Tell me you love me. Maybe I'll let the fire take you."

"I never told you I loved you," I said. "Not once."

"Why not!?" he exploded. His eyes watered. Not because of smoke. "What did I do wrong? We were happy, Pam."

I willingly breathed in smoke and heat. No running. No turning back.

"My name… is Beverly!"

I lurched towards Owen. Slow, burnt, bled-out.

In it.

It meant nothing. Owen swept away my lazy harpoon slash, but he didn't use his own blade in return. He punched the burnt side of my face, bursting blisters, pulverizing raw flesh, and leaving me sprawled flat on my back. The harpoon tumbled out of my hands.

Black spiders gathered at the edges of my sight, but I fought to stay awake. The heat didn't help. One side of the kitchen was totally ablaze, but the effect was like a warm blanket lulling me to sleep. I had one more trick to try, but it was stupid. So fucking stupid. This was better. Call it a day. Good try.

Get the fuck back up right now, bitch.

Right... right. Back up. I spat a tooth, another for the pile, and rolled onto my stomach. I started crawling.

I heard a low clatter from behind me. I looked over my shoulder. Owen had picked up Mama Charlize's harpoon.

I groaned. "At least use your own knife you fucking mama's boy!"

"Shut up!" Owen yelled. "You've made this hard enough!"

I kept crawling away, trying to get out of the kitchen. "Oh yeah? Well, I'm used to it. Always my job to make it hard."

Elbows. Knees. Elbows. Knees. Not even crawling. Writhing. Like a worm. I crossed the threshold into the living room, and it got a little easier. The smoke wasn't so thick.

But the wall was so far away.

"Always me," I said. "Me on top, me stripping for you on the boat."

I kept talking, always surprised that I finished another word. I kept waiting to feel the harpoon between my shoulder blades. Kept waiting to be spiked to the floor like a butterfly on a board, but so far it hadn't happened yet. "You can talk about loving me all you want, but love is action. And I did all the work."

And then, miraculously, the wall. I'd made it. The mahogany expanse of it loomed in front of me like the side of a New York City skyscraper. I was there.

So was Owen. He flipped me over. His stance straddled my waist. Sweat plastered his hair to skin splotchy red from heat and fury. He had the harpoon high over his head.

"You want me to do the work?"

Thunk.

He buried the harpoon in the wall. My heart surged, afraid he'd ruined everything. But no, I still had a chance.

"Well, tough shit. This isn't work. Not for me."

He dropped down on my torso, making no effort to take any of the weight as his bulk dropped down my diaphragm. I coughed up smokey air.

"Never let it be said I only cared about your looks."

He wrapped his hands around my throat. His big hands didn't waste any time crushing my larynx down to a cocktail straw.

"The safe word is, 'deep fried,'" he said.

I couldn't even croak. I barely had any air left after he sat on me, and nothing was making it past the grip on my throat. The black spiders were back, spinning dark webs over my eyes. I couldn't push him off. He was too big. Too strong. My fists pounded relentlessly, but not against Owen. I beat at the wall over my head. I hit the wood paneling again and again with whatever force I had left. I couldn't hear the sound of it, not with the blood rushing in my ears, but I felt the vibrations with every strike of my fist.

BANG.

BANG.

No results. No change. If Owen knew what I was doing, even he thought it was too stupid to interfere with. But it was the only card I had left. Nothing to do but keep trying.

Bang.

Bang.

I could barely see Owen. The darkness in my own eyes was getting thicker, but so was the smoke in the living room. It was possible that he would die anyway. The fire was totally out of control now. He might not be able to get out at all, even if he wanted to.

But I doubted it. Owen was a survivor. And either way, I wanted to be here to see it, damnit.

Wishful thinking. I couldn't see anything now. Owen had finally faded into blackness.

No, Mom. Cat's voice. *You're the one in the black.*

Blind. Deaf except for the hammering of blood trying to get out of my ears.

No sensation except for my fist, moving even when the rest of my body couldn't. Weak as a girl scout going door to door with cookies, but still going.

Bang.

Bang.

And then even my fist quit; abandoned the hammering against the wall. It would have been bad enough if it just lay there, but my hand spasmed of its own will. Clutched desperately at the air for a life preserver that would never be thrown. Panic-reacting like any common victim.

No! I raged in the silence of my own head. *NO!*

Yes. I could hissy fit all I wanted, but I was dying. Dying as shamelessly as anyone else. Dying in the black nothing. No bright lights. No last memories of Cat or Anthony. Just darkness. Darkness and Owen's hands still wrapped around my throat. Tighter. Tighter.

And then, even that was gone.

CHAPTER 41

The only feeling left was the heat. The undeniable, scorching reality of fire. My entire body felt the way your hand did when you held it too close to a campfire for an unbearable second. There was a bare moment when I considered that, maybe, there really was a Hell and I was already in it.

And then I remembered I was in the middle of a fucking house fire.

I coughed. I actually could cough. No more bear trap grip clutched around my throat. With tremendous effort, I deadlifted my good eye back open.

Two different sets of eyes stared back at me. Owen's dense green and, looming over his shoulder, eyes of the darkest black. In both pairs of eyes, firelight danced against the glazed, unblinking surface. The twist of color in two pairs of dull marbles.

"Auntie," I croaked. "Nice of you to join us."

Auntie didn't answer. She just stayed right where she was.

Upside down.

Her antlers sticking out of Owen's back.

I let my head roll back and gazed up at the wall. I could see the gouges where the screws holding the antelope head to the wood had ripped loose.

That had been my only hope. Try to send enough tremors through the wall to loosen the anchors holding the mounted antelope head and drop it down on top of Owen. Even just knocking him off balance would have given me a chance.

244 | S e a n   M c D o n o u g h

What must have happened instead was the antelope head flipped perfectly upside down, and the horns had punctured through Owen's back. Deep enough that the top of the antelope's head was pressed against his shoulder. Dead eyes, side by side.

But it wasn't the eyes I noticed as much. It was Owen's mouth that held my attention. It had been fury on his face as I drifted to black, but that wasn't what I saw now. It was a clenched grimace of remorse I saw frozen on the face hovering over mine. It was regret that he'd felt in those final moments, not anger.

I cupped his cheek. It was still warm in the fire raging around us.

"We were happy," I whispered. Not that there was anyone to hear it. I was alone except for the flames steadily devouring the manor.

"Last ones out," I said to Auntie. I didn't bother trying to wrestle Owen's dead weight off of me. I was impaled. Burned. Barely holding it together from all of the damage Reese and Luke had done. I'd put Owen on the barbecue first, but I wasn't far behind him.

I closed my eyes again and laid back. I thought to myself that more noise machines ought to offer crackling fire as a setting. I'd always loved fire. I listened to the wood snapping as the fire consumed it. The house groaning as the beams started to weaken. This wasn't so bad.

Not so bad at all.

And then a door screamed open. Fresh oxygen made the fire leap and growl for more.

"Mom!?" a voice called.

I heard Cat cough. "Oh God," she muttered. Then, again, "Mom! Mom where are you!?"

My eyes snapped open briefly at her entrance, but I closed them just as quickly. I fought to stay silent. Let her not see me. Let the smoke and fire be too thick to see through and let her think she'd tried her best, but I was gone. She needed to go.

And then her hands on my shoulders. Shaking me gently. "Mom! Mom, can you hear me!? Please wake up!"

I couldn't fight the cough clawing at my throat while she was shaking me like that. A muffled wheeze slipped through my clenched lips.

I opened my eyes and they immediately teared up at the encroaching smoke. Cat was coughing too, but she was determined. She put her shoulder against Owen's body and muscled it off of me.

"Can you move?" she asked me.

"I told you to leave," I rasped.

"You told me to make my own decisions. Now, come on. Sit up."

She didn't wait. She got underneath my arms and hauled me into a sitting position. I screamed.

"I'm sorry, mom. I'm sorry." But she didn't stop. She shimmied in front of me and draped my arms over her shoulders. "Hold onto my back. Don't let go." She dropped to her hands and knees with me draped over her shoulders and clinging to her neck.

My daughter crawled forward, and all I could do was just hang onto her.

———————

We made it to the porch. Fresh, clean, crisp air. For a time, all either of us could do was gulp it down by the gallon.

Then, something structural screamed inside of the manor. The house didn't have long.

"Mom, there's a railing here. Can you stand?"

I just panted. All I could do was feel every stab. Every burn. Every missing drop of blood.

Then I felt Cat's hand in mine.

"It's here. Right here." I reached up and felt the smooth wood of the banister. And then Cat behind me, lifting me into enough of a crouch where I could cling to the banister and stay up. She guided me down one step. Two. Three. And then the crunch of gravel. I looked ahead and saw a car parked at the head of the driveway. Exhaust drifted out of the tailpipe from the still-running engine.

"We can do it," Cat said. "A few more steps."

I let my daughter help carry me away from Paxton Manor. To the car that she'd somehow commandeered and drove here from the hotel despite never once being behind the wheel. The whole excruciating journey, her voice was in my ear.

"Come on."

"We can do it."

"One more step."

I took one final look over my shoulder. There was no saving Paxton Manor. The entire building was up in flames. All that remained of the last few years would soon be ash.

Anthony was buried somewhere in a shallow ditch. Gone too.

So were my parents. My best friends. Everything.

Cat tugged me forward. "We're almost there, Mom. Don't stop now."

We made it to the car. Cat got the door open and gently ushered me into the passenger seat.

"We'll get you some help," she assured me. "Somehow. *Somehow.*" Not really talking to me anymore. Already thinking of all the angles. How to get someone brutalized like me to the ER without an ID. How to do it without getting the police involved.

I hope she was thinking of what she'd do if I didn't make it that far. The seat below me was already saturated with my blood. My face was a writhing nest of fire-ant bites. The harpoon wound through my torso was a black hole of agony.

Strangely, the scar in my palm didn't hurt at all.

Cat closed the door. I was alone in the car as she made her away around to the driver's seat. I sank deeper into the seat. My hazy vision drifted up to the rearview mirror.

There was a woman reflected there. She was sitting up in the back seat, still wearing her motel uniform. It was the woman I'd talked to while she was sweeping the front entrance.

There was a barbecue skewer still sticking out of her ear.

Cat got into the driver's seat. She reached across my lap to buckle my seatbelt and then leaned over and kissed me on the cheek.

"I love you," she said.

END

BIO

Sean McDonough is the author of 5 novels, three published short stories, and one season of reality TV. He lives in New York with his wife and two daughters. Look for him on Instagram @houseoftheboogeyman and on Facebook at Sean McDonough-Horror Author. You can also look for him at your local horse racing track or horror convention.

A B O U T T H E
P U B L I S H E R / E D I T O R

————————|————————

Dawn Shea is an author and half of the publishing team over at D&T
Publishing. She lives with her family in Mississippi. Always an avid
horror lover, she has moved forward with her dreams of writing and
publishing those things she loves so much.

Follow her author page on Amazon for all publications she is featured
in.

Follow D&T Publishing at their website, **www.dt-publishing.com**,
or search for their Facebook Group

Or email here: dandtpublishing20@gmail.com

Beverly Kills Again by Sean McDonough

Edited by Tasha Schiedel

Cover Art by Ash Ericmore

Formatting by Ash Ericmore

Made in the USA
Middletown, DE
27 July 2024

58003390R00146